A Little Place in France

Signed First Edition

No.

35

Of 200

Barbara Hammond

Barbara Hammond

A Little Place In France

www.brightsparkpublishing.co.uk
www.bargainbooksonline.co.uk
www.bargainprintonline.co.uk
www.scotlandswritersoftomorrow.co.uk
www.getitpersonalised.co.uk
www.self-publish-for-free.co.uk
www.selfpublishforfree.co.uk

A Little Place in France

Barbara Hammond

DEDICATION:

To Lynn Pertoldi, without whose help and support
this book would never have been written.

This Book was published by BrightSpark Publishing, 2110.

First Edition.
© Copyright 2010.

The Author, namely Barbara Hammond, asserts the moral rights
to be identified as the author of this book.

Designed, typeset, printed, and bound completely in-house
By BrightSpark,
21 Commerce Street
ELGIN
IV30 1BS

www.brightsparkpublishing.co.uk
Telephone 01343 208286
Or mobile 07967 178224

CHAPTER ONE

1

I raised my champagne glass and toasted the future.

Warm sunlight filtered through the plane trees surrounding the Place de Darnetal. I felt confident, clever and triumphant.

It was a feeling that was not destined to last.

A man I had noticed talking to the waiter walked up to me and asked if he could join me at my café table. Without waiting for permission, he sat opposite me. He signalled the waiter, who appeared promptly by his side. He ordered a panaché for himself and a second glass of whatever I was drinking.

I was a little taken aback by his cavalier behaviour... but, on the other hand, he *was* tall and obviously muscular beneath his smart tweed coat and fawn slacks. His most striking features, however, were his long dark curly hair and neatly clipped beard and moustache. He looked a bit like an old fashioned pirate.

"Madame..." he began, taking off his cap, "my name is Théophile Colbert. I was named after a relation, now long dead. Please call me Théo." He smiled briefly. It made him look younger and a lot less formidable. He was, I imagined, in his mid-thirties. He had the very dark blue eyes that are sometimes found in the black-haired Celtic races, with long curling lashes. I approved of what I saw.

"You must know," he continued, "that in all small towns there is a gossip network that ensures nothing remains secret for very long." He twisted his cap in his hands. Having screwed up his courage to accost me, he was now obviously at a loss as how to proceed. I decided to give him some help.

"I suppose you've heard that I inherited the house in the rue du Château from my great aunt?"

"Oui, Madame. I heard from Monsieur Olivier at Chez Henri that you were thinking of converting the old place into a hostel. He thought we might be of use to one another."

It was a few weeks before this encounter that I had inherited the house. Located in the little town of Montreuil-sur-Mer in Northern France, it was a legacy from an unknown aunt who had intended to leave her property to my late mother. On little more than a whim I had decided to keep the large rambling structure and turn it into a business venture. It was only that morning that I had mentioned my proposed plans to Henri at my hotel.

"Madame," he tried again, "I have a small construction business. I am a time-served mason and carpenter. I can also provide most domestic requirements such as electrical work, plumbing, painting and decorating. I live here in Montreuil and know the area. I worked for several prestigious companies in Lille, Rouen and Arras before setting up on my own."

I was intrigued. He was very good looking. "Several companies, Monsieur?" I queried.

"Yes..." He looked uncomfortable. "I had a small problem." He indicated his untouched shandy. "That is all over now, I can assure you. I am always careful."

Common prudence might have ended the conversation there and then, but I reasoned that here may be an opportunity to get a good job done cheaply. The man was obviously having difficulties finding work if he was reduced to approaching strangers in the street. My decision to listen further had nothing whatsoever to do with his indigo eyes, with their lovely lashes, his shy smile, or that very sexy beard.

I agreed that we would view the property together first thing the following morning. Théo stood up and made a very graceful bow for a man of his size. He paid the waiter for both my drinks as well as his own and then strode away.

As I finished my second glass of Champagne my thoughts went back to the morning the letter arrived. It had been a dull, grey morning, and getting up had seemed more than usually onerous. I had padded into the bathroom and looked at my reflection. I'll be forty next year – and I felt it. My skin did not show too many lines, but my eyes, which could look green or brown depending on the light, were sad. I had recently had my hair cut from the coiled braid, which, when loose, had reached nearly to my waist, to a short modern crop. The style made me look younger, even though the hair itself did need some occasional discrete help to keep the grey out of the brown.

I am tall for a woman – five feet ten inches – and I pride myself that I can still fit into a size fourteen dress. My waist has thickened slightly in recent years, but my stomach is flat, and I have been told I have good legs.

I heard the post flop onto the mat, so I and went to see what the postman had brought. Amongst the usual bumf of advertisements and a couple of bills was a thick, cream envelope with a French stamp. It was addressed to Mlle. Edith Calamier, which was my mother's maiden name.

I decided that work could wait, and slit open the heavy paper with just the slightest feeling of apprehension.

The letter was from the office of the Notaire in Montreuil-sur-Mer in the French Pas-de-Calais. It advised of the death of their client, also a Mlle. E. Calamier, in the family home in Montreuil. In her will she left all her worldly possessions to her niece.

The bald statement was followed by all the usual lawyerly clauses. If the niece died first the property could descend to any direct heirs. Mlle. Calamier was requested to contact the office at her earliest convenience.

I rang my office and left a message saying I had urgent family business to attend to and would be taking a day's leave. They would understand. I had been forced to take quite a lot of time off one way or another that year.

Since I was a small child I had known my mother was French. It was the family joke that Dad had brought her home as a souvenir at the end of the war – quipping that she was more practical than a German revolver and longer lasting than a bottle of wine. Mum would always respond by chasing Dad with whatever was in her hand. This could be quite spectacular when it was her big chopping knife, but it always ended in kisses.

My mother had never mentioned any living French relations, neither had she ever gone back to France. "Geneviève, ma chérie, Scotland is my country now," had been her standard reply to childish curiosity. "Did I not have to marry three times to secure your fickle father and my place here?"

Mum would talk fondly of the double church and civil ceremonies that had been conducted in France, with the whole wedding party, led by the bride and groom, walking all round the square from the old church of St. Saulve to get to the Mairie that was actually situated just round the corner. Then, when the war ended, Mrs. Richard Sinclair – formerly Mlle. Edith Calamier – had been shipped to Scotland. "Like a very disreputable parcel!" had been her favourite phrase.

As soon as she had arrived in the small town in Scotland's central belt that was to be her home, my father consulted a solicitor. This individual, with more than a trace of disapproval for what he considered my father's rash behaviour, had advised a UK ceremony.

"That is if you really would like to secure the long term future of this person as your wife in Scotland," he had said with shuddering xenophobia.

So, my Mother's story went, the dress, the hat and the shoes came out once more. They had, however, to buy a new bouquet as the original one had been left on Mamie's grave in France. This was always said with such a tone of regret that I remember wondering if my parents would have brought the flowers with them if they had known a third marriage would be required.

In the years that followed, Dad took advantage of the educational opportunities on offer to returning servicemen. He qualified as an accountant, and became a Fellow of his Institute. Mum taught French to private pupils, and did some dressmaking. After the war, women, especially 'foreigners', were not welcome in the world of work. It was admitted, however, that being French was not quite as bad as coming from the incomprehensible, unpronounceable and by then nonexistent countries of Central Europe.

Mum suffered several miscarriages in the first few years of her marriage. My parents were warned that further attempts to have children were not a good idea. The lost babies caused both of them deep grief. I can only be grateful to them for not blighting my childhood with the ghosts of my dead brothers and sisters. Then, when they thought that conception was no longer possible, and being parents was an impossible dream, I came along. I was delivered safely, and disturbed their Darby and Joan equilibrium forever.

From earliest infancy I spoke two languages. Mum criticised my French to the day she died. Her favourite phrase was, "You speak French like a Norman peasant and have no more grammar than his cow." She never seemed to realise that my accent reflected her own.

Mum developed cancer in the Spring of 2005, and died after a mercifully short illness. I was surprised by how well Dad seemed to accept it. Within weeks he was laughing and joking as usual. To keep himself occupied, or so he said, he started on an extension to the kitchen. When that was completed, he followed it up with some general repairs and maintenance. Finally he redecorated the whole house, top to bottom.

A year after Mum died, Dad too was dead. I found him in his favourite armchair, Mum's photo in his hands. All his affairs were in such excellent order that his old sergeant major would have been proud of him. The death certificate quoted a cardiac malfunction: no doctor would state 'broken heart' on a death certificate. It would look so unprofessional.

It was six months after Dad had passed that the letter came from France. I decided to take it round to Jeremy Buchanan – he was the solicitor who had helped me sort out my parents' wills and the sale of their house. Jeremy, who had not been qualified very long, was struggling as the most junior recruit in a branch office of a large national chain of solicitors, and in a very difficult area at that. He was both friendly and efficient. I suppose I made a welcome change from maintenance claims and drug charges.

"My condolences on the death of your great aunt," he said after I had stated my business.

I made a small negative gesture. "I never knew her," I explained.

"Well, Ms. Sinclair, this seems quite straightforward. I will get in touch will these people, explain the circumstances and then we can work out the next steps."

A couple of weeks later a reply arrived which we jointly translated from French legalese. I was Jeremy's last client of the day. We sat in the stuffy, overcrowded office looking at the letter from the Montreuil solicitors.

"It's surprising the amount of assistance this French Notaire is prepared to extend. He will sell the house and contents for you – he already has a buyer lined up – and transfer all monies to your account in Scotland," Jeremy said, running his fingers through already disordered hair.

"On first sight, and subsequent checking, all this is all tremendously helpful and easy. The proposed solution is the best for you, both for your convenience and financially. I have consulted with colleagues who have far more experience than me. Their advice is for you to grab the settlement with both hands."

I considered a while. "And you, Mr. Buchanan, what do you think?"

Instead of replying directly he asked, "Whereabouts in France is Montreuil-sur-Mer?"

"It's about thirty miles south of Boulogne. Despite the name it's about ten miles inland from the little fishing port of Etaples. It's one of those towns from which the sea receded a long time ago." I replied; pleased to show off my knowledge of an area I had never visited.

"I've heard of that. Isn't there a big military cemetery somewhere in the area?

"That's right."

"Just over the channel, in fact."

I waited; he obviously had something in mind.

"To be honest, it's too good, too accommodating. Nothing I can put my finger on…" There was a pause and, another attack on his hair. "But it's the sort of deal I might put together if I wanted to achieve a quick settlement because something big was brewing in the background. My advice would be, if you have the time and inclination, go over yourself and have a look at your inheritance. Decide then if this settlement is your best option."

I thought about it. I had not taken a holiday for almost two years. I had taken a lot of time off work, yes, but that had been to deal with my mother's illness – then the deaths of both my parents – so that hardly counted. And that had been largely covered by generous amounts of compassionate leave from my company, so I still had holidays due. I certainly could afford to go away. The whole idea of a fortnight in Northern France exploring my Mother's old home seemed very attractive.

Within a week I was bowling along the long straight roads of Northern France in sparkling sunshine. I had the hood down on my small Peugeot 306 convertible and felt freer and more confident than I had in months.

I wondered how much of the attractive, gentle landscape would have been recognisable to my parents. Quite a lot, I decided, as Montreuil still looked very much as it would have done when Napoleon marched there. I passed through the narrow gateway in the town wall and drove up the cobbled main street, flanked by grey, narrow windowed houses.

My hotel was in the upper part of the town, fronting onto a tree-lined square graced by an ornate fountain. Chez Henri had a faintly seedy charm about it. The decor looked as if it had not changed since the 1930s. Threadbare mats made the polished wooden floorboards treacherous. The walls were painted a dull brown, which reflected little of the light from the minuscule bulbs, and timer switches ensured that even this dim illumination was extinguished at unpredictable intervals, leaving you in the dark if you lingered too long on the stairs or along the tortuous corridors.

On the other hand, I had a large double room to myself with private facilities at a very moderate cost. Neither was there anything amiss with the food when I went down for the evening meal. The accent was on seafood, as one might expect for an establishment so near the coast. I started with a tasty fish soup made substantial and warming with croûtons, cheese and a spicy roulade.

The hotel manager was a jolly man: large and bald, with an expansive stomach that strained at his informal check shirt and baggy jeans. He showed me how to spread my croûtons with roulade, sprinkle them with cheese, then send them floating across the surface of the soup.

There was an intermediate course of a gratin of mussels that was served at blistering heat. The main dish was a fat red mullet with chips served on a separate plate so one could dissect the fish with greater ease. Cheeseboard and tart were served in the reverse order my mother had always insisted on at home. A long meal, but at the end I felt comfortably replete but not bloated.

I took coffee and calvados into the lounge, where I listened to the locals standing at the bar. They were discussing the coming fête, and saying some slanderous things about the town's politicians. I felt remarkably at peace, as if I had come home.

2

The next morning I had a ten o'clock appointment with M. Xavier LeFrançois. Tall, well groomed and silk suited; he was the very image of a prosperous businessman: the sort of person I dealt with every day in the course of my work as an engineering buyer for an international chemical company. He immediately put my teeth on edge by insisting on guiding me into his office with his hand on my back. He, in turn, was mortally offended when I stopped short and requested him, in a voice perfectly audible to his staff, not to touch me.

Things did not improve when he started to call me his "dear young lady". I responded by calling him my "dear old gentleman". After a bout of such verbal sparring, we finally achieved a businesslike if tense relationship.

"I very much regret that you have put yourself to the quite unnecessary trouble and expense of a journey to France." Monsieur looked at me severely.

"No trouble at all, I assure you," I smiled sweetly. "I shall enjoy a little holiday whist I am here. It is a very lovely part of the country."

"As I stated very clearly in my letters to your solicitor, your aunt's house is quite dilapidated. Ordinarily it would be extremely difficult to sell." Mr. LeFrançois repeated. "It just so happens that I have another client, a local business man, who wishes to develop in that part of town. His offer is not only fair but generous."

"I accept all of this Monsieur," I said reasonably. "I simply wish to see my inheritance for myself."

I often dealt with characters like the pompous Xavier in the course of my work. At such times I bolstered my self-confidence by telling myself that I was not just me, Sinclair, but the representative of a multi-million pound company. On this occasion, however, I was acting purely for myself, so I steeled myself and tried to inject into my voice and demeanour all the certainty of respect I can command in business dealings.

Twice he got up to show me to the door. I remained seated, politely smiling and absolutely adamant. If I left his office without the key, I would never regain the impetus to obtain it again. I would be railroaded into the sale, and would only have myself to blame. We returned to the arguments.

"My dear, erm, Ms. Sinclair, I have to inform you that I am far too busy to escort you round the property today."

"Monsieur that is no problem, in fact, I would prefer to go alone."

"I have indicated to you already that the house is not in a safe condition."

"Yet my great aunt was living there until a few months ago. It cannot be all that hazardous."

"Many people do not like to go alone into a building where someone has died."

"I am sure my relative would wish me no harm, and any building over a certain age will have had someone die within its walls at one time or another."

"I really cannot approve," Monsieur said eventually, "but if you insist I cannot prevent you." He went over to the safe in the corner of his office and produced a heavy, old fashioned key with a brown label. "You will return this to my secretary before the close of business today."

I did some more polite smiling, though under my calm exterior I longed to punch the pompous charlatan on the nose.

M. LeFrançois bowed me out of his office and I walked briskly off in the direction indicated. I soon found the house, in a quiet street not far from the ruins of the old castle. My aunt's former home was tall, three stories plus an attic but quite narrow. The building did have an air of neglect. Brickwork, woodwork, guttering, tiles all looked as if they could do with some attention.

I unlocked the door and entered. It was evident that some cleaning and tidying had been done, but there was still a lingering smell of cats and commode. I turned from the long hallway into the front room. Mantelpiece, dresser and numerous occasional tables were all quite innocent of ornaments. I wondered how many friends and neighbours had helped themselves to a souvenir or two. They were welcome to their mementoes.

The house was narrow but it was three rooms deep. At the end of the hall was a handsome staircase leading to the upper floors, while a more functional set of stone steps led to the nether regions. I tried up first.

Clearly there had been money at one time. There were old fashioned but functional bathrooms on both first and second floors. The bedrooms had a strange empty feeling, as if they had not been used in a long time. I supposed that in her last illness the old lady must have set up a bed in the lounge downstairs.

Edith Calamier had died here. I hoped her departure had been peaceful. As I had told the Notaire, more than one person must have died in a building that had certainly seen Napoleon, but if their ghosts roamed the rooms then they were quiet ones.

I sat on a linen-bound mattress on one of the wrought iron bedsteads. It protested noisily under me. This was my inheritance. It seemed as big a white elephant as I had been led to believe, though not quite so dilapidated. If there had not been so much pressure brought upon me to sell, I think I would have taken the key back like a good little client, accepted the money and salted it away for my own old age. Part of my character was what my Dad had always called 'the Calamier streak' – stubbornness in a normally placid temperament which, when roused, could verge on the destructive. I was not going to let this shabby house go.

But on the other hand, what was I going to do with it? The reduced ferry services in and out of Boulogne had decreased the need for overnight accommodation in the surrounding area for those travelling to and from Britain. The house wasn't really suitable for turning into a holiday home – a Gîte de France. So, what...?

I wandered back downstairs and smiled to myself. With its handsome reception rooms and multiple bedrooms it would make an ideal brothel! Alas, I did not have the least idea how to recruit either the staff or the clientèle for such an establishment.

Pocketing the borrowed but now purloined key, I decided on the good old delaying tactic of sleeping on the problem.

Unfortunately, neither that night nor the next brought any revelations. I did, however, enjoy myself just being on holiday and seeing some of the many sights recommended by my Michelin guide.

Slowly, an idea crystallized in my mind. Girls! No, not prostitutes – school girls! What I would do is provide specialist holidays in France for small parties of sixth-form students. There was ample parking in the main square for either cars or minibuses – I didn't have sufficient rooms to take coach parties.

It could appeal to those wishing to improve their French, their knowledge of European history, or the politics and economics of modern France. Montreuil had more history both ancient and modern than perhaps any other corner of the Fair Lands. Yet almost all the British thought of the area as a place to be driven through as quickly as possible on the route to more desirable destinations. Even well-travelled young people would not know the region intimately.

The trips I envisaged could be tailored to focus upon a particular period of history: Medieval, Napoleonic, Belle Époque, or the First and Second World Wars. Education would be coupled with a true taste of modern 'Vie Français'. My brain was buzzing with possibilities.

To keep costs down, the standard tour would be five days, taking advantage of the cheap travel options offered by both the ferry and shuttle companies. Students would put up with and might even welcome same sex share, which would also increase the number of paying guests. Teachers, however, would be tempted by top-class single accommodation. I allowed for one member of staff to six pupils. The teacher's costs being divided amongst the kids. Food would be well above the package holiday norm. Wine was to be included: a glass for the young people, a bottle for Miss.

The more I thought about it, the more I was sure it would work. There would not be any seasonal restrictions as educational trips invariably took place in term time. During the school holidays I could always have my name down with the local Tourist Board as willing to put up the odd benighted traveller. The facilities might be a bit basic, but a godsend compared with a night in the car.

I realised that I had been restless for some time. My job as an engineering buyer had not been giving me the same satisfaction since my mother's illness. I felt ready for a new challenge. My company did offer its senior staff the opportunity for career breaks. I would investigate the possibility of applying for one. Work in the department had diminished with the recession. Management might be quite happy to be relieved of paying my salary for twelve months. If my proposed scheme failed then the sale of the property would cover the cost of my year's adventure.

It was a fail safe plan, especially as I had inherited my great aunt's savings as well as her house. Not a lot, but enough to pay for the necessary alterations and refurbishments. Until clients began to appear I could live off the interest accumulating from my prudent parents' insurance policies and the sale of their house.

This last thought gave me great sadness. It was their frugality that had allowed me this measure of independence. For a moment I passionately wished them back with health restored. That was not a possibility, of course, but the pain of their loss was still sharp within me, and always will be.

Shaking myself back to practicality, I calculated that at the end of twelve months the project would be showing signs of success or failure. If I could not make a go of it, I would sell up, return to the UK and resume a business career. If it *was* a success, then I could continue to run the business myself if I was enjoying it – if I wasn't enjoying it I could put in a manager and go back to purchasing electrical equipment and maintenance services in the industrial world. That decision could only be taken nearer the time.

The next day I asked my own hotelier, Henri, if could spare me some time. He was friendly and far from busy. Once breakfast was over he was happy to chat with me over a fresh pot of coffee. I laid out my plans for the old house and was slightly surprised to find him very enthusiastic.

"Chére Madame, we need not be rivals. Indeed, we might become colleagues." He waved an expressive hand towards his restaurant. "Too often these days my tables are empty. You say yourself that you will not have the kitchen to serve lunches or dinners, but your clients must eat somewhere, n'est-ce pas? Why not here? We could come to an arrangement on costs."

It was a very good idea, but M. Olivier had not finished. "Teenagers are not going to go meekly to bed at 9:30. Some good looking English girls in my place would certainly attract the local young men. I have a nephew who runs a disco. The local chanteuses are always looking for somewhere to perform. The young people would be able to enjoy themselves." He placed a large finger against his nose. "I would keep a friendly eye on them. It would be much better than them roaming the bars."

This was an aspect I had not yet contemplated, but he was right, of course. Yes, Henri's scheme might very well suit us both, I decided. So, with thoughts of a potentially booming business buzzing through my brain, I made another appointment to see Monsieur LeFrançois. I had not looked forward to telling him that I was going to keep the property, but in the event the interview did not go as badly as I had feared. I calmly insisted that I would take possession of my inheritance when the legal formalities could be completed, following the old adage 'never apologise, never explain'.

My decision was greeted with barely concealed exasperation. This came as no surprise, but Monsieur seemed to accept my decision and promised to start the necessary paperwork.

It was later that day, as I was treating myself to a celebratory glass of champagne in the town square, that the rather dishy Théophile had approached me.

3

The following morning Théo was waiting for me as I came down to breakfast. He joined me for coffee and croissants as I explained a bit more about my plans for the Calamier place. We then wandered over there. The tour of the premises took a few hours, with Théo making notes on the back of an envelope.

Whilst I did not trust M. Le François, I would have been foolish to have ignored his advice simply because I disliked him. I needed to be sure that the structure of the house was safe, the wiring and plumbing in good order and so on. My great-aunt had been very old, and had not been in good health for some time, and therefore would have had little or no inclination to deal with such practical matters.

Théo asked to borrow my key whilst he made a more detailed survey. He promised a proposal before I was due to return home. He was as good as his word. We had dinner together the evening before my departure. Théo accepted a glass of wine but mostly drank mineral water. Through seafood salad, roast chicken with cream sauce, cheese and a slice of another of Henri Olivier's fruit tarts, Théo expounded his plans.

"You, as a client, would like a fixed price contract." He began counting off the points on his large fingers. "I, as the renovator would of course prefer costs on a time and materials basis. I cannot afford to take a loss if things become trickier than I expect."

He looked so serious. I wished he would smile again and then chided myself for the frivolous thought.

"I therefore propose a step-by-step plan. First to clear the house and sell at auction those items you do not want to keep. This would be on a 15% commission basis. This would pay for my time and ensure I get the best possible prices because it is in my interest as well as yours."

The proposal was open to abuse, but my examination of the furniture had led me to believe it wasn't worth much, however it was handled. The household sale would give me some idea of the man's enterprise and honesty.

"Then the work on the house. It needs complete rewiring, and the plumbing has to be brought up to Ministry standards for hotel grade accommodation. The structure is basically sound but I have found a spot of dry rot in the cellar. After that I will give you a fixed price quote for the smaller jobs – renovation of the windows, guttering, tiles, pointing, and dealing with the dry rot. If this is acceptable we can attend to the other tasks, such as refurbishment, alterations and redecoration."

With a mental reservation to get alternative quotations if costs began to escalate, I decided to go along with him. I stood up and offered him my hand. He did not so much shake it as clasp it within his own. His grasp was firm yet gentle, the skin of his palms warm and pleasantly rough. I enjoyed his touch.

I smiled and said, "Before you get too enthusiastic, I have some bad news for you." He looked concerned but waited for me to finish. "I shall be taking a career break from my work in Scotland. This means I will be on hand to supervise, interfere and change my mind at unpredictable intervals"

Théo's reaction was totally unexpected. "This is wonderful news!" he bellowed. I was treated to a great beaming smile before being pulled into a huge bear hug and given three fat kisses on the cheek, French style. I suddenly wanted to respond. Feelings that I had considered long dead and buried began to show that they were not: they had only been lying dormant, like a seed waiting for the first sunshine of spring.

I pulled away with what dignity I could muster, scolding him gently for his roughness. He looked so abashed I had to laugh. I suggested we order coffee before we scandalised the restaurant. Looking round the empty dining room, Théo said with a perfectly straight face. "Yes, indeed, French tables and chairs are easily shocked." This caused me to giggle like a schoolgirl. I began to like this gorilla of a man more and more.

"Where will you live during the restoration?" He asked. "You can't stay here in the hotel. It would be far too expensive and not very convenient."

"I had hoped to live in the house. The attics are going to be converted into a self-contained flat for the use of the eventual manager. That should be one of the first jobs."

"Certainement, but it must come after the rewiring and plumbing that will disrupt the whole house." Théo chewed on a knuckle for a moment. "My mother has a holiday home in Equires, which is only a couple of kilometres from here. It is a small chalet-type building at the top of her garden. She thought it would bring in a bit of useful income. Unfortunately the impoverished Parisians who used to rent the place became so much of a trial that she decided it was not worthwhile."

Théo gave me a quick grin. "How she used to envy her neighbours who had a similar Gîte. They managed to secure some shy English tenants who came regularly, paid promptly, were almost invisible during their stay, and left nothing but a large collection of wine bottles in the dustbin when they left. The tales Maman could tell you about the Parisians would make your hair stand on end! But I ramble." Théo became more serious again and continued. "What I wanted to say was that I am sure my mother would be prepared to lend you her holiday home at a prix d'ami whilst your flat is being prepared."

It made excellent sense and I asked him to make the arrangements with Mme. Colbert. Next day I returned to Scotland.

4

I should not have been as surprised as I had been that the arrangements all took far longer than they should. Initially the Notaire dealing with my great Aunt's will had been tremendously helpful. That however was when it looked like I would sell the property. Now I was no longer co-operating, the French legalities were drawn out to interminable length.

My young solicitor, Jeremy Buchanan, had been a tower of strength. He took on his own shoulders the battles with his French equivalents, alternatively cajoling and threatening recourse to the French equivalent of the Law Society. When all was complete I asked him why he had gone to so much trouble on my behalf. This resulted in a ruffling of his always unruly hair and a mumbled, "It will look good on my CV when I finally move on from this crummy office."

It was only as he held my hand as we were saying goodbye and he asked me to keep in touch, that I even began to comprehend there might have been another reason.

My company dithered over granting me a career break. It was only the intervention of my Union Representative that actually got them to take me seriously. She pointed out that I had suffered three bereavements of close family in a very short period of time. This was a slight stretching of the truth: mother's death from cancer and that of my father from grief had devastated me, but the passing of my mother's aunt had not affected me too much as I had not even been aware she was alive until she wasn't – if you see what I mean!

My Union Rep. insisted that I needed a complete break for the good of my health. I was proposing to take time off without pay. If the sabbatical was not granted, the Rep. told my company, I might have to take a considerable amount of time off on fully paid sick leave. After that morsel was brought to their attention, the decision became a foregone conclusion.

During the weary weeks and months it had been pleasant, almost comforting to have long chats on the 'phone with Théo Colbert. We talked about everything and nothing: local gossip, the weather, the ups and downs of his precarious business... On his advice I retained some of the larger pieces of the old fashioned furniture. They would give my hostel some authentic atmosphere and would definitely appreciate in value if cleaned and restored.

It was late autumn when I put my own furniture in store, gave up the tenancy on my flat, and set off for France with my car full to bursting with all the things I could not bear to leave behind.

Gulls screamed, and a fitful rain blew against the windscreen of my car as I waited to board the ferry. My stomach was fluttering with apprehension that had nothing to do with the imminent voyage over the Channel to France.

It was early evening when I arrived, weary from the journey, at Mme Colbert's. The old lady came out to welcome me as soon as she heard my car pull up. She invited me into her own home for an aperitif before I set about moving in. I would really have preferred to start transferring my luggage straight away before exhaustion set in, but I did not want to appear rude.

"I live here on my own for I have been a widow a good many years," she said with a sigh. "Théo is our only child, and he came late."

"He doesn't live here then?" I asked.

"My son lives in La Calotterie, the village in the valley. He bought an old farmhouse down beside the river Canche. He does it up when no other work offers. When it is finished he plans to sell it and move into another ruin. That is no life for a young man. It will be good to have you as a neighbour if only for a while."

I heard this with a degree of apprehension. The reasonable rent would prove very dear if I had to spend half my time entertaining Théo's mother.

Mme. Colbert smiled. Some of my thoughts must have shown on my face. "Don't worry, I shall not be a nuisance, I realise there is a lot to do when you are first setting up a business. Théo has had to do it several times. You know of his troubles I suppose?"

"Théo told me himself," I said sharply.

"Then let me tell you what I expect Théo has not, before he comes to see how you are doing." She poured more wine into our glasses and settled back in her chair. "Théo was on the eve of taking his final examinations. He had known Brigitte almost all his life and they had been engaged for about a year. It was planned that they would marry just as soon as he was out of his apprenticeship. But one day, quite unexpectedly, she went away, leaving a letter saying that she was going to Paris and intended marry someone else.

"He took his exams and passed, but not perhaps with the marks his tutors expected. There then followed a very wild time. I was at my wits' end. He did not listen to me anymore. He was drunk every night and had a whole succession of jobs, each a little bit more down-market than the last, until he could not find work anywhere."

Madame Colbert's bright eyes watched for my reaction. I was clearly being assessed. I did not reply immediately. Then I said simply that I had known something about Théo's background, but not the details. In fact I had found out more about my renovator in the last half-hour than he had disclosed during the previous six months. Théo was singularly reticent when it came to talking about himself.

Madame Colbert continued: "Eventually our priest managed to get through to Théo – how he did so is a story for another time. However, my son finally agreed to go for counselling, and it seems to have worked. He has settled down and is now building up his own business."

She looked at me steadily. "He is a good man at heart." Madame Colbert assured me. "I would not want to see him hurt again." It was a statement from a loving mother, but perhaps with a soupçon of a warning thrown in.

Quite suddenly I realised that seeing that Théophile Colbert was not hurt again was important to me too.

CHAPTER TWO

1

Just as I felt that duty was done and I could get on with setting up my new home, there was a squeal of brakes, and a few moments later Théo bounded into the room. He stooped to kiss his mother then came over to wring my hand. Then covering my hand with both of his he clung on whilst he looked at me carefully.

"You look tired, Mademoiselle," he said eventually. "I will help you get your things into the Gîte then I will take you to dinner."

I started to protest as I did not want to be taken over in this fashion. Then the thought of trailing all my boxes and cases up the short steep path from the car to the chalet on my own intervened, so I accepted, thanking him for the offer instead. For such a big man he moved with grace and economy. He was also very strong. My car was empty within ten minutes.

The Gîte was shining clean. Fresh flowers graced every room, and all the shelves and drawers in the kitchen were freshly lined with gay flowered paper. The oil-fired cast iron heating stove was lit, and a basket of basic provisions stood on the old-fashioned polished wood dining table. Mother – and possibly son – had ensured me a warm welcome. Théo put away as much as he could then promised to come back for me at eight o'clock.

At last I was alone. I explored my new domain. A small glassed-in veranda led into the large single ground floor room. This had dining room furniture at one end and a sofa with easy chairs grouped round a coffee table at the other. A wooden staircase gave access to a platform-like bedchamber directly under the sloping roof. A tiny attic window in the bedroom overlooked the garden.

It had just enough space for one comfortable double bed and two chests of drawers. There was no wardrobe. On the other hand there was a huge armoire in the main living area that would hold my clothes and anything else I cared to put in it.

A small annexe off the living room contained kitchen, shower room and WC. Not by any stretch of the imagination luxurious, but I thought I could be happy here for the weeks until my own flat was ready.

I looked at my watch, if I was to be washed and changed by 8 o'clock I had better get a move on.

Théo was on time to the minute. I appreciated that. I practice and expect promptness. I was also glad I had changed. Théo was sporting a smart navy blazer and cream slacks, looking very tasty indeed. The outfit looked so very freshly pressed that I wondered if it had been purchased in honour of my arrival. The thought gave me a little frisson of pride and pleasure.

I began to feel like royalty. Madame Colbert waved us away, standing on her own front doorstep. In Montreuil, M. Olivier from the hotel greeted us as old acquaintances, and indicated a quiet table by the window, garnished with a small posy of late roses. A glass of champagne was on the house. I noticed that the glass offered to Théo was more slender than my own and barely half full. This man had good and caring friends.

The journey was beginning to catch up on me and I hoped the meal would not be too heavy. I need not have worried. A small plate of oysters was followed by sole, a warm goat's cheese salad, and tiny tarts of wild strawberries. Théo was served a glass of white wine to keep me company but it was hardly touched. Mostly he drank mineral water. I admired the man's restraint and the way he made no issue of his problems.

When the meal was over, Théo asked me if I would like to stroll round to see the house before going back home. I agreed readily as there had been little chance so far to indulge in private conversation. The cobbled roads gave me an excellent excuse to link my arm in his, which I found very nice.

We spoke seriously about the renovation. The final authorisation had only been signed a month previously, so just the first phase of the work had been completed. Théo was urging me to put both thought and money into the 'manager's flat'. It would be my home if I finally decided to live there, and I would want some luxury. Equally, if I decided to put in a supervisor I would not get the calibre of person I needed to make the project a success without the incentive of comfortable personal quarters.

This line of reasoning made sense, and I was just going to go into further details when the roar of revved motorbikes drowned our conversation. Two enormous machines filled the narrow street and effectively pinned us into a corner. The leather suited, space visored riders and pillion passengers dismounted and swaggered towards us in silence. I am not into macho stoicism. I screamed at the very top of my lungs, "Au secours! Voleurs! Voleurs!" It seemed to make them pause.

The lead biker muttered, "Scrag the woman!" Théo shoved me behind him against the rough wall. I shrilled again and thrust my hand into my bag. I thanked God that the first thing my fingers clutched was my rape alarm, which I activated to add to the general mayhem. Throwing aside the device, which was still giving out its ear splitting whistle, I searched in my bag once more. My fingers connected with the steel pen that had been a gift from some long forgotten business contact. I raised it, knife-like, in my clenched fist. The street light glinting on the metal caused at least one of the bikers to back up a step. I screamed with all the power at my disposal once again. Lights were going on in the neighbouring houses, some doors were being opened, which made the bikers retreat to their machines and roar off into the night.

The Gendarmes joined us, but their help was too little, far too late. Their cars' flashing blue lights caused further disturbance, along with their blaring sirens. Our story was greeted with extreme scepticism. We were 'requested' to accompany the officers to headquarters. We were breathalysed: Théo's level was okay, of course, but my count was doubtful – on the other hand, I had been on foot and had no intention of driving a car so it didn't matter. We were questioned for the third time before being finally allowed to go, with the instruction not to cause any further breaches of the peace. Us! I was absolutely livid. I cursed, swore and called down the wrath of heaven on villains and police equally.

It was only when we returned to the quiet shadow of my chalet that I realised the peril we had been in and anger gave way to bitter tears. I trembled so much I could hardly stand. Théo held me in his massive arms.

"You have been very brave, my dear. You have nothing to reproach yourself with. You saved us both by your presence of mind. Sleep in peace now and we will meet again in the morning."

I let myself out of the car and hurried into the chalet, but it was a very long time before I could sink into welcome oblivion.

2

As the days passed, the memory of that night gradually became less vivid. I explored the area, making detailed notes on trips and visits for my prospective guests. I raided the library, and talked with the staff at the local museum, who gave me the names of a few experts who lived in the area who might help with my research. What I wanted to offer was not just the major attractions covered in all the published guidebooks, but some extras that would give an edge to Calamier tours. I needed local history, anecdotes, stories, legends; things that put flesh on the dry bones of monarchs, dates and political legislation.

I was just returning from a day trip to the First World War sites of Vimy Ridge and the huge French Military cemetery at Notre Dame de Lorette. It was riveting but utterly heart-rending history in the raw. I was particularly glad to see Théo's battered van standing outside his mother's house. I quickly searched my mind for an excuse to visit Madame Colbert.

No excuse was needed, for as soon as I pulled up Théo came bounding out of his mother's back door and crossed to my car. He was so obviously excited that I wondered what could have possibly happened.

"Where have you been? Where have you been? I've been waiting for you for hours."

I took his two large hands into my own.

"I am here now, calm down and tell me what has been going on."

I led him up to the chalet and poured a tumbler of fruit juice for Théo and a glass of wine for myself.

"Mademoiselle, as you know I have been working on the spot of dry rot in the cellar. The cement lining the floor was rotten and crumbling. I had been scraping away all the broken rendering and guess what I found?"

"I have absolutely no idea!" I was beginning to catch some of Théo's urgency. "Just tell me!"

"A trap door."

This did not seem very exciting. "And…" I encouraged.

"I lifted it and there was a second cellar underneath. It was completely empty, unless you count dirt and cobwebs, but when I examined that floor it was flagged. One of the flags held the remains of an iron ring – there is yet another level even further down!"

"Well, what did you find?"

"Nothing, yet, I have been waiting for you to come home so we could explore together. It is your house, after all."

Bless the man. I doubted I could have been so restrained. Caught up in treasure hunters' fever I raced up the stairs to my bedroom and changed into sweatshirt and old jeans. I also wound a cotton scarf round my head. I am not afraid of either dirt or spiders, but I would rather not have them either of them in my hair if I could help it.

As I changed I thought about Théo's discoveries. The series of chambers one on top of the other was remarkable but not extraordinary. Montreuil-sur-Mer is built on the summit of a hill. I supposed the inhabitants of the town must have excavated over the years trying to build more and more secure hiding places for their valuables as the armies of Europe fought over the strategic ground. Would there be anything to find in this long forgotten hidey-hole? We scrambled into the van and set off for town.

"When do you think the basement you found was created?" I asked.

"It must have been before 1800," Théo replied. "The earliest plans for the house date from the time of Napoleon. There is no mention of either of the lower cellars in the deeds. It could be hundreds of years old – the

Good Lord alone knows when Montreuil was first inhabited."

I could not resist a little showing off. "I have learned during my talks with the local historians that there are two distinct theories about the origins of the town." I pontificated. "The most widely accepted is that the original inhabitants occupied the lowlands to the west around the time of Clovis."

"And when would that be, Madame la Professeur?"

I ignored the sarcasm

"Around 500CE," I had been doing my homework. "The abbey of St. Saulve was founded on the hill about 200 years later, followed in 900CE by the first citadel. There is a second theory however, mostly held by the local unqualified historians and scorned by the academics who have prized theses to protect."

"Come on then, what is that?" Théo really sounded interested.

"The people from the region think that Montreuil was the original town from pre-history. It spilled over into the western valley in a time of both prosperity and low water tables, then retreated back up the hill after a few hundred years after floods and demographic change."

"So do you think we will find cave paintings in your sub-basement?"

Théo could be a pain. I decided to play straight man to his comedian.

"Not a chance. The best we can hope for is some artefacts from the sixteenth century when the castle was constructed in its present form."

"You know so much in so short a time." Théo sounded impressed. "I was born here and I have never heard half of this. What made you do all this research?"

"I have not really studied the history of the area in depth." I demurred. "I still need to do quite a bit of reading before I start my tours. It would be disastrous to be caught out by my more knowledgeable clients any more than I can help."

Perhaps the sub-cellar could contain proof one way or another of the town's origins. Would living on top of such archaeology be an asset to my business? Now here was a thought: would some academic foundation be prepared to buy my property at an inflated price?

"Was there any evidence of previous excavations when you located the sub-cellar?" I asked.

"No, nothing, it looked as if it had not been touched since the house was built," Théo sighed and looked a bit put out.

"This is all speculation and academic wrangling," I protested. "As far as I can tell nothing has been actually proven one way or another. I came across these facts because M. Errard at the bookshop can't stop talking not because I am an accredited historian. I can assure you I know almost nothing about Livingston where I was born. I presume it had a past before the Industrial Revolution but I have never looked into it." I caught a faint glimmer of a smile under the beard. I reckoned that in the not too distant future I would learn more about Livingston than I really wanted to find out.

"Who have you told about this?" I asked to change the subject.

"I have told my mother. I did not ask her to keep it a secret, but neither is my mother addicted to gossip," Théo answered stiffly.

"I never thought for a moment that Madam Colbert was a gabby lady," I assured him quickly. "I was just checking who might know of this find besides ourselves."

There was rather a long silence.

"Paul from the timber yard was delivering some new joists just about the time I came across the sub-cellar. I might just have said something to him."

I didn't think that a timber yard driver would have much interest in a cellar dating back to the middle ages, and was therefore confident that we might be able to keep the discovery to ourselves for a while.

I was wrong.

We left the truck in the narrow street just outside the front door. It partially blocked the road, but Théo did not seem to care. (The French really are abysmal parkers).

Théo led the way down into the bowels of the house. The top cellar had skylights looking out on the back yard. Although still in the process of renovation, it looked as if it would give me useful extra storage space. I wondered if laundry facilities could be located here. Now was not the time to ask, as I was being urged down a wooden ladder into the second cellar. Théo lit large oil storm lantern. A warm glow reflected off the walls of a room that reminded me rather of a dungeon: roofed, walled and floored with stone slabs.

The stone with the iron ring was just slightly off centre. With a heavy mallet, Théo knocked away the remains of the ring and attached several lengths of stout electrical flex. The archaeologists might have a fit, but even they would have to get into the sub-cellar one way or another.

Théo lifted the stone, festive now with its bunch of coloured wires. The ease with which he hoisted the massive slab gave me fresh admiration for his physical strength. The lantern illuminated a set of stone steps, which led down into the darkness below. Théo had a coil of rope ready.

"I think you must go down first, Mademoiselle," he said

I must have looked as apprehensive as I felt.

"I can support your weight and bring you back up if all is not well," Théo said quietly.

I looked again at the solid muscle under his tee shirt, and knew it was no idle boast.

Théo wound the rope round my waist and shoulders and tied it with a complicated knot. I prepared to go down the stairs. Very, very gently he placed a finger under my chin, raised my face to his.

"Down you go, ma petite. Rely on me, I'll not let you come to harm."

I believed him for far more than the descent of a flight of stone steps.

The stairway was in remarkable condition and quite dry. It descended for about ten metres and then led into a narrow corridor that sloped gradually downwards. The walls and floor looked as if they had been tunnelled from the solid rock. The air was cold with a slightly earthy tang, but quite fresh. I called back describing what I had found.

Théo descended the steps and I moved forwards. After about twenty meters the tunnel was blocked by a pile of stones.

"The roof must have caved in, are we in danger?" I called.

Théo did not answer at once. He crouched down, examining the debris.

"No, look, Genèvieve, these dark gritty blocks are very different to the smooth limestone of the floors and walls. Someone has brought this material down here."

Suddenly there was the most terrifying sound I have ever heard. A crash of metal on metal was followed by the unmistakable thump of stone on stone.

We raced back. Théo's tool bag had been thrown down the stairs – and the stone trap door was firmly back in place!

CHAPTER THREE

1

Théo mounted the stairs two at a time, placed his massive back under the stone and heaved until I swear I could hear his muscles tear and his bones crack. It refused to budge. Théo cursed violently and colourfully. I was too numb for language pious or profane. I stared at the slab as if I could remove it by will power alone.

Théo sat on the top step and put his head in his hands. Then suddenly he started to laugh. Not the hee-haw of hysteria but the merry sound of genuine humour. He held up a bottle. It was cheap aqua vitae, the clear spirit that French housewives use to preserve fruit. There was another in the shadowy corner of the steps.

"I can see the headlines now." Théo crowed, "'Drunken revellers in basement tragedy'."

"Stop it, Théo," I shouted. "Have you gone mad?"

"Not mad, but I'm very, very angry. I promise someone is going to pay for this." For a moment Théo seemed murderous.

"Stop it!" I shouted again. I could hear the panic in my voice.

"Let us think the matter through calmly." Théo said. "Come, sit with me and consider."

Unwilling to provoke him further, I moved onto the bottom step.

"The slab did not close of its own accord," he said slowly. "Even if I had been foolish enough to leave it unsupported, the tool bag and bottles indicate the presence of a third party. So someone has trapped us in this cellar."

"But why should anyone do such a thing?" I was whining, but couldn't help myself.

"There are two reasons why. One I can fathom; one I cannot."

I found myself getting furious, but didn't stop myself as I knew it was a better feeling than sheer blind panic.

"I think our mysterious friends secured the opening by jamming the slab with one of the joists I brought in to replace the wood with dry rot. They hope that we will be tempted into drinking the spirit – sooner rather than later, knowing my weakness. Eventually they will return, reopen the slab and 'erm, complete what they came to do," he finished lamely.

Only by now I did not need Théo to tell me the scenario. The story would be clear for the police to read. Me, battered to death and the only possible culprit a drunken Théo. I felt physically sick.

Théo regarded me kindly. "Please don't worry, Chérie. First I am not at all tempted by their crude spirits. At the very least they could have sent us to our doom with a decent cognac. Second, I have a secret weapon." He rooted in his tool bag and brought out a battered mobile phone.

"Will there be a signal this far underground?" I worried.

"It is essential for my business that I stay in contact. I bought the very finest model on the market."

I stared at the grubby item dubiously. Théo gave it a wipe on his trouser leg.

"Unfortunately it has to live in a tool bag, so it looks as if it works for its living, but it is robust, n'est-ce pas? If a signal can be received, this petit garçon will get it. Also remember we might be deep under the streets of Montreuil, but this is ground level for the inhabitants of the low town of St. Josse." Théo switched it on and showed me a not full but reasonable reception.

"Our villains are malicious but not particularly intelligent. Now, before I call for help, shall we try to discover what our friends want so very much to hide?"

I nodded a little uncertainly. We returned to the rock pile with a couple of crowbars from the tool kit. Slowly at first, then with more ease, we jimmied the rocks loose and sent them rolling down the corridor. Within half an hour we had excavated a reasonable space at the top of the pile. Théo took a powerful torch from his tool bag and shone it into the cavern. There was the secret we would have been murdered to protect.

Grey with dust and mould were four bodies: two adult sized and two the size of children. In one corner was a great iron chest, open and inverted, lying just as it had been discarded. Immediately behind the bodies was a rusted metal grill and beyond that a bricked up door.

"I think I know where we are," said Théo. "See the carving on the stone lintel over the door? Those are angels. This must lead into the crypt of the church in St. Josse. From the church we would be within a few metres of the Boulogne Road."

We scrambled through the opening and peered down at the bodies. The smaller of the two adults had been a woman. A great quantity of long hair was adhering to the scalp. There were still scraps of fabric covering the bones; it was obviously the remains of a long full dress. It would take a forensic archaeologist to be certain, but I suspected 18th Century. Still entwined in the woman's fingers were the beads of a pearl and ebony rosary. I touched nothing.

The story was as clear to read as if the unknown woman had been able to tell it to me herself.

"What happened here?" Théo whispered.

"I think our dead family were aristocrats, in fear for their lives at the height of the Revolution," I responded. "A trusted servant must have offered them a way of escape through an old medieval tunnel in the basement of the house of some friend or relative.

"Imagine them at dead of night climbing down into this cellar, carrying their most valuable possessions in that iron chest. They would have been promised a carriage and flight to safety in return for generous payment. Instead they were betrayed, robbed and murdered just at the moment that they thought they were going to escape. The aristocratic gold and jewels have gone to form the basis of the family fortunes of one of the present day notables in the town."

"It appears that their descendants are every bit as tricky and ruthless as their peasant ancestors," Commented Théo.

"I agree. And revelation of the ancient crime would do the present generation no good at all," I replied.

"No, Chérie, especially if they had a career in the legal profession such as Monsieur Le Francois."

"We don't know it was him," I protested.

"Any journalist worth their salt could ferret out who lived in this house in the 1780s, and where their descendants are now."

"It could be my mother's ancestors," I countered.

"It could, but I would bet next year's salary it's not."

We watched the pitiful remains a moment longer. Ever since the light first touched the ancient corpses I had felt neither horror nor disgust, just an overwhelming sadness.

"The men who committed this crime are way beyond the reach of temporal justice," Théo said thoughtfully. "If we cleared out everything here and then invited your friend at the bookshop to come and view the empty cellar as a historic curiosity, I believe the attacks would cease."

"Yes, I think so too," I replied.

"Some people in a position to do you a lot of good would have cause to be very grateful," he persisted. "You have two choices. One, I can ring the police and ask them to rescue us and at the same time declare the bodies we have found and then let the law take its inevitable course."

"What's the alternative?" I asked.

"I could phone a couple of mates and ask them to let us out. Then for a generous pourboire they would help us empty the corridor discreetly."

I indicated the grey bodies. "What about the..." I hesitated, "...remains?"

"Our Aristos would be no worse off wherever their bones lay. If it would help, we could even find them a spot in consecrated ground, albeit unofficially."

They would still be denied a Christian burial, I thought. I looked again at the woman. She was on her back, her arms spread wide. The bones of the smallest child were behind her. She had vainly tried to put her own body between the killers and her baby.

"Ring the police," I said.

It took an unconscionable time to convince the Gendarmes that we were not making a hoax call. However once they were mobilised, they were remarkably efficient. They retrieved us from our cellar prison, inspected our grisly find and called for reinforcements.

Théo and I sat for hours on hard, straight backed chairs in the kitchen of the Calamier house. Whilst space suited technicians removed the ancient remains, we made statement after statement until I was faint from exhaustion. They could not have been more thorough if the murders had been done that night, instead of generations ago.

Eventually they had to let us go, although I was warned not to leave the country without prior consultation. Théo picked up his tool bag and led me out to his van. As he set the bag down in the back, I heard the faint clink of bottles. I glanced at him in surprise. Théo grinned.

"My mother makes excellent preserved fruits; it seemed a shame to waste the spirit."

I was able to raise a smile. The guy was an ace.

2

For The next two days I stayed close to my chalet home, wandering round the garden, eating and sleeping little or not at all. I had chosen to go public and I did not regret it. Now I needed to decide whether to try to carry on here in France or give up and go home. The choice was not proving easy to make.

On the third day I saw the familiar van draw up outside Madame Colbert's house. Théo had come to discuss the find in the cellar. I went indoors at once. I really did not feel ready to talk to Théo. For one mad moment I actually considered hiding in the great armoire, but immediately dismissed the idea as both undignified and useless.

I was not mistaken, for after the usual five minutes for him to greet his mother, the large figure was striding up my path.

"Geneviève, ma chère!" he called, "enough of this lurking round your chalet like an anchoress practising for sainthood. I have come to take you to the forest of Crécy for a picnic."

I regarded him with absolute misery. I felt that I could not accept his kindness when I was on the point of running away. It would leave him without the work I had agreed he should do and force him to face the ire of our enemies on his own.

Théo smiled at me with sympathy.

"Chérie if you are troubled in your soul or have some important decision to make, there is no better place than amongst the old trees. They have seen generations come and go. They think their own slow thoughts. You will find calm there and, I think, comfort. Come."

Like a child, I picked up my coat and followed him down the path to the van. Within half an hour we were in the woods. Théo parked near one of the forester's roads and we set off through the trees. It was not silent; nature is very rarely completely still. The dry leaves rustled with the intermittent breezes, birds called to one another, and there was the steady pop and crackle of dead twigs beneath our feet.

Théo was right, however – there was quietude about the place that was calming to the heart. Blown leaves drifted down from high branches in a constant gentle rain. The autumn colours this year were sombre rather than fiery. Burnt browns, ochre yellows and deep rusty reds all mixed with the late season green-black of the conifers. This forest had been old when twenty thousand Frenchmen had died here under a hail of arrows from the English Archers of Edward III.

There was a sudden crashing in the undergrowth and Monsieur Le François stood before us. He was almost unrecognisable. His fussy business suit had been replaced by a hunting jacket and breeches. Dishevelled hair fell over his flushed face and his whole manner was wild and unrestrained. In his hands was a hunting rifle pointed directly at me.

"All the work my grandfather and my father put into our practice will be destroyed overnight," he raged. "I could kill you. We offered you twice as much as that mouldy old dump was worth, but you wouldn't stay in Scotland, you wouldn't sell, you wouldn't keep your stupid nose out of what doesn't concern you! Well, now you're going to be the victim of an unfortunate hunting accident."

"Xavier!" Théo took a step forward. "Don't be more of a fool than you can help." The rifle swung towards Théo.

"Think, man" Théo shouted "With all your little pals on the town council, you can prove your ancestors were miles away at the time the Aristos disappeared: in the army, fishing for cod, working in Paris – any old thing. Tell everyone the Calamiers were responsible, she doesn't care. In fact it could even help her business, attracting the crazy Rosbifs to stay in her place. You commit murder and you will find yourself without a friend. Your mates will all be covering their own cute little backsides and you will be standing naked in the breeze. The Flics aren't stupid. We've got them out of their beds twice now after being attacked. They're not going to go for any hunting accident garbage."

With each point Théo jabbed a finger towards Le François and took a cautious step forward. The man was putting himself between the rifle and me. By the all the saints, two could play at that game. Before I could move however, Théo made a prodigious flying leap forward, placing himself inside the reach of the long barrel of the gun. LeFrancois was sent stumbling backwards, sitting down heavily. The gun discharged with an almighty bang, but the bullet whistled harmlessly into the whispering trees.

Théo wrenched the weapon from the notaire's grasp and buried it barrel down into the soft mulch right up to the trigger guard.

"Think about it, you stupid man," he said viciously, "before you make a bigger fool of yourself than you actually are."

Théo grabbed my arm and practically ran me to the van. We drove back to the Chalet without speaking. I dropped silent tears onto my twisting hands. Théo was audibly grinding his teeth in anger and frustration. At the chalet we both got out of the van. He disappeared into his mother's house, leaving me with the bitter words, "Oh, God, I want a drink!"

3

Golden October gradually gave way to grey, wet November. The bodies of the ci-devant Aristos were buried after a simple but touching ceremony in the parish church. The service was conducted by a visiting dignitary, gorgeous in cope and mitre. To my surprise old St. Saulve's was full. I saw Monsieur Le François, back in his dapper glory but looking distinctly uncomfortable. He greeted me with a neutral, "Most unfortunate affair, my dear young lady." It was as much of an apology as I was going to get – but more than I had expected.

Théo and his mother were also present. After the church service he waited for me outside, twisting his cap in his hands. I walked up to him.

'I'm so sorry,' we said together.

I met his glance and smiled. "You saved my life and I have never even said 'thank you'," I said.

"I took you into danger and never even apologised," he replied.

I offered my hand, which he took as usual in both of his. "We must talk soon," I said

"Yes," he agreed.

We parted as the crowds milled about without any more being said.

I had made my mind up to return home. Routine, safe, dull boredom seemed suddenly very, very attractive. I walked away from the church and went towards the house that had caused me so much trouble and upset.

It was still in a state of semi-renovation. Perhaps I could make it a condition of sale that Théo finished the restoration work? I walked through the rooms. They were dusty, quiet, oblivious to murder, theft or coercion – just rooms waiting for the return of people to give them life and purpose.

On impulse I lit the oil lantern and went down through the layers of cellars to the dreadful corridor of death. The police had cleaned up very thoroughly. There was nothing left. Just as I turned away something sparkled in the lamp light. I went to see what it was. In the far corner near the bricked up door lay some beads. I examined them more carefully. No, not just some beads, a rosary. The ebony and pearl rosary that I had last seen firmly entwined through the bones of the Countess's fingers.

Bending down, I picked it up. Surely this must have been taken away with everything else? It was impossible that it could have been left behind. Yet there it was, smooth, cool and dust free in my hand. A light breeze fluffed at my hair and was gone.

Slowly, I climbed the stairs back to the outside world. The malaise and depression that had lain so heavily on my heart for weeks was suddenly gone. I felt younger, happier than I had since my mother had told me the dreadful news about her cancer.

I had come to a decision. Théo would finish the renovations here. There *would* be a Calamier Hostel to give young people an introduction to France. And I would be its Directrice.

Before any of that happened however, I was going to go to a half renovated old farm house in La Calotterie – and take a certain Monsieur Colbert out to dinner.

CHAPTER FOUR

1

Four weeks later I was once again prowling through the rooms and corridors of my hostel, but this time as resident. Théo had put in eighteen hour days, and called in various favours from friends and acquaintances to get the work finished. Madame Colbert had helped me with the refurbishing. Now all I needed were some guests. There had been a good response to my advertisements and approaches to schools in southern England, but realistically I could not expect much until the New Year. Still, it gave me time to make my final adjustments and work out a new advertising campaign.

It was just after nine o'clock in the evening, and. I was bored: French television held no charms, Théo was getting some well earned rest, and Monsieur Olivier would be busy with his pre-Christmas parties. I contemplated an early night with one of the new books I had recently ordered from Scotland when the telephone shrilled into my loneliness. My first thought was Théo, but the voice that answered my greeting was not his.

"Madame Sinclair?"

"Oui"

"This is the Sous-Préfecture in the rue d'Hérambault."

My heart sank as I had seen enough of the police in the last few months to last me for quite some time.

"We have a bus here full of vieux garçons. They belong to some sort of British veterans' association. They are on their way home from a regimental reunion in Arras. They say they were booked into the Hotel Vauban, but there is already a group of Royal Engineers in there."

"How can I help, monsieur? My hostel is not open yet, and even if it were I don't have the facilities to cope with a coach party."

"Madame, their driver has been touring the country for hours. There is nowhere else." The desk sergeant lowered his voice: "Some of these characters are in their eighties, and looking a bit green around the gills. If someone is not kind to them soon, there might be nasty consequences, if you take my meaning. I think I can get you some help."

What could I do? "Bring them round, I'll do my best," I said.

It was not until then that I realised how many friends I, a newcomer and a foreigner, had in Montreuil. I managed to borrow from my French neighbours' some spare beds, camp beds, blankets, pillows and linen. The veterans stumbled out of their bus, and we packed then into the rooms somehow. Certainly far beyond the numbers the fire regulations would have allowed. On this occasion I thought the ever vigilant Sapeurs-Pompiers would not give me too much trouble as they had provided most of the camp beds.

My new guests were hungry, thirsty and tired. Here was another problem. I had intended to provide bed and breakfast only in my hostel. I was not equipped for mass catering. On the other hand, I could not send the men out into the night again, even if there had been a restaurant with places available at that hour and willing to accommodate them.

As the coach was unloading I contacted Madame Couroyer from the bakery. She was desolated, she told me, but there was no fresh bread available at this time of night. The point made, she found she could provide me with a dozen of her better keeping brown country loaves and some biscuits. She arrived not only with the bread but two enormous plum tarts. No obligation she assured me, but if I wished to serve 'un bon dessert' they were at my disposal. I refrained from kissing her as she has a moustache to rival that of Lord Kitchener.

We agreed that she would send round a morning order of bread and croissants for the relevant numbers the next day. I must have been gripped by a kind of hysteria, because I found myself ordering pain au chocolat, pain aux raisins and a batch of brioches as well. In the cold light of reason, I rationalised this recklessness by telling myself that the old guys would more easily pay for their scrappy accommodation if they had a good breakfast to send them on their way.

At this point, Théo arrived. I don't know how he had heard of my problems, but he was surely welcome. We got Monsieur Binet to open up his charcuterie and loaded Théo's van with his entire complement of readymade main course dishes, which had been intended as the following day's speciality dishes.

Montreuil housewives, who had planned on serving a quick hot lunch to their hungry families courtesy of the charcuterie, were not disappointed, however. M. Binet, enterprising as ever, cooked up a huge cauldron of mashed potatoes, which he offered with some barbecued Breton sausages he had been trying out. Complete with a garnish of watercress and sliced tomatoes to tempt the appetite, it was a success fou that he has kept in his repertoire ever since.

As luck would have it, all the potential main courses I purchased were kind to old teeth. There was chicken in cream sauce, tongue in a piquant tomato sauce, and beef braised to the consistency of jam in old red wine. All served with a mountain of yellow saffron rice.

As we were stacking the containers, Mme. Binet touched my arm.

"Will you need some cheese, Madame?"

"Yes, most certainly," I replied. A wheel of brie, a ball of mimmolet, and a roll of the local goat's cheese were swiftly boxed and added to the load.

"Sale or return," Madame whispered into my ear, "but what about wine? You must offer some wine!"

That was certainly true. Madame, of course, could help me out!

"Take a few cases," she insisted.

She saw I was looking alarmed: "Sale or return," she repeated, "an arrangement between colleagues."

Even so, I thought it was a bit opportunistic when her son brought out six cases of mixed red, white and rose wines plus a case of champagne and a selection of spirits. As it turned out there were very few returns!

As we were unloading back at the hostel, the distinctive van belonging to the multistar Hotel Napoleon drew up beside us. Les Gendarmes had told all the hotels in the area of our predicament. Yet out of the eight or so establishments serving food only the snooty and isolated Hotel Napoleon had responded.

They had sent along a huge dixie of soup intended for next day's lunch. It was just what was needed. My visitors could warm up on that whilst the rest of the food was reheated in the ovens. The Director of the Hotel Napoleon has also loaned me his sous-chef Edouard to help me out. Edouard in turn had brought his girl-friend, Rosine. She was a diminutive young woman who looked about ten years less than her real age of nineteen. She had a head of bubbly dark curls that exactly matched her personality. Her happy nature easily communicated itself to our guests, even those who had minimal or no French.

I was amazed at the veterans' resilience. Once they had a base, however simple, they rapidly recovered from their exhaustion. This had been mostly due to the disappointment and depression brought about by their rejection from their expected accommodation and the subsequent abortive tour of the countryside. They started on the case of champagne – after which the fun never stopped.

After dinner they insisted on a sing song. Fortunately several people called round to ask how we were managing. They were immediately roped into the impromptu celebrations. Card schools were set up, which lasted into the early hours of the morning. I put my foot down at gambling for money. As a result, imaginary stakes of millions of Euros were being wagered with sweated seriousness before the tables finally broke up.

2

The next day we waved the old boys away to their ferry. I set about putting my hostel to rights and returning all the borrowed kit. The invoice that I put into the tour company was paid promptly and without query, and set my venture off on a decent financial footing.

It had been an adventure, but I was prepared to put it to the back of my mind and get on with everyday life. I had misjudged my soldiers. The following day the florist's van arrived with an enormous elaborate arrangement of hothouse flowers with a small card with a regimental crest and the single word, 'Merci'.

Sometime later there followed a letter in elegant copper plate script from regimental headquarters expressing formal thanks for my help. The most lasting result, however, was a regular stream of veterans' groups and associated women's organisations and youth groups from all over southern England wanting to book more orthodox visits. They sometimes made the proviso that as part of the package they would like a 'stranded travellers' dinner'.

My friend Henri Olivier, from the hotel in the upper square, happily took over the catering arrangements. The venture I had started almost as a whim had taken its first step towards success.

One thing the unexpected invasion had taught me was that I could not cope alone. Some sort of assistant would to be necessary if I was to have any time to myself.

I was pleased when a few days later Rosine came to see me. She was dressed in a smart suit and had tamed her curls into a severe style that made her look older but not as much fun.

I invited her into the parlour and offered her a cup of coffee, which she declined.

"Madame," she began. "I very much enjoyed working here the night les vieux garçons arrived so unexpectedly. I noticed then that you had no assistant. Such a person would, I think, be very useful to you in the running of this establishment."

I formally agreed that this was so.

"I find myself at liberty at the moment, and perhaps could be persuaded to join you if we could agree terms."

Rosine's face was creased with concentration as she struggled to remember the lines she had learned with such diligence. Whilst I admired the effort she was making I preferred the laughing, chattering girl I had met some nights before.

"How is it that you find yourself 'at liberty' so near Christmas?" I asked.

"I knew you were going to ask that," Rosine said in a far more natural voice.

"Any employer would," I replied. "So what's the answer?"

"I've known Edouard all my life," was the unexpected reply. "There has never been anyone else for me. When he secures a decent position we're going to get engaged. I've tried shop work, a job at the sugar factory, I even did a stint in an insurance office but I did not like that too much. Sooner or later one of the types in charge tries to change my job description. Well, I'm not that sort of girl! So I move on. One day Edouard and I are going to have our own hotel – Michelin stars, rosettes in all the guides, the lot. I thought it might be good to get some experience in a little hotel like yours, and you being a single lady, I thought there would be no funny business." She gave me a quick grin.

I assured her there would be no trouble. We agreed salary and hours, and I said she could start in January as I was not going to open officially until after the New Year Celebrations. We shook hands, and I found myself looking forward to working with Rosine.

On Christmas Eve I went round to Madame Colbert's house. I had bought Madame a cashmere jumper and Théo an Aran sweater from a little outlet shop I knew from when I lived in Scotland.

"Christmas has lost its magic," Madame Colbert sighed as we enjoyed a glass of Pinot de Charente in front of the blazing fire in her lounge. She had carefully placed my gaily wrapped parcels under her tree then persuaded me to stay for a drop of festive cheer.

"All the bustle of effort and burden of expense means that no one really enjoys Christmas any more." She was quiet for a moment and I wondered if she was remembering the Christmases of her youth.

"Yet in the middle of this year's rush I thought of something," Madame Colbert continued. "I don't know if you know, my dear, but the Parish Committee of old St. Saulve runs a party on Christmas Eve. Plans and preparations are made months in advance. They're an old fashioned lot and the celebrations don't change much from one year to the next.

"The Committee hires the main hall of the Mairie, and a couple of days before the event the decorating team sets about transforming the place. Every year Monsieur Delcroix, President of the Council, declares, 'it rivals the Ritz in Paris!' Better in fact, for all our decorations are natural and lend their own special fragrance'. Well that's as may be, he doesn't have to sweep up pine needles for six months afterwards!

"Everyone in the town contributes towards the buffet. Don't worry, Geneviève, they'll be asking you next year, count on it. The grand Hotel Napoleon presents a huge boudin de Noël Anglais, the Butchers' Guild send a mountain of black and white puddings, and all the ladies donate their own specialities. I have to say that every year there are embarrassing amounts of food left over. Monsieur Delcroix runs the games and everyone is expected to join in. There are simple games like musical chairs for the children and more complicated ones involving balloons in unlikely places for the adults. The highlight of the evening, however, is the Grandmothers' cookery quiz. I tell you it's played with an intensity not seen outside the deep gaming tables at Le Touquet. There is stronger partisan support for the contestants than there is at a five nations' Rugby match.

"A few years ago things didn't go quite according to plan. Just before 10:00pm a bunch of bikers in black leather with their spiky haired girlfriends gatecrashed the party. Monsieur Delcroix was outraged, as you can imagine. He went striding over to tell them to leave, in no uncertain terms. Madame Binet from the Charcuterie was all for sending for the gendarmes. The intruders, however found they had a rather unexpected champion – old Mlle. Vernay. She's as thin as a stick and has dressed in nothing but black since the death of her parents thirty years ago, and hovers on the edge of most public gatherings, never saying very much to anyone.

"Suddenly, she hobbles up to Monsieur Delcroix, shakes her stick at him, and says, 'Shame on you Monsieur Le President! Don't you know that the Boite de Nuit has been closed? Their cellars were flooded last night. Everywhere else has been booked up for months. Read your Sainte Histoire before you tell them there is no room for them here.'

"Well, old man Delcroix gave her a black look, but had to let the bikers in. He gave them strict instructions to behave themselves. Well, they fell on the food as if they had not eaten for a week. Still, there was more than enough – even for Heavy Metal appetites!

"So, radiating disapproval, Monsieur marches off to introduce the quiz. A formidable number of grannies enter every year, but a lot of them are past it. The rules say that every lady has to be accompanied by a youngster – they're needed to relay questions into failing hearing aids or act as scribes for arthritic fingers.

"Would you believe it? One of the bikers separated himself from his turkey leg long enough to ask the thin old biddy who had stood up for them why she was not going to play. 'Je suis celibataire,' Mlle. Vernay said. 'I have no family to act as my aid.' The lout who's wearing low slung jeans and an extremely rude tee shirt says, 'I'll support you Grand'Mere, if you'll have me.'

"We all thought that Madeleine Vernay would have a fit, but the old lady turns to the boy, gives him a look and says, 'Oui my son, I'll have you, but not in that tee shirt.' So there's a bit of a kerfuffle, and within a few seconds there he is, in a blameless white but noticeably tight shirt.

'Bien,' she said, and they both went forth to do battle.

"As the contestants were introduced, the various families shouted their support. You can't imagine the noise created by the bikers for old lady Vernay, and she's lapping it up.

"The first questions sorted out the ladies that were no longer very 'with-it', and they were duly returned to the bosoms of their families. Only three women remained: Mme. Le François, you know - the mother of your 'friend' the Notaire; Veuve Delcroix, M. Charles' respected parent; and Mlle. Vernay. Every answer was precise and correct from each of the contestants. Honours and marks being equal, a tie breaker question was proposed. It was: 'What is the essential requirement in fish soup?' "

"Mme. and La Verve debated at length about the inclusion of crab, or the need for Mediterranean fish such as Rascasse. But Mlle. Vernay just laid her fingers on the wrist of her champion. When the tumult was at its height, he declared in a voice used to carrying over wind and engine noise. 'The fish must be fresh!'

"Well, the bikers screamed their approval at the tops of their voices. The judges had no choice: they reluctantly declared Mlle. Vernay the winner. Now not a lot of people know this, but I was standing right behind the pair of them after it was all over. Madeleine put her hand on the boy's arm and said, 'Thank you, my son. This is the first time I have ever been able to enter, having no kin to support me.'

"The boy swaggers, 'that's no big deal, missus – I ain't got any relatives either.' 'It's a shame when a young man has no family to impress his young lady,' said Mademoiselle, to which the boy says, not giving an inch, 'Neither is there anyone to disapprove of his bird!'

"Mlle. Vernay said, 'I live at 5 rue de Dieppe. I would be perfectly happy to disapprove of any young woman you cared to bring to see me – unless it happened to be the right one,' she said. Then the two of them stand there, holding hands. Well, the party starts up again, and he goes dancing off. But at a quarter to twelve, M. Le Cure leads the congregation across the road to celebrate the first Mass of Christmas, and bless me, but don't the bikers go too? Whilst everyone was in church, the weather changed from a hard dry frost to a whirling white snowstorm, and when the folk came out though the great oak doors all the roads and pavements were covered with a fresh clean layer of snow. And here's the thing," Madame Colbert laughed, "for the first time in *sixty years* Mlle. Vernay left the Christmas party on the arm of a young man!"

As I made my way home, smiling at the story, I wondered if what she had told me was true. If it wasn't, it should have been.

CHAPTER FIVE

1

The following months went by quietly enough. I settled to my new life, ceasing to fret during the weeks when my rooms were empty or the times I had to refuse custom because they were full.

It was about the middle of May when I found myself pacing the floor of my private sitting room in increasing agitation. Miss Horsfall should have returned hours ago. Of all my guests, no one was more regular in their habits or more considerate for her host.

My concern had been engaged when she had not returned by seven in the evening. When eight o'clock had come and gone I tried to convince myself that the simple mistiming of a visit had caused the delay. Nevertheless, I called my colleague Henri Olivier at the hotel where my guest regularly ate her evening meal to see if my missing visitor had gone straight to the restaurant.

"No, ma chère, she is not here. She had a reservation for 7:30, but so far no sign of her. This is most strange; she is usually punctual to the minute."

I thanked him, and rang every other restaurant in town to see if anyone matching her description – a tall, thin, English woman in her sixties, with white hair done up in an old-fashioned braid – had called in that night. Miss Horsfall spoke good grammatical French but had a distinct accent.

I considered contacting the police, but held off from doing so as I knew they would not be amused if I called to say a sane and mature guest was missing – especially as it was only ten o'clock at night. Yet some inner demon was telling that all was not well.

Théo sprawled in an armchair by the fireplace. He watched me stride about with increasing concern.

"Call the police, my friend," he advised. "It is better that les flics grumble at you for disturbing their rest than they begin to wonder afterwards why you did not call them sooner."

Relieved to at last be doing something, I dialled the number of the Sous-Préfecture. It was some time before I could get anyone to actually take me seriously, but when I asked for the names and badge numbers of the officers who were passing me from one to another, the night shift became a little more professional.

They still thought I was panicking unnecessarily, but they promised to send an officer round in the morning if my missing guest did not show up for her breakfast.

"Who is this woman, chérie?" Théo asked. "And why are you so concerned?"

"Edna Horsfall was one of the first people to come to the hostel. She brought a select group of sixth formers from the girls' school at which she is deputy headmistress. They were cultured, sensible girls doing either European history or French 'A' Levels. We must have done something right, because within weeks she returned with a group from her Town's Women's Guild. They were not so serious, and had very little French, but they seemed to manage to have a good time."

"Yes, I think I remember that party – very jolly." Théo smiled into his beard.

"I had a phone call a couple of weeks ago asking if I would take her as a private client. Well, it's the English half-term and bookings are a bit thin, so I said yes. The visit has been quite a success until tonight."

"What has she been doing with herself?" Théo asked.

"I don't exactly pry into my guests business," I bridled.

"Of course, chérie, but you must have some idea," Théo coaxed.

"She is a dedicated walker that I do know. She also said something about Joan of Arc. I think she is preparing some sort of talk for her Guild. Apart from that, I don't know very much about her at all."

That is where we had to leave it. I didn't sleep very well that night and counted the minutes until I could phone the police again. As agreed, they sent an officer round to take a statement and search the potential victim's room.

There was a distinct change of atmosphere when a drawer in the dressing table was found to contain a passport, ferry ticket, sundry other essential documents, plus more than enough Euros to cover both hotel and restaurant charges. This was obviously not the usual 'hotel skipper'.

An examination of the luggage revealed a small amount of good quality clothing. Items for laundry were stored in a separate plastic bag. There were all the usual accessories of a person spending a week away from home, but nothing out of the ordinary.

I was told that I was obliged to keep the room available for the week reserved. After that, if Miss Horsfall had not returned, I could empty her room but should keep her effects in safe storage.

"The authorities simply seem to be going through the motions rather than taking the disappearance seriously," I railed to Théo.

There was slightly more interest when the burned out remains of a Vauxhall Astra were found in one of the more dubious suburbs of Lille. The car was eventually confirmed as that belonging to Miss Horsfall.

It was illogical for me to feel so guilty, but that was how I did feel. No friend or relative from England had enquired about the missing woman. The hotel bill had eventually been settled, and the personal possessions claimed by the representative of a firm of solicitors. It offended my sense of honour that after a lifetime of service no one seemed to care about the missing woman.

After a few days of snapping at everybody and pacing my living room floor in frustration, Théo said, "Chérie, if you are so concerned, stop wearing out your new carpet, and come and sit down. I will make us both coffee, pour you a large glass of Calva, and we will seriously consider how to unravel this mystery."

I gave Théo a black look, which he totally ignored. There was no sign of either sarcasm or mockery in his attitude. I sighed. How often I underestimated this great bear of a man, with his piratical beard, long curly dark hair, and the softest, most gentle eyes in the world.

I perched uneasily on the edge of one of the chairs. He resettled himself in the arm chair and began to enumerate all those questions that the police should have asked but had signally failed to do.

"Did Mademoiselle Horsfall give you any indication whatsoever either at breakfast or the night before of what she planned for the day she disappeared?" Théo put up one sausage-like finger.

I swirled the high octane spirit in my glass and watched the way the fluid teared on the smooth surface, before slowly running back into the main body of the liquid. My thoughts went back to the last time I had seen Edna Horsfall.

"She had dinner at the hotel. I saw her come in just after ten. She said she eaten a very pleasant meal."

Théo held up his hand. "Chérie, if you can, please try to remember her exact words."

I scowled at him and then nodded, recognising the sense of the suggestion. After a few seconds of further thought, the words of that final conversation came quite easily.

"She greeted me and then said, 'Dear Monsieur Henri excelled himself tonight. I am sure he gets better and better, although I do wish he would not serve chips with every main course. They are more than I can cope with these days, yet young Valerie his charming assistant is so concerned when I send them away uneaten. Do you know, when I was a student, we used to be tantalised by descriptions of French vegetable dishes. Alas, they must be the province of private homes, because most restaurants I can afford seem to rely on the inevitable plate of frites. Well, good night my dear. I would like breakfast about eight o'clock tomorrow morning as I have rather a full day planned.' Then she wished me goodnight again and went directly to her room."

"Next morning," I continued, "she came down stairs in a jumper, walking britches and stockings but with the ordinary soft shoes she would drive in. She kept her walking boots in her car out of respect for the hostel."

"Did you serve breakfast yourself, or did Rosine do it that morning?"

"It was Rosine."

"Then tomorrow let us see if Rosine can give us any further clues."

2

Rosine showed no surprise when I cornered her next morning with questions about a casual conversation with one of our guests that had taken place weeks ago. The smooth forehead wrinkled in concentration. She walked into the breakfast room and placed herself at the table nearest the window. A heavy swag of lace curtain gave at least the appearance of privacy from passers-by in the street.

"Mademoiselle sat here," she declared. "I asked her if she was going walking as she had on the costume des randonnée. She replied that she was, but she was also going to have lunch by the sea."

"Did you see which map she was studying?" I asked, eagerly.

"Oui Madame, it was the blue one showing the great forest of Crécy."

A trip to the Maison de la Presse brought the unwelcome knowledge that at least four of the local maps showed parts of Crécy woods. We bought all of them, and took then back to the hostel. Théo spread them out on the floor and I badgered Rosine into tears, but she could not remember which one she had seen at the breakfast table.

"Chérie," said Théo, "this is not getting us anywhere. Let us look at the problem from another angle. Your guest wanted lunch by the sea. Let us work out where are the most logical spots. We looked at the map again. There were only two towns within reasonable driving distance for someone who wanted to walk in the woods and eat at the seaside – Le Crotoy and St. Valery-sur-Somme."

"Voila! Tomorrow let us go to the seaside and try to find someone who remembers your vielle fille."

"Théo!"

The big man made a mock moue of repentance at his disrespectful phrase. Théo's house restoration business had grown so rapidly over the last few months that he had employed a couple of labourers, which meant that he could take the occasional day off, although he rarely did so. I had staying in the hostel a small party of war veterans who, whilst completely harmless, much preferred to be attended by Rosine and her very pretty younger sister, the shy Marie-Liesse, than myself, so I would not be missed for a short spell... Besides, the old men loved vying with one another in paying the pair extravagant compliments in very passable French, and then pretending to see the young women blush. I suppose they reminded the old gents of the girls they had flirted with more than sixty years ago.

3

The next day was grey and cold. Théo called for me in his van and we headed south. As we turned from the main N1 towards the coast, we were met by a spindrift of sea fret. It smeared the windscreen as the wipers tried to waft it away. We were left in a misty world that made the lagoons and marshes on either side of the road look slightly sinister.

We came to a T junction where we had to choose left or right. There was no traffic on the road, and we had time enough to pause and toss a coin. Heads, left for St Valery; tails right for Le Crotoy. Heads won out, so we turned left, and began following the route of the tourist steam railway.

Soon, we crossed the ornate bridge over the Somme on the outskirts of St. Valery and parked in the large car park by the marina. From there we walked into the centre of town. It was the start of the new tourist season, so the restaurants looked fresh, and appetising smells drifted through the streets.

No one from the two fat, motherly ladies at the Auberge des Amis to the stringy waiters in dinner suits at the Hotel Henri IV, had any recollection of a white-haired English woman in walking clothes.

Dispirited and disappointed, I could not face lunch. We walked in silence along the deserted promenade, looking out at the grey sands of the estuary until we were thoroughly cold and depressed. Finally, Théo tucked my arm into his own and propelled us both back into town and the brightly lit welcome warmth of a Salon de Thé. There he ordered two mugs of hot chocolat viennois and two sugar pancakes. The chocolate came topped with a mound of whipped cream. The comforting food and pleasant atmosphere soon put new heart into us both. Théo called for a second round, and we started to plan our next day's excursion with renewed energy.

The following morning brought a marked rise in temperature and a few fitful rays of barely warm sunshine. We parked in Le Crotoy, overlooking the sea opposite the prestigious restaurant of Chez Mado. We spent a few minutes watching the leaden waters of the bay of the Somme occasionally turn to silver as the sun showed through the clouds.

Our enquiries met with no more success here than they had in St. Valery. Heartsick, we eventually we returned to the van.

"Come now, Chérie, as we are here, let's treat ourselves to a good lunch," urged Théo, indicating Chez Mado.

Without much enthusiasm I allowed myself to be led through the hallowed portals of the famous restaurant. Inside, despite enough game trophies on the wall to stock a minor Scottish castle, the atmosphere was welcoming and friendly, even for two windswept and slightly scruffy travellers such as ourselves.

A Kir Royal for me, Suze for Théo, and anchovy topped warm flaky pastries, soon raised our spirits. Almost by reflex, Théo asked the waiter who took our order if he had seen the missing woman.

The waiter thought for a minute or two. "Yes, a woman such as you describe was in here a few weeks ago. She had chosen a seat at a table for four, right here near the window overlooking the sea. There was a bit of a fuss when we had to ask her to move to a smaller table because she was on her own."

The young man was startled when his previously well-behaved guests, hooted with laughter, clapping one another on the shoulder and changed their wine order from a modest Gros Plant to a bottle of champagne.

Over the expertly cooked meal, we tried to work out our next step. In the end, we decided to drive to the forest of Crécy by the most direct route. It led us straight to one of the parking areas provided by the Forestry Commission.

It was as good a starting place as any. We parked the van in the first and most convenient spot. Under one of the great trees at the edge of the car park was a notice board with a map showing the recommended walks. We went to examine it. Of course I got out of the van on the side that would have been that of the driver in a British vehicle. As I swung my legs out to avoid a puddle, I caught sight of a brightly coloured scrap of paper in the mud.

I stooped to retrieve it, and found that it was the wrapper from a variety of British sweet, of which Miss Horsfall had been particularly fond: a sprinkling of tiny screwed up toffee wrappers had been the old lady's only weakness, and as such the more endearing. Wordlessly I showed my find to Théo, whose dark visage looked even blacker than ever.

"Do not build too much on this chérie; it could have been left by anyone," he cautioned.

Locking the van, we followed the forestry walk that starts from that particular car park. Following the round yellow paint splashes that designated the official pathway, we made our way into the depths of the forest. From the well worn track we peered into the mysterious woodland maze created by foresters and the natural denizens of the timberland.

Clouds had closed in once more and the light was not good. A person – okay, I'll say what was on my mind, a *body* – could be hidden anywhere in there and an army of searchers would not find them. We came to a sign indicating the way to one of the great trees that are the showpieces of the forest. It was called 'Le Seigneur, a massive oak some distance from the path we were on. We strolled towards it. It was of truly heroic proportions in a forest of huge trees. Théo rested his hand on the rough bark.

"Let's look at the map," he said. "I remember from the plan in the car park that there is a forest pool near here."

I followed his thinking. The forest has a lot of visitors, most of whom stick to the forester's paths. If Miss Horsfall had taken ill suddenly, or even had an accident of some sort, she would have been found by now. That left the possibility of foul play. She was not a big woman, but neither was she as light as a child. If someone *had* murdered her, they would not have wanted to carry her body too far.

"Let's go and look," I replied.

The pool was a deep depression overhung with the solemn weeping branches of the trees. Dark rhododendrons clustered thickly to one side. On the other, bramble tendrils stretched out to trip the unwary, and dead branches spread their skeletal fingers to bar the way.

Nevertheless, there were narrow paths to the water made by the forest creatures. Théo knelt by the edge of the stagnant pond, and reached for a suitable piece of wood, with which he started to stir the murky depths. The water swirled and eddied. I watched in fascination as the peaty water almost seemed to take on a life of its own. Then, amidst a torrent of silver bubbles, a shrouded figure slowly rose to the surface of the aphotic water. Argent hair streamed like weeds from enveloping folds of dark cloth that wound a body like a shroud. I screamed in horror.

We had found our missing guest.

CHAPTER SIX

1

Théo called the authorities on his mobile phone then stood vigil by the pool. I went back to the car, ostensibly to meet the police and direct them to the crime scene but also to recover some composure.

Recovery of the body and subsequent interrogation took hours, but eventually we were dismissed. There was a warning, however, that we should be prepared to make ourselves available for further questioning.

Two evenings later, Théo was again filling my private sitting room in the old house, a huge mug of coffee almost eclipsed by his massive hands. The door bell sounded. The hostel was empty, as the veterans were out at an official reception which would probably last until the early hours of the morning. I expected no one else.

Théo rose and indicated that he would see what the visitor wanted. I was glad to rely on his strength, but curiosity impelled me to follow him down to the front door. The man who stood in the doorway had authority stamped on him like a brand. He was tall, thin to the point of emaciation, with pale skin that looked sickly in the street light. The over-long black hair swept back from his face emphasised his sharp, slightly crooked nose. It was the Inspecteur de Police who had questioned us in the forest. This time he introduced himself by name, M. Delavoie. I somehow got the impression that he and Théo already knew one another.

"You are a hard man to track down, Monsieur Colbert. Your mobile phone is switched off; your staff inform me of your movements, but each time I try to find you it seems that either you have not arrived or have just left wherever you were supposed to be. Fortunately for us, your mother was able to indicate where you might be found tonight."

Théo did not look very perturbed at this litany.

"I am always at the disposal of our admirable Policiers. If you had left a message, I would certainly have contacted you." Théo turned to me. "May I invite him in Chérie?" he asked.

"By all means, bring Monsieur Delavoie upstairs," I said hurriedly.

When we reached my private apartment I indicated I would go into my bedroom to leave the men alone. Théo held out a hand to stop me.

"This is your home, Chérie. It would be a gross impertinence to use it as my private offices. Besides, I would prefer it if you stayed and heard whatever Monsieur le Inspecteur has to say to me."

The detective looked uncomfortable. "Are you sure you wish Mademoiselle Sinclair to be present, M. Colbert?"

"Quite sure, Monsieur," was the stolid reply.

The detective took out his notebook. "The body in the forest was indeed the missing guest from this establishment, one Edna May Horsfall," he began. "She was identified from dental records sent from England. Her niece and nephew refused to travel to France." There was disapproval in every line of the officer's stringy body. "The cause of death was gunshot wounds. The first shot fired from a distance – it could be interpreted that it was a chance shot by a careless hunter hit the woman. This was followed by a double barrelled shot at close range. The accident was then covered up with murder."

"By Our Lady!" exploded Théo. "The woman was on a tourist path, who on earth would be using a shotgun there?"

"You know where she was walking for certain, do you?" the detective said quite pleasantly.

"As near as damn it," Théo responded vehemently. There were a few moments of silence. "What do you want? Why are you telling me this?"

"The woman was wrapped in an English jacket – a Barbour. The coat was almost new at the time of immersion, our technicians inform us. The admirable Mademoiselle Sinclair is English."

"Scottish," I interrupted, but they both ignored me.

"You, Monsieur Colbert, have just celebrated your birthday. The jacket was size extra extra large." He looked at Théo. "You are size...?"

"Extra extra large, as you know."

"Where were you on the afternoon Miss Horsfall died?"

I tried to interrupt, to say that I had bought Théo a watch for his birthday gift, but both men waved me to silence. I realised I could not prove that I did not buy a coat – it's impossible to prove a negative.

Théo reached into his coat and brought out the small diary he used as an appointment's calendar. He flicked through the month of May.

"I had an arrangement to see Monsieur Khane in Arras." Théo thought for a moment. The detective seemed willing to give him all the time in the world. I had the most awful premonition. "M. Khane cancelled at the last moment," continued Théo. "I decided to go home and complete some paperwork." He brightened. "My neighbour Mme. Teillier was just leaving to go shopping in Montreuil. I remember greeting her and her little girl, Rita, as I passed them. Mme. Teillier might very well remember."

"The lady remembers very well," the detective smirked. "I might suggest a very different scenario," he said, his voice suddenly vicious.

"You had no intention of doing any so-called paperwork. You decided to give yourself a holiday. You took your gun, drove into the forest of Crécy, and went banging away at anything that moved. You shot, perhaps first by accident but then in cold blood, the guest of your lover, Mademoiselle Sinclair. When even your rotten conscience could take no more, you helped find her body. And the reason why you were able to so conveniently find her is because you are the one who put her in there in the first place!"

Théo seemed to remain unmoved. After a few moments of silence he asked mildly: "Do you wish to charge me with this crime?"

The detective did not reply directly. He picked up his coat and prepared to leave. Just before he opened the door he said, with mockery clear in his voice, "Don't leave the country, Théophile."

Théo stood motionless with his eyes closed until we both heard the bang of the front door and the sound of heavy footsteps fade into the silence of the night. Théo drove his great fist again and again into the plaster of the wall until the blood ran freely from the broken skin of his knuckles. I ran and placed myself between Théo and the wall.

"No, no more!"

His arm was drawn back for another tearing blow, but when he perceived my presence all the fight went out of him. As the giant slab of a man collapsed onto his knees and sobbed, I gathered his head onto my breast and comforted him as he let out his frustration and rage. Slowly the sobs ceased as I stroked his hair, gently.

Finally he said, "I am so sorry you have become involved in this, Chérie, and that you have been subject to such rudeness."

Rudeness? The detective had been unpleasant, but rude? I realised that he must have meant the crack about my being Théo's lover. It had hardly registered, let alone hurt.

"You, me and Le Bon Dieu know the truth. No one else matters."

"Chérie, I hate to ask, but I need your help," Théo muttered.

"Anything, I will do anything at all," I cried with fervour.

"Les Flics have got me in the frame for this killing. They are not going to look any further than me. If I am to clear my name we must find the wretch who did it."

"My most excellent friend, we will find him and he will go to the guillotine," I promised.

Théo gave a very ragged sigh, raised his head and took my hand in his. He kissed each one of my fingers very gently. I felt a rush of warm feelings for the man, but this was not the time to think about romance.

"Chérie, France abolished the death penalty in 1981, and the last man to face the guillotine did so sometime in the late seventies."

We reseated ourselves by the fire. "What do we know that will help us in our search?" I queried, all practicality.

"The man is at least as big as me if he takes an extra extra large jacket," Théo said, counting the points on his thick fingers.

"He has some connection with the UK, because of the Barbour coat. They are not readily available here in France," I added with enthusiasm. His second finger joined the first.

"He fancies himself a sportsman, but he is not very good, or at least ill disciplined. No one with any sense would go loosing off shots in the public parts of the forest." Théo thought for a moment. "The best person to help us is Monsieur David in St. Riquier. He owns one of the most popular sports shops in the region. He is also the President of the League of Sporting Clubs this year. He knows everyone, and not much in the hunting world gets past him. I would like you to come with me."

"We will go together or go in convoy, because you are not going without me," I smiled into Théo's worried face.

"When this is all over, Chérie, we will have a long talk. But now I have to go. My mother will be concerned after the visit from the detective. I should put her in the picture myself before gossip spreads the word."

I must have looked sceptical, because Théo continued seriously: "I would not put it past our petit copain in the Police Department to deliberately leak the rumour himself, to put pressure on me to confess. The trouble with rumour is it easier to spread than contradict. A shadow of this sort could ruin my business, yours too, Chérie – by association if nothing else."

I could not say anything to this; it was all too obviously true. I took his hand for a moment and then he let himself out into the dark street.

I did not sleep well that night. My dreams were full of the sombre shadows of trees, behind which even darker images menaced.

2

I don't think the next day ever did dawn properly. There was just a change of shade from dark grey to lighter grey. The wind howled outside the window and the rain lashed down relentlessly.

We travelled through the sodden countryside until we came to the signs for St. Riquier, driving down the narrow but handsome main street of the old town to park in the abbey square. We looked towards the beautiful flamboyant Gothic church of cathedral proportions. It was light and elegant against the leaden sky. The former monastery was now a prestigious local museum. Scholarship and worship made a poignant counterpoint to our present grim task of hunting a murderer.

The sports' shop was only a few streets away, but we were both dripping water by the time we reached it. I was surprised by it: I had expected at least a double fronted emporium, but the shop seemed to be the converted front room of an ordinary town house.

M. David himself was a little gnome of a man, perched on a stool amongst his gun racks and cabinets. Every inch of wall space that was not taken up with merchandise was covered with posters advertising sporting events and ball-trap competitions. As we entered, the old man got up and formally shook hands with both Théo and me.

"I must tell you, M. Colbert, that I was interviewed by the police immediately after the body of that unfortunate woman was found. There are very few people in this region that fit the profile of the killer, and none as well as you, monsieur. I do not wish to wound you, but your aim has never been more than adequate. I, myself have always known you as a prudent man, but who has not taken an ill advised shot in his lifetime?"

Having delivered himself of this unwelcome speech the sportsman rammed an ancient pipe into his mouth and clamped his teeth round it.

"It is not a bad shot we are looking for M. David," I said slowly, giving my racing thoughts time to catch up, "it is a bad hunter. The first shot, the one fired from a distance, was remarkably accurate. We have all forgotten in the horror of finding our friend wrapped in that wretched dark green Barbour, that Miss Horsfall was wearing a brown tweed jacket with a white scarf." Now I could not get my words out fast enough, I was starting to gabble. I deliberately slowed myself down.

"Let us take another scenario," I continued "A good shot but not an experienced hunter. Someone who is not familiar with the great forest or particularly aware of the Forestry Service tourist walks. A man, who knows he is hunting in deer country, sees a brown shape with just a flash of white moving through the trees. He raises his rifle and fires before he has time for thought."

I gestured frantically to the posters. "It could be a man who came for one of the clay pigeon shooting competitions. The most logical wearer of British clothes would be someone from the UK."

The two men looked at me in consternation. Then M. David unclamped his pipe and said "Brava, Mademoiselle, you are without doubt un vraie Sherlock Holmes." He searched for a moment then unearthed a sporting calendar from under a mound of magazines and catalogues. "There were four ball-trap competitions that are possibilities in the weeks just before and just after the murder. I am acquainted with the organisers and if you will permit, I will telephone and ask if one of their competitors was a Rosbif of trés grand taille."

"You are very kind Monsieur," Théo said stiffly.

"Théo my boy, do not be offended." M. David cajoled. "Admit it; you would have had doubts if you had been in my place. The police officers made a very good case against you."

"No, I do not blame you for your suspicions Monsieur, but I do think you were very harsh in your opinion of my shooting skills. I think I shoot very well for a business man who has little time for practice.

I looked at Théo's hurt, rigid face, then at M. David and doubled over with laughter. After a moment or two M. David also began to chuckle and, finally even Théo gave a reluctant grin.

"When this is all over, young Théo, we will shoot together." M. Davis promised. "I will show you some little tricks that will bring you up to Olympic standard."

We all became serious again as the old man began to telephone the various club secretaries. He started with the competitions that had taken place before the crime. The first said they had no foreigners at their May meeting. The second said they had had visitors but none of them could be described as big men. A third club had cancelled due to lack of support. I could feel anxiety clutching like a claw round my heart as M. David dialled the fourth club.

A few pleasantries were exchanged then M. David asked the now familiar questions. I could see by his face that he was not receiving good news. I suddenly had a thought. "Was there anyone who was expected but did not turn up?" I hissed. The question was asked and an answer received. We had to wait through what seemed like endless good-buys before we learned that four members of a small club in Kent had registered to shoot but had been no-shows on the day. The Secretary did not know them personally, so could not say what they looked like. He would, however, look up their addresses and fax them to St. Riquier.

"You have a fax machine?" I queried in surprise.

"Not here," was the amused reply. "But my good friend the curator of the museum lets me use his when I need the service."

We thanked the old man and made our way back to the square. Turning into the brightly lit and welcoming café Théo ordered a glass of Grog au Rhum for me, and a viandox, the French version of Bovril, for himself. The grog was steaming and fragrant with cinnamon. I warmed my hands round the glass and watched the rain fall steadily into the already large, dark puddles in the street.

"If one of those missing visitors is our man," I said at last, "I could well understand him wanting to duck out of a shooting competition just after he had committed murder. But it doesn't really explain why his friends didn't turn up either."

Théo thought for a moment, his eyes narrowing in concentration.

Then he smiled but with little amusement. "We are forgetting the car, Chérie. Miss Horsfall's car – it was found in Lille. It is, of course, possible that the car was stolen from the forest car park by louts. Or perhaps the murderer drove the vehicle all that way before abandoning it and returning to the woods for his own wheels using public transport – a long and tedious journey with a long walk at the end of it. Neither of those ideas seems very likely."

Théo raked his hand through his hair. "If he had friends, friends with whom he was sharing a car, then they could follow him and pick him up when he had abandoned the incriminating vehicle."

"Why Lille? Why so far?" I asked.

"The city does have a certain reputation for unsavoury areas."

I knew from my own researches that there was a direct motorway link from Lille to Dunkirk, which had the cheapest ferry fares across the Channel. It was beginning to make sense.

"Are you going to take this information to the Police?" I asked.

There were a few moments of silence. Eventually Théo said: "I am convinced, because I know I am innocent. I have to realise that all we have is surmise and speculation. I don't think what we have found out today would persuade our friend the detective."

"So what do we do next?" I asked.

"It means, Chérie," he said, looking ruefully out of the window, "that you must contact the cold wet lands of England." The moment of humour was gone almost instantly. "I am going to need your help once more. My English extends to ordering a coffee and asking the way to the gents."

"Any help I have to give is yours," I said. I could see Théo was getting emotional, so I searched for something to lift the atmosphere. "After all, you were quite right in suggesting that this problem could affect my business. Who would want to stay with me, if it becomes known I let my friends murder my guests?" It was a joke, but there was a distinct atmosphere of hurt pride almost all the way home.

3

M. David telephoned the next day with the names and addresses of the four missing contestants, plus the phone number of the club secretary. I thanked him profusely and then felt almost sick with nerves as I prepared to dial.

"What possible reason could I have for wanting to know the size of the men in his club?" I asked.

"Chérie, considering the reputation of French women in England, he will think it a perfectly natural request."

I made a face at him, but the moment of laughter had given me the confidence I needed. I spoke in English but allowed my voice to take a strong French accent.

"I'm Madame Calamier," I said, "Je suis l'assistante to the organiser of the spring ball-trap competition at St. Riquier. One of our members 'as decouvert zat 'e 'as picked up a jacket that was not 'is – vous comprenez?"

I was assured the secretary did comprehend.

"Zee jacket was a Barbour extra extra large – could it belong to one of your team?"

"My dear young lady, it most certainly could!" was the enthusiastic reply. "Neil Watmough was on the team that went to France in the spring. He must have a fifty inch chest at least. Come to think of it, I don't think I've seen him in that coat since. I'll ask him at the next club meeting."

You'll probably give him a heart attack to boot, I thought as I put the phone down after thanking him.

"What do we do now, go to England?" I asked Théo.

"You forget, Chérie that I am forbidden to leave the country. No, we will present all that we have discovered to the obnoxious Inspecteur. Beside which, I think we will find we have done enough."

As it turned out, Théo was right.

Interpol did their role by gathering our evidence and passing it on to Scotland Yard, who in turn arranged to interview the man in question. Before they could do so, he committed suicide with his target rifle somewhere deep in the Kentish woodlands. The French police announced that they were not looking for anyone else in the case of the death of Miss Horsfall.

M. Delavoie reluctantly told Théo he was free to go about his business.

CHAPTER SEVEN

1

One of the highlights of the social Calendar of Montreuil-sur-Mer is Le Bal des Sapeurs-Pompiers, the Fireman's Ball. The business community all buy sheaves of tickets, not only in recognition of the men who had and would again put their lives on the line to protect the goods and property of their neighbours, but also because it is an excellent night out.

A couple of weeks before the grand event, which always takes place in the last week of July, I sat round the kitchen table with Rosine, Marie-Liesse, and Edouard. We had already bought our tickets and offered to put up visiting firemen on a cost-only basis, which was in effect free-of-charge. I wanted to make a more visible contribution, one that would confirm my place in the community.

The multi-starred Hotel Napoleon was going to provide a large cauldron of its famous fish soup – the marmite des pêcheurs. The butcher's guild promised a side of well hung beef for the rotisserie. The association of local bakers gave bread and patisserie, and the charcuterie was responsible for the pâtés and salads.

Most of the licensed hostelries had put their name down to donate beer, wine and spirit. The supermarket provided bottled water and fruit juices. There did not seem to be a lot left.

"Cheese," said Marie-Liesse.

I shook my head. "No, the new cheese shop in the Place De Gaulle will want to show off their selection." They really did have the most marvellous cheeses – I had started offering a slice of the local mimmolet with my breakfast platter. It had gone down very well.

We lapsed back into silence.

My thoughts drifted to Edith Calamier, my mother's aunt. The answer to the problem came quite suddenly. I turned to my bookshelf.

"Edouard," I said aloud, "I have an old book in the collection I inherited from my great–aunt. It's an Edwardian lady's guide to party giving. One of the entremets it describes is called 'Delice d'Enfer' – devil's delight."

I found the recipe without difficulty. The description ran: 'A light cake masked and decorated with red icing, the centre cut out and filled with an iced compote of red fruits with a maraschino cream, served with a sauce of burning brandy'.

"Edouard, do you think you could devise something along those lines?" I asked. "My idea is that it would be produced as the centre piece at the midnight supper after the fireworks. I'd like you to give it an individual touch. We might call it gateau Sapeurs-Pompiers."

Edouard looked serious. "Peut-être, Madame," he said at last. "Please give me a few days to think about it."

Rosine was about to protest, but I touched her hand in quick warning. Every chef worth his salt likes to show a little temperament.

The young man stood, made a small half bow. "I assure you, Madame that I will do my best." Then, tucking my book under his arm, he let himself out of the kitchen, leaving us all staring after him.

There was silence for a few moments, and then Rosine said, "I think we might very well have the seeds of a success."

Edouard did manage to work out how to make the desert. The plans were so spectacular that I was sure it would be the crown of the evening's entertainment.

I telephoned M. Delcroix, President of the Committee and tentatively made the suggestion that 'Calamier Holidays' supply 'The grand Desert'. There was no hesitation – our contribution was IN.

2

The night of the ball arrived all too soon. The event was to be in the open air and was held in the grounds of the Chateau. A planked wooden square had been laid over a section of the grass for the dancing. The day had been hot and sunny and the evening was warm and thankfully dry. At first my enjoyment of the evening was somewhat affected by a degree of nerves as to the general public's reaction to the cake. As the evening wore on however, I stopped worrying and threw myself into the waltzes and old fashioned polkas. Disco dancing might be de rigueur for the Boite de Nuit, but the citizens of Montreuil liked to get up-close and personal.

At Midnight the fireworks began to burst their way into the night sky. A small team of fire fighters were on hand in professional kit to deal with any emergencies. My nervousness returned now there were only minutes to go before the entrance of my surprise. I clung to Rosine's arm.

"Nothing will go wrong Madame," she whispered.

The fireworks ended in a torrent of red white and blue sparks whilst the band played 'The Marseillaise'.

A roll of drums heralded the entrance of the dessert. Edouard had excelled himself. The cake had been shaped like a great fire-engine. It was bursting with scarlet fruits and decorated with red cream. The chef made a pass with his hand and lit the brandy sauce. The whole dish seemed to flare. There was a gasp from the audience, a shout from the duty fire men followed by the pounding of boots. Next thing my beautiful cake was being sprayed with foam from a battery of fire extinguishers. Suddenly the young officers realised what they had done and began to look sheepish.

Someone in the crowd laughed, then others found it funny and joined in, suddenly we were all convulsed by the ridiculous farce.

Everyone except Edouard, he gave an anguished cry of "ma delice!" Then bunched his fists and set off in the direction of the firemen. It could have been a disaster, not least because the officers were all two meters tall and had shoulders like rugby forwards; Edouard was a full head shorter and weighed about sixty five kilos.

A familiar shape appeared out of the crowd and circled the young man with his massive arms. With seconds the fight went out of our chef and he began to sob on Théo's shoulder.

Privately I determined that next year I would stick to giving a contribution and putting up visiting firemen.

CHAPTER EIGHT

1

The long hot days of summer slowly faded into golden October and the mists of November. Théo had come round to spend the evening in my house on the rue du Chateau. He sprawled in the huge old armchair by the fire he had claimed as his own. He's a big man, well over six feet in height with the heavy shoulders and forearms of a working mason. He did not actually overwhelm my little flat at the top of my hostel, more like comfortably fill it.

"Chérie," he said, taking a sip from the glass of alcohol-free aperitif he preferred, and holding the elegant stemmed piece of crystal with a gentleness and grace that at first seemed at odds with his massive form and piratical beard. "I have been given a piece of news from a cousin of my mother who works for the estate agent."

Théo restored old houses when other work was thin on the ground. Friends and relatives always gave him titbits of information they thought he might find useful. He did not always pass them on with such formality.

"The old boy who owned the big house on the Arras Road has finally passed away in the Maison de Retraite. It will be put on the market in a couple of months once the legal paperwork is done."

"Théo, that place has been empty for years! With those overhanging trees and mock medieval turrets it looks more ready for occupation by Count Dracula than wealthy Parisians."

"Apparently that is what the heirs think, too. I approached the manager of the agency and he has let me have a look around. It is in better shape than anyone can guess from the outside."

"Are you interested?" I asked.

"Naturally I am interested, and there are a few options open. I could do a deal with the heirs, a couple of great nephews who live near Amiens. I could do it up before they sell it and take a proportion of the increased selling price. Certainly they have no money to pay for the work up front. If that does not appeal, or they need a quick sale, I could present myself to the new owner as a potential renovator."

Here Théo shifted slightly in his chair, which made me wonder what on Earth could be coming next.

"There is another possibility," he paused. "We could buy the place ourselves!" It was said in a rush.

I had not seen that coming at all. Théo spoke into my silence.

"You lose quite a bit of business here because the accommodation in your hostel is very basic. Agreed, it is superior to the Auberge de Jeunesse, but most people want a degree of comfort, an en-suite bathroom, a bar, a restaurant. This is a unique opportunity to expand."

Théo was now sitting upright, emphasising the points he was making on his thick fingers.

"My business is solid, and I could raise a certain amount of capital with the bank. My mother has a little nest egg she is prepared to hazard. If you could put up some money too, we could expand Calamier Holidays as a joint venture. You did at one time have the intention of putting a manager in here to run the hostel. You could continue with that plan, and whilst I am creating the Chateau du Roi Soleil from Castle Dracula you could give some thought to filling its corridors with, if not the crowned heads, at least the full wallets of Europe."

I felt a frisson of fear. I did not have the background or the knowledge to run a grand hotel – it was beyond my scope. I opened my mouth to pour scorn on the whole idea when other thoughts came rushing in to stop my tongue. After a few moments I said simply:

"I can't commit myself now, but your idea is interesting. It certainly can do no harm to go and look at the place. I've always been intrigued by it."

I changed the conversation by telling Théo about the minor problem of one of my guests who insisted on smoking cigars at breakfast. The two ladies at an adjacent table complained the smell made then feel sick. My sympathies were with the women, but my attempts to keep the peace by having one or both parties take breakfast in their room was not meeting with much success. I looked forward to the day when smoking would be illegal in public places and I could blame the law for enforcing a no-smoking policy.

Théo did not stay much longer, claiming that he had a mountain of paperwork to get through. He kissed me on the cheek as he left, much as I had seen him salute his mother. The flat seemed very empty after he had gone. I took a last look round the building; assured myself that all my guests had safely returned from what flesh pots our sedate little town could offer.

I then settled down to an hour with my own paperwork, occasionally disturbed by the lingering scents of freshly sawn wood and Gitanes that were the constant companions of my missing friend.

2

The next day I took a walk up the Arras Road to have a closer look at the mansion which rejoiced in the name 'La Cloche Blanche' – the White Bell. There was no pavement at that point on the road, but the garden wall was set back a little way from the main highway. The grounds were skirted by a low wall on which were cemented high rusted railings. Low branches of trees wept over the metal spikes, and convolvulus twined thickly up the uprights. The gate was shut, but when I tried it I found it was not locked; it swung open with a rusty screech. A weed-choked gravel drive led up to the house, ending in a half circle before the front door.

The house itself was quite magnificent. A mini-chateau built by some nineteenth century industrialist who wanted, as every true republican does, his own castle. My first practical thought was parking – my guests would not want to leave their Mercedes and Jaguars on the road side. I caught the mental slip and determinedly rethought the phrase as 'The hotel's guests'.

I went round the back of the building and there was the answer: a row of tumbledown structures full of the accumulated rubbish of half a dozen generations. They must have originally been stables. It should be possible to obtain planning permission to turn them into a set of secure garages for guests' transport. Although a less tricky access route would have to be devised.

At the front of the house there were definite possibilities for a pleasant fine weather 'terrasse', but the garden was a mess. Ground ivy choked everything, but it was just possible to see where in former times there had been a lawn and flower beds. It looked as if one lonely rose bush clung tenaciously to life. The easiest answer to the garden might be to grub everything up and start again.

Suddenly I was conscious of the smell of perfectly foul pipe tobacco. I looked round and was surprised by the appearance of a short, old guy. I had heard no one approach. He had a fierce moustache, and it positively bristled at me. His hair, in contrast, was thin and lank, and patches of pink scalp showed through. Hair and moustache were white but stained yellow with tobacco smoke.

He was obviously a countryman. His heavy cord trousers were tied with raffia round the ankles. His grubby, collarless blue and white striped shirt was covered by an old-fashioned brown waistcoat engrained with a multiplicity of stains. He had no coat.

"Bonjour, Monsieur. My name is Sinclair. I'm just looking at the old house. I have permission from the estate agent to enter the grounds as I might have an interest in buying the place."

He did not say a word but make his intention clear by shaking his stick at me, I was not welcome.

"Monsieur, I assure you I have a legitimate reason for looking round the house and the authorities know I am here."

The watery blue eyes glared at me and his whole face went a mottled blue-red. I had never seen anyone become puce with anger before. It was quite fascinating.

I allowed myself to be shooed out of the garden and back onto the road. When I was safely out of the gate he turned on his heel and stumped off behind the house. It did not strike me until I was quite a way down the road that despite the fellow's fierce demeanour and obvious hostility, I had not been the least bit afraid.

That night I mentioned my visit to Théo. He was visibly pleased and eager to hear my thoughts.

"It looks as if it might have possibilities," I said. "But I need to see inside before even trying to come to a decision."

I then spoiled my careful lack of commitment by talking about using the old stables as a lock up garage. I could see Théo wanted to continue the subject, but I changed the conversation slightly by asking who the fierce little guardian was. Théo twisted the end of one of his moustaches, a habit he had when thinking.

"I don't know, Chérie. The heirs won't have put in a caretaker – it's not worth the effort or the cost. Your character isn't one of the immediate neighbours, either. In fact, I don't recognise him as anyone from this area."

"Well, he can't have come from very far away – not in this weather without a coat."

Théo agreed and promised to have a word if he saw the old boy. He was much more interested in getting my opinion of the Cloche Blanche and the direction I wanted our new joint venture to take.

"Théo!" I exclaimed, "It isn't a venture at all – let alone a joint venture!" My protests were interrupted by the sound of the front doorbell. Late evening callers were rare, and Théo accompanied me to the front door when I went down to answer the summons.

It was M. Delavoie, the local Inspecteur de Police, and he was accompanied by one of his uniformed officers. He began to push his way in slightly before I had bid him to enter.

"I require a few words with you, Mademoiselle, on a matter of urgency," he stated brusquely. "We are searching for two children." He glared at Théo and me. I returned his gaze, somewhat mystified but willing to let him continue with his explanation.

"The children are Dutch; two girls, one seven the other five." M.

Delavoie produced a picture of two fair haired charmers, smiling into the camera. The taller of the two wore her hair in two tight braids; the other had a very bushy ponytail.

I looked at the picture for a few moments then said: "I very rarely have children as young as this staying at my hostel, and certainly none at the moment, Monsieur. If these children are Dutch why look for them here?"

"They have been taken from the home of their paternal grandparents, we suspect by their mother. She was born near Dunkirk. Every Gendarmerie in the Pas de Calais has been asked to look out for them, especially in seedy hotels and lodging houses."

I was so astounded by the gratuitous insult that I could only stare at the man. He waited a moment to be sure the affront had been taken, and then continued: "There has been an unconfirmed sighting in Le Touquet. They may or may not have been a man with the party. If you see any children who match the description of these girls, I expect you to contact me immediately. This is not an occasion for you to practise your amateur detective work."

He left a few leaflets on my coffee table, and walked out without further explanation or leave taking.

"Quel emmerdeur!" I exploded. "Do you know, I don't think I have had one pleasant conversation with that... *canaille* since I set up in business?"

"You and everybody else," grinned Théo. "Unfortunately you get the deluxe treatment through mixing with disreputable characters, like me."

When I first met Théo, he had given me a candid history of his recent past, which had included heavy drinking and unemployment. Since then he had said very little about himself, although his mother had added a few details – whether in warning or explanation, I had never been sure. Now I felt that Théo was ready to tell me a bit more about himself.

"Well, come on," I encouraged, "let me into the secret, too."

Théo settled himself back in his armchair. "It happened a few years back when a newly promoted Onesime Delavoie came to Montreuil to shake us all up and prepare his path if not direct to Paris then to some prestigious office in Lille. I was pretty low by then. I had just been sacked from a minimum wage labouring job, for being incompetent, by a guy who would not know one end of a mallet from another unless he dropped it on his foot.

"I was with a bunch of guys in Chez Henri. Delavoie came in and was rousting out Henri about some infringement of the under age drinking laws. It was all rubbish, of course, he knew Henri was gay and just wanted to hassle him a bit."

"Henri is gay?" I interrupted, amazed. "What about Valerie, his assistant? I thought they were..." I searched for a word, "...close."

"They are, but not sexually. Valerie was a bit – a *lot* – wild as a girl. She wanted to go straight. She needed a boss who would not capitalise on her past; Henri wanted a bit of cover. You have seen for yourself that in an old-fashioned town like this, all sorts of peccadilloes are accepted, provided that people at least attempt to be discreet. It was an ideal set up, and suited them both perfectly. Valerie has a home, a steady income and can sleep alone, which suits her, while Henri can 'erm sleep with... whoever he wants."

"Anyway back to the story. The boys and I barracked Delavoie until he had to back down and leave. Later, though, Delavoie came round to my mother's house and asked to speak to me – outside! He said something to the effect that if I thought I was so tough why didn't we sort it out man to man? The next bit is not funny, as it probably blocked the man's promotion.

"We agreed to meet on the Saturday somewhere private. Well, on the day I had a glass or two to give me courage, then a glass or two more. By the time we met, I must have been as drunk as I have ever been without passing out. To be honest I don't remember much about it except that I completely lost my temper. When the verger came to open the old church of St. Saulve on Sunday, Delavoie's trousers were found wrapped round the statue of St. Expedit, his jacket was round the shoulders of St. Therese, Our Lady had his shirt and tie over her arm, and his underpants flew from the weather vane."

"What happened?"

"It was all hushed up, of course. When I went to confession I tried to explain what had happened. Old Father Vincent, God rest his soul, was utterly furious. He gave me penances I will never forget. The mildest was that I should go for counselling. That was the turning point of my life. I should be – I *am* – grateful to the man. I have apologised more than once. Unfortunately, every time Delavoie sees me he also sees his drawers flying from the church roof!"

Théo looked so solemn and serious, I clamped my teeth into my bottom lip, determined not to smile. Then Théo's lips twitched and I could stand it no longer. I laughed until my stomach ached and tears ran freely from my eyes. Théo put an arm round my shoulder and we were an inch away from a kiss. I shyly turned my head away. Théo gently kissed my cheek then left without any further words.

3

Two days later Théo telephoned to say he had the key to the old Cloche

Blanche, and asked would I like to see inside. I said that indeed I would, so we agreed to meet at noon.

The first thing I noticed about the place was that Théo had obviously done some initial clearing, because the place was empty of furniture and fittings. The reception area had high ceilings and was of handsome proportions. My first thought was that the place would cost a fortune to heat. The kitchens were unexpectedly large and spacious. Properly fitted up they could make the base for a real *cordon blue* chef. As we toured round we found a number of additional pantries and sculleries that could be used for storage and house ancillary services such as laundry.

We went up to the first floor. The large bedrooms would convert easily to en-suite apartments. The second floor had smaller rooms plus several garrets in the decorative turrets, certainly enough space for a viable number of guests and some live-in staff. Back down the stairs we ended up in the splendid dining area that led onto the garden terrace.

"This is not 'The Grand Hotel', Théo," I said flatly. He looked a bit crestfallen. "Don't look sad," I chided, "because that's a fact that's in our favour. I don't have the knowledge or experience to run a Michelin rosette hotel, and if I did this place would not be of interest. Where could we locate the sauna, the Jacuzzi, the hairdressing salon? Don't forget, the Hotel Napoleon struggles for half the year. There is not the business for two such prestigious hotels in such a small catchment area."

I walked round the ground floor again.

"What I could aspire to, what this place lends itself to perfectly, is a more modest establishment of two or three stars in the hotel guides. We can grow and learn together. You yourself said that my hostel was losing those visitors who wanted a degree of comfort.

"Here is my suggestion. Calamier Holidays mark two, with bathrooms, restaurant, and perhaps some visiting experts to give lectures on French history. We would, of course, also be open to the usual hotel trade of business people and tourists"

I walked to the French window and outside, once again, was the old man.

He was standing in the middle of the weed infested former lawn staring at us and shaking his stick!

Théo was instant attention, but before he could wrest open the ancient doors, my former antagonist had disappeared. Théo looked around the grounds, but eventually returned alone.

"The old blighter can move; I'll give him that. He looks familiar, though. I know him from somewhere, but I can't think where. Perhaps one of the neighbours is having grandpa to stay for a bit. I'll ask around."

CHAPTER NINE

1

In the next few days I began to sort out my finances. I could fund my half of the purchase price of the Cloche Blanche from the monies I gained from my deceased parent's insurance policies and the sale of their house. I had also been pleasantly surprised by a gratuity from my former employers. When I sent in my resignation at the end of my sabbatical year the management had made me redundant rather than accepting my termination of employment. It was an unexpected and much valued 'thank you' gift for my years of service.

Once my capital was committed, it left me without a life-belt, so to speak; however, some of the money could be recovered by the resale of the property if all did not go well. The big problem was the cost of refurbishing. What was the value of the labour that Théo would contribute? Did the ideas and plans I put in have any monetary value?

We went to see M. Le François. I had thought long and hard before consenting because of the trouble he had caused when I inherited the Calamier house. The old lawyer simply chose to forget about his attempt on our lives and finally we were glad to do the same. We were at the end of what had seemed an interminable afternoon in the notaire's stuffy office. The dapper lawyer suddenly turned to me and declared:

"You do realise don't you that it would be so much easier if the two of you were married? I could draw these papers up in half the time and with half the cost to yourselves."

I could feel the blood rushing to my face. I stood, made a grab for my coat and stammered: "Monsieur le Notaire, you go too far!"

I fled from the office with M. Le François and Théo staring after me as if I had taken leave of my senses. I was too worked up and embarrassed to go back to the hostel. Instead I crossed the square and took the path onto the ramparts of the old city, intending to walk round, cooling my burning face and emotions. As I looked out on the grey skies, dull frozen farm fields and leafless trees of the countryside. I felt as if the geographical landscape matched my own barren heart.

Before long I heard the thump of running feet behind me. I was apprehensive until I saw the huge form of Théo come pelting along the path, his scarf tails flying and breath steaming into the cold air. He dropped into a walk beside me, and for a few minutes we ambled in silence.

"The man is an ass, Genèvieve you know he is. I would have expected you to protest, laugh in his face even, but I can see you have been really hurt. Please, ma petite, tell me about it. Is it something from your time in Scotland? I know so little about you before you came here and put the colour back into my world. Why did a woman as attractive as you suddenly want to uproot herself and make her life in another country?"

"I told you!" I said sharply. "My parents both died within months of one another."

"Yes, *il était tragique*," he said, softly, "but before that they were healthy and you had a life of your own."

"I had a very demanding job,"

"Chérie," he said very gently. "Tell me."

We walked in silence for a few minutes longer. A thin mist was rising over the marsh land which skirted our hill top fortress. My thoughts went back to Scotland and all those wasted years.

I started to tell Théo the sad story.

I joined a large international chemical company straight from university. My college days had been great fun, but none of the friendships I made then proved especially strong or long lasting. All our promises to keep in touch remained unfulfilled as each of us began our new careers in different parts of the country.

In common with most new starters, I was a bit disorientated and lonely in a company where everyone seemed to know everyone else, and I felt like the odd person out. Then one of the senior chemists – let's call him Andrew – came to visit my office and singled me out for conversation and attention. I felt very flattered.

There was something very, very attractive about him. When he asked me out I was thrilled. He was, of course, married. His wife had suffered from a slight stroke a few years previously, and there were other medical problems. They no longer had a married life, or so he told me, but he could not leave her. He probably also told me his wife did not understand him. I don't remember. Though why I might have baulked at this cliché, when I had accepted so many others as gospel, defies comprehension.

I moved from my parents' house into a flat so that we would have somewhere private to meet. I was besotted with him. After the first couple of occasions we rarely went out anywhere. Andrew stressed to me that with our old-fashioned Chief Executive it would harm both out careers if our affair became known within the company.

We drifted on in that way for years. I knew he took out other girls;

he could not resist making a conquest. The girls never lasted very long, they were only flings, or so I told myself. The end came as no surprise to anyone but me.

Andrew finally met a blonde with hair down to her waist and legs up to her armpits. The long suffering wife was divorced. He simply stopped seeing me – the now redundant mistress. Any possible unpleasantness at work was avoided by him transferring to another division of the company. Our affair was over with a vengeance. The one brief protest I made was dismissed as hysterical nonsense. Mostly my erstwhile lover made himself 'unavailable'.

Over those years I had not made any other close friends, and to a large extent lost the communication skills necessary to take me back into society. So I carried on staying in my flat until my mother became ill and I moved back into my parents' house to help nurse her.

"What do you think of this Andrew now?" Théo asked carefully.

"I wish him well," I replied positively. "It hurt at the time, there were a few tears – no, there were rather a lot of tears. I was bitter, lonely and disappointed. On the other hand, he had never made me any promises. If anything, it served me right – I was 'the other woman', after all. What consideration did I have for the cheated wife? Perhaps the most surprising thing is the smallness of the gap it left in my life."

"Don't be too hard on yourself, Chérie." Théo was quiet for a moment and then asked, slowly, almost shyly, "How do you see us?"

"Whatever do you mean, Théo?"

"Chérie, I come round to see you in the evening when I don't have a rush job or I am not going to the gun club. We don't go out together much."

"Théo, we are friends and business colleagues, it's not the same thing at all. Besides," I said, trying to lighten the atmosphere, "I'm assured you are not married."

"No, Chérie, I am not." He said it quite solemnly. Then, with a characteristic gesture, he tucked my arm into his. "If we stay out in the freezing fog much longer, Mademoiselle Geneviève , we might come down with pneumonia and have to share a joint hospital bed – and what would that do for your reputation?"

Théo laughed, but it seemed less at his joke and more as if he had suddenly come to a decision. We walked back into town. When I attempted to turn into the street that led to my hostel, he marched me forward into the main town square and into the little patisserie and café near the supermarket. It was a place that was a great favourite with all the mid-afternoon shoppers. Some of the town's most notable gossips spent a fair bit of time there. Théo ordered lemon tea for two and a plate of their finest cakes.

"After our session with M. Le Francois, I think we deserve a treat!"

We did indeed, and so we spent a very pleasant half hour devouring the delicacies. Whilst we lingered over our éclairs and fruit pastries, several matrons for whom Théo had done work in the past came up to pass the time of day and mention their plans for further extensions or renovations. I knew what Théo was doing – and I found it did not displease me.

When we finally arrived home, Théo left me at the front door and walked off to find his van. Rosine and her boyfriend Edouard were waiting for me. They sat side by side like two school children attending on the headmistress. Edouard stood up nervously as I came in and asked if I could spare them a few moments of my time. I was intrigued and led the way up to my flat. We sat facing one another whilst Edouard played with a folder he held in his hands and stammered about how good it was of me to see them. Rosine finally lost patience and interrupted.

"Madame, we are aware you are about to expand your business and turn the old house, La Cloche Blanche, into a hotel." After having delivered her first firecracker she stopped to gauge my reaction. I was interested but slightly mystified. I indicated that she should go on.

"You know that Edouard and I have planned for some time to improve ourselves and eventually run our own hotel. We would therefore like to apply for the positions of Head Chef and Hotel Manager in your new establishment." Rosine was breathing hard as if she had been running. They both looked a bit pink faced and were gripping each other's hands with a ferocity which must have been painful. I tried to relieve the tension by pouring us all a glass of wine. I then gave myself some thinking space by asking the standard questions about Edouard's qualifications and experience. The boy had some very impressive diplomas, as well as excellent references from the hotel Napoleon.

The career jump from Assistant to Chef was not easy to achieve. I could see why this shy young man was having difficulties in persuading prospective employers to put him in charge of the most critical part of their operation. Tiny vivacious Rosine, who looked young enough to still be at school, would have problems in convincing anyone who did not know her that she was capable of running a hotel. Yet she had proved herself an efficient manager, and well able to please and handle guests, albeit in a small operation.

I was unsure how to proceed, and so took refuge in delaying tactics.

"We have not even signed the sales agreement. When the legalities are complete it will still take quite some time to complete the restoration. Hence I have not yet contemplated staffing the hotel."

This was true, and a serious lapse on my part. There was also the consideration that if they eventually wanted an establishment of their own I could find myself a few years down the line looking to replace the team who had made my hotel's reputation. The worst possible scenario would be that Rosine and Edouard take my clients with them.

"Madame," Rosine said quite firmly, "if the Cloche Blanche is a success then you will wish to expand to a more prestigious hotel, and who better to open it than the tried and tested team who have succeeded before? If we look in to the future we might very well see a Colbert, excuse me, a Calamier chain of hotels with Edouard and myself as directors in the company with responsibility for the culinary and hospitality policy and hands on control of the flagship of the enterprise, wherever that might be.

"If this is too ambitious, chère Madame, please forgive us our dreams. More practically, contracts could be written to allow such notice of termination and conditions of handover that any change of management would be seamless to the client base."

I was astounded. It sounded so possible, yet the substance was pure fantasy.

"This is not something that can be decided in an instant, my dear Rosine. Let me think a little more about the shape of the hotel I have in mind. I must also consult with M. Colbert, who is my partner in this enterprise."

Rosine nodded and she and Edouard left my apartment. She knew and I knew that what I had said was pure prevarication.

I put The Cloche Blanche and all its problems on hold as I prepared for the run up to Christmas. I had guests up to December the 23rd, mainly shopping expeditions. This meant that I kept my refrigerator and freezer as empty as possible of my own foodstuffs because during the week or so before the great day they would be filled by numerous carefully marked parcels belonging to my guests.

From Christmas Eve onwards, however, we were all on holiday for a month. Last year, Henri Olivier had held a huge Christmas party over at his restaurant, Chez Henri. It had been enormous fun. All the restaurateurs and hoteliers in the town had contributed not only to the food and wine but also to the work. It had been like a giant house party, and had lasted for several days as people took time off from their own concerns. This year, Henri was going to visit his mother in the Auvergne. She had not been well for some time, and Henri wanted to have one last Christmas with her whilst she was active enough to enjoy it. No one else had offered to take on the task of organising such an enterprise, so there would be no communal party this year.

I found myself feeling a bit low. It's all very well saying Christmas is a time for families, but when you don't have any family at all, you can feel very much like a spare part. About a week before Christmas, Théo called round during the afternoon. I walked into the breakfast room to find him whispering with Rosine. They jumped apart as guiltily as if they had been kissing. There was a lot of blushing and stammering before Théo told me he had brought some greenery to decorate the hostel. His van was full of holly, mistletoe, strings of ivy and pine branches. The scent was delightful. One of the members of Théo's gun club was a forester in Crécy Woods, and a certain amount of 'pruning' was one of the perks of the job.

I left Rosine and her sister Marie-Liesse to do the decorating whilst I took Théo up to my apartment for a cup of coffee.

"What was all the whispering about, Théo?" I asked, curious and feeling just a tad left out. Théo tapped the side of his nose with a grubby finger.

"*Une grande surprise!*" he said. "I am sworn on my mother's life not to reveal it." He rolled his eyes in mock horror. "Don't worry, Chérie, it is all very harmless."

I had not realised until that moment that I was worried.

"Here, I have a surprise I *can* tell you about." Théo produced two tickets from inside his jacket. "There is to be a Christmas Eve Concert in the old church of St. Saulve. They have secured a soprano from Paris, a string quartet from Bruges, and our own M. Delcroix and his son are to perform a couple of trumpet and organ pieces."

"How will the distinguished soloists react to the local competition?" I wondered cynically.

"Come, Chérie, and judge for yourself."

I agreed quite willingly. My musical taste tends very much towards the classical, and I had not attended a live concert since coming to France. It surprised me that Théo would be so keen. I had not suspected his musical tastes ran in that direction. Perhaps I had underestimated my friend, just as I had apparently underestimated the talent of the local Montreuil musicians.

2

Next day, towards the end of the afternoon, Mme. Colbert arrived at the hostel. She claimed to have been doing some last minute shopping in town, but her arms were empty of parcels. I had always been on amiable, if slightly distant terms with Théo's mother. When I first moved to France, I had stayed in her holiday chalet whilst the hostel was being refurbished; we had been companionable but not intrusive neighbours. Now despite the fact that Théo shuttled between our two homes, we were still not intimate.

Nevertheless, I welcomed her in and showed her the artistic

decorations courtesy of Rosine and Marie-Liesse who had added their own glass balls and ribbons to Théo's greenery. The old lady was suitably complementary, and we went up to my flat where she accepted a glass of aperitif.

"This year I expect both my brother and my sister with their children and grandchildren for the Christmas holiday," she began.

"How very nice for you," I murmured.

"Yes, we visit each other's homes in rotation, and this year it is my turn. I will be doing all the traditional dishes – oysters, a turkey and, of course, a chocolate log."

As much to get away from this catalogue of treats in which I would have no share as any real interest in her relations, I asked, "Do you have a large family, Madame?"

"I am one of five children," Madame continued comfortably as I topped up our glasses. "My parents were considered old-fashioned, even by their contemporaries. In the old days the theory was that every married couple should have a large family. You gave one boy and one girl to the church and kept the youngest girl at home to look after you in your old age. The wishes of the young people played no part at all in this strategy, which was why the plans of their parents went awry so often."

"I can well imagine," I replied."

"In fact, my oldest brother did become a priest. He has never had a parish, but lives as a monk in one of the stricter communities. It does not permit women over the threshold and will not allow the inmates out, even for a family visit. Ma Mère was not at all pleased at not having a newly ordained priest to show off to her neighbours."

Mme. Colbert said this with so much satisfaction that I was shocked. It must have shown. She smiled at me.

"My father, my brother and Théo have all been to visit Brother Simeon. He is as happy as it is given any of us to be in this life. My sister Marie also embraced the conventual life with enthusiasm. As Sister Emmanuelle she has nursing, midwifery and teaching qualifications of the highest order. Her convent sent her all over the world to set up daughter houses. She has retired from field work now, but has a most influential position in Rome. She writes to me dutifully, but I can't pretend to understand more than half of what she says. That wasn't quite what Maman planned, either.

"My youngest sister, Claire, when she realised what her role in life was supposed to be, became pregnant and got married – unfortunately, in that order – as soon as possible. The fellow was a loser, my poor sister did not have a good marriage, and even before he died, little Claire had lived on her own for many years."

"What happened to the child? I asked.

"Sometimes I doubt there ever really was a child. She told me she had a miscarriage. Anyway, there was no baby. Later, before Claud – Clare's husband – disappeared entirely from the scene; there was another child, Marie-Claire. She has a doctorate in French Literature and lectures at the Sorbonne. Marie-Claire and Théo were almost brought up together. Claire was on her own, I had Théo so late and my husband was far from well even then. We supported one another."

Suddenly, I didn't want to know any more about this clever cousin.

"What about your other brother?" I asked

"Henri was a dutiful son and went into the army as my mother had always intended. He did very well, and Maman at last had a child she could boast about. Poor Maman! Henri was posted to French Indo-China, and brought back an exquisite oriental bride. My parents never recovered from the shock. Not long after Henri's return Maman had the first of the series of strokes that eventually killed her. Papa, on the other hand, seemed to just become more and more vague until he eventually slipped away."

"If my parents had been able to look beyond the end of their noses they would have seen that Precious Jade was a cradle Catholic, just like we were. My brother and his wife raised three of the finest boys any grandparent could have been proud of. They became a doctor, an advocate and another career army officer."

There was silence for a while and I refilled our glasses.

"You are doubtless too polite to ask about me," Madame said directly. "I was to be the one to provide the next generation. I married my childhood sweetheart, a young man who was supposed to inherit a substantial local farm. We were married in the parish church, and a flock of white doves were released to celebrate our nuptials. The problem was that the expected grandchildren did not appear. My husband's relatives lost control of their land through poor speculation. When Théo came, long after my parents were dead, and everyone including myself had despaired of my ever having a child, there was nothing for him to inherit."

"Chère, Madame," I said, embarrassed. "Thank you for your confidences. It could not have been easy for you to tell all this to a stranger."

"My family history is well known. You would have found out long ago if you talked to the village gossips. I know that listening to tattle-tale is not your style, and that is no reflection on your excellent French. I am telling you these stories to illustrate that parents do not always know what is best for their children, and the best laid schemes can go astray – as your own poet tells you." Madame Colbert finished her wine and put the glass to one side.

"You have indulged an old lady far too much. What can be more boring than a recitation of old stories?"

I demurred politely. In fact, I had found her revelations fascinating.

"The object of my visit was to invite you to join us all after the concert on Christmas Eve and stay through Christmas Day and St Etienne. I know your hostel will be closed, and there will be more than enough going on at my home to prevent you being bored."

I felt a sudden sinking in my stomach. This was just the kind of family party I had dreamed of, yet how could I, a virtual stranger, intrude on their celebrations? With great regret I said, "Thank you so much for your kind thoughts, but I can't impose on you in this way." I felt as if I was cutting myself in two as I mouthed the polite phrases.

"Chère Mademoiselle Sinclair, I do not invite you because I fear you will be lonely without us. You are invited because my beloved Théo will either be lonely without *you* or more likely he will desert us to spend most of his time here in your hostel. Much better that you join us, I think – after all, we are not all that terrifying, n'est-ce pas?"

Madame got up and buttoned her severe black coat. "I shall expect you for supper after the concert. Bring your case with you, for you will be staying two nights at least, bonsoir Mademoiselle Sinclair."

With a gracious inclination of her head, Mme. Colbert let herself out of the flat. I had the feeling that I had just been hijacked.

CHAPTER TEN

1

The last of the guests were waved away on the morning of Christmas Eve. Once the kitchen and bedrooms had been put to rights, I paid Rosine and Marie-Liesse their Christmas bonus and sent them home. The big old house seemed empty and a little sad without its complement of staff and visitors. I returned to my flat to finish wrapping the gifts I had bought for Théo's extended family.

It was just about dusk and I was contemplating having a bath and getting ready for the evening when I was surprised by a clamour of knocks and rings on the front door. I made my way down stairs to find a pair of eyes peering at me through the letterbox. I opened the door to be confronted by a tall, arrogant young man well aware of his own good looks. Beside him stood a rather faded blonde, they both wore black leather jackets and jeans. Behind the pair were two little girls. They wore their fair hair in braids, and looked to be about eight and ten years old. They stood closed to the woman, looking nervous and apprehensive.

The man stared at me for a moment or two. I felt as if I was being mentally undressed. "Genèvieve Sinclair?" My name was as much a sneer on his lips as a question. I acknowledged the fact, more puzzled than angry.

"The old bat at the bakery said you run a cheap boarding house. We need a room just to get us over the blasted Christmas holidays."

He made to push his way in but I blocked the door.

"The hostel is closed," I said firmly. "The Coq d'Or on the far side of the upper square is remaining open, I suggest you try there."

"The Scraggy Chicken finds itself unable to take us. Travelling with children can be a first class pain in the behind."

I watched the woman flinch and realised that the statement had not been made for my benefit but as a rod for her back. I don't know when I have detested anyone so quickly. I was about to close the door in their faces when the older of the two girls whispered, "Maman, I need to go to the toilet."

The reaction of the young man was instant and vicious. He hit the girl across the face, one hard automatic slap with the back of his hand, without warning or comment. The youngster put her hand to her head and moved a little nearer her mother. I could see her teeth clamped into her lower lip and tears start from her eyes, but not a sound escaped her lips.

Suddenly I thought of the police alert for two girls. I wondered if these could be the hunted fugitives. If I let them go, M. Delavoie would have another grievance against me. Reluctantly, I let them in. I showed them to a pair of connecting rooms on the first floor.

"I said I wanted a family room. I'm not made of money," the lout said belligerently.

"Pieter!" The woman said under her breath.

This earned her a glare that boded ill for when they were left alone.

I wanted to separate those children from the brute, if at all possible, but I feigned indifference. "If the accommodation does not suit you, then you are perfectly free to go elsewhere." I said indifferently.

My comment brought on more smirks, and an attempt to stroke my arm. The latter I prevented by the expedient of catching his thin wrist and removing the offending digits from my person. I could almost feel the wave of anger that followed my action, but he contained himself. They must have been in greater need of shelter than I had realised.

"My hostel provides bed and breakfast only." I explained carefully. "No meals are to be taken in the rooms. And I will require a deposit for your proposed stay of three days."

I waited until the money was produced, then made my way back to my own rooms. Only then did I realise what I had done. I had effectively ruined my own Christmas. I would offend Théo and his mother, possibly beyond all forgiveness. I settled myself in front of the telephone. My first call was to the Gendarmerie. M. Delavoie was not available – where are policemen when you want them?

My second call was to Rosine. I half hoped, half feared, that she would not be at home. She answered the telephone herself on the second ring. I hesitantly told her how I had committed myself. There was no need for further information or even a specific request.

"Mademoiselle Geneviève, I will gladly stay at the Hostel over Christmas. Edouard is working, so I had nothing planned. It would be such a shame for you to miss the family gathering at Mme. Colbert's."

I wondered briefly how Rosine knew about the invitation from Théo's mother but was too grateful for her help to cross question. There was, however, one consideration which did need to be voiced.

"Rosine, the children are charmers, but the boyfriend is poison. It would be as well if Eric could stay with you. I would be most happy to pay for his time. Tell him I have a new game on my computer."

"Bien sûr Mademoiselle, I believe you have made his Christmas!"

I flung on my coat, grabbed my bag and hurried into the town centre, thinking about Rosine and her siblings. Mme. Bonneau had four living children. Rumour hinted at several other miscarried pregnancies. Rosine, Marie-Liesse and their little brother Pierre were all small dark and of keen intelligence, although Marie-Liesse and Pierre both lacked the sharp wit and outgoing personality of their older sister.

However, the well-loved Eric, the first born, was a changeling. Well over six feet in height and weighing at least eighteen stone, he had thin fair hair and wide innocent blue eyes. Educationally he was very challenged, to the point that I doubted he could read or write. Quiet and placid, he still lived with his mother and probably always would. Some income came from odd jobs in the community. His strength was prodigious and his stamina legendary. He was accepted and liked by the town's people of Montreuil as an enormous child who would never grow up.

The only blot on his character came from an incident that had happened a couple of years before I came to Montreuil. The story ran that a group of louts from Paris, who had been staying near Le Touquet, had come inland on their motor bikes looking for a little fun with the 'rustics'. They had seen Rosine and Marie-Liesse crossing the square and began to circle them on their bikes, making obscene remarks.

Accounts vary from here on. The one sworn to in court, by possibly the largest number of witnesses to volunteer their statements at one time, said that Eric happened to be near at hand, observed what was happening to his sisters, and went to their rescue, gently pushing the cyclists out of the way.

Other stories which circulated subsequently included several expensive motorbikes piled up in the fountain in the main square and a number of leather clad riders being thrown through plate glass windows. The exaggerations about men and machines being held over the town ramparts until the louts begged for mercy, I really discounted. It would be impossible to hold a man let alone a motorbike over the hundred metre drop.

When the case came before the magistrates, the young men involved admitting to teasing the girls but seemed to forget what happened after. However they offered to pay in full for the windows that had unaccountably been broken. In the end, both youths and Eric got no more than a severe caution and were bound over to keep the peace. Eric has done that most amicably ever since – though it's doubtful if the same can be said for the louts.

The young man's only skill is an absolute wizardry at computer games. Unfortunately, even the most complex scenarios do not satisfy him for long and the family cannot afford to buy packages at the rate he can master them. I doubted that the good natured creature would need a bribe to watch over his little sister, but a new challenge would keep him from under her feet, at least for a little while.

I went to the video shop to buy a couple of the latest releases. The assistant knew Eric very well and was able to advise me on items he knew the boy had not seen and would tax even his formidable powers. Seized by a sudden rush of Christmas spirit I crossed the square to the book shop and bought several children's books. Madame asked me if they were for a gift, then proceeded with simple artistry to turn the practical parcels into true 'cadeaux', with gaily patterned wrapping paper and coloured ribbons. I doubted if mum and the boyfriend (she wouldn't have been stupid enough to have married the beast, surely?) would have much for the girls, and I hate the thought of any youngster being without gifts on Christmas Day.

When I returned I found that the telephone was ringing in my flat. I leaped on the phone and managed to catch the caller before they hung up. It was M. Delavoie from the Gendarmerie. I explained about my unwelcome visitors, recounted the description of the girls and the casual if not cruel attitude of the bravo, who could by no stretch of the imagination, be their father. M. Delavoie expressed himself with a degree of courtesy I had not experienced before. He listened without interruption until I had finished, then asked a few pertinent questions. When I had given as much information as I could provide, he even went as far as to praise me for my public spirit. I felt as if I had received the Legion of Honour!

I went downstairs to make a last check on the premises before changing for the concert, only to be cornered on the first floor landing by the man I nicknamed 'Gypsy Pete'. The guy looked as if he had been poured into his tee-shirt and jeans. I wondered if he stuffed tissues down his pants to achieve the required effect. He stepped close to me, invading my personal space and looming over me.

"Hello, Petite Proprietaire," he smirked. "Are you going to be all alone on Christmas Eve?" Moving even closer he leered, "Would you like a little company?"

"No, Monsieur," I replied. "I intend to go to church. However there will be staff here to care for my hostel."

A dramatist could not have staged the timing better. The front door opened and Rosine called out a cheery greeting. I stepped forward and planted my heel on the lout's instep. Out of the corner of my eye I saw his fists curl. I raised my voice and asked, "Rosine, my dear, is Eric with you?"

There was no direct reply but suddenly and silently a huge shape appeared at the top of the stairs. Even though I knew the poor young man was harmless – even more, that he had affection for me personally – I felt a thrill of fear. Pete stepped away from me with alacrity, wished me a very rapid "bonsoir", and disappeared into his room.

Eric no longer seemed so menacing. He shambled forward to kiss me very gently on the forehead and mumbled, "Genny".

I don't like diminutives as a rule, but Eric was an exception, as any speech at all gave him trouble. I clasped both his hands within mine and told him how glad I was to see him. Rosine followed her brother up the stairs. She took one look at me.

"Mademoiselle, what are you thinking of?" She shrieked. "Monsieur Théo will be here within minutes to take you to St. Saulve and you look more ready to scrub the floors than go to a concert!"

I was propelled back into my own apartments. With Rosine's help I was showered, changed and more or less presentable by the time Théo came to pick me up. We walked over to the old church, the upper square was festive with coloured lanterns and the first of the evening's revellers were congregating before dispersing to the various restaurants already blazing with light and loud with music.

The church was full to bursting. A couple of heavyset farmers checked tickets as the cream of Montreuil society shuffled to their seats. On the dot of seven-thirty the massive porch doors were closed, the choir and orchestra took their places, candles were lit, electric lights dimmed and the music began.

That night the congregation were treated to a performance that could not have been bettered in any concert hall in Europe.

The local choir followed the overture. It was obvious that they had courageously chosen a piece that was at the furthest limits of their capability. The whole audience was on the edge of their seats with heartfelt support. When they finished the last exultant 'Gloria' their friends and neighbours were on their feet applauding with enthusiasm and ecstasy.

During the rest of the concert the listeners remained exuberant and inclined to clap early and at length. I worried on behalf of M. Delcroix and his son. How would they compare with the imported soloists? As the first glorious notes of the trumpet and organ voluntary soared into the vaulting, I rejoiced with them. The quality, sensitivity and sheer passion of their music caught the whole audience in its spell. When the piece came to an end there was a few seconds of absolute silence as the magical spell unwound, then there was a storm of applause to rattle the plaster saints in their niches.

To my mind, that silence was as much a tribute to the music as the subsequent applause. All the soloists then performed an encore. The electric atmosphere seemed to inspire the artists to something more than the conventional lollipops. The ushers had opened the great church doors in preparation for the usual after-concert rush. As the soprano commenced the old war horse 'Panis Angelicus' not only did the early leavers pause, but a small crowd of revellers passing through the upper town car park went suddenly quiet and approached the church door to listen. As the final notes died away, the unofficial admirers did not know whether to draw attention to themselves by applauding or simply slip away. The soloist never knew how much pleasure that final almost unconsidered trifle had given.

I left the church on Théo's arm. I was amazed at the number of people who greeted us friends, business acquaintances, neighbours, people I did not actually know but saw regularly about the town... There was a real, warm sense of belonging that I had not known since my father died.

Théo did not go directly towards his van but urged me gently towards the town's ramparts. Very soon we were away from the crowds, yet we were not without illumination. There were a mass of bright stars that night. In the valley we could see the headlights of cars on the Arras road and the reflections of street lamps in the night sky.

We were, however, very much alone. Théo took off his jacket and wrapped it round me. We stood for a long moment my back to his chest, his arms encircling me.

"I love you very much Genèvieve. I have liked you and respected you right from our very first meeting in the square. I don't think I have ever met anyone equal to you for your honesty, enthusiasm or loyalty. Even so, for love there must be something more; a man-woman attraction. I was so anxious to get your goodwill, your business, that I purposely suppressed every intimate feeling. Chérie, the time has come for more honest dealing. I love you, emotionally, physically and by our sweet lord Jesus I would love you passionately" He put a finger to my lips. "Don't give me an answer now. Over the holiday I want to show you more of me, more of my family than you know so far. I also realise that from this point there is no going back to the way we were."

So saying he turned me around with infinite gentleness in his huge, powerful hands. Then he kissed me. It was a lover's kiss, as deep and strong and positive as he was himself, and just as sweet. I gave no verbal answer, for none was needed.

I returned the kiss, as if I had come home.

CHAPTER ELEVEN

1

Nothing is ever as dreadful as we imagine it will be, and sometimes things can be a lot better than we anticipate. When Théo and I arrived at Mme. Colbert's house, most of the expected guests were already there. The younger children had been put to bed, but an occasional sleepy head would appear from time to time to check on the adults.

Madame's brother, Henri, a large, jovial man, had assumed the role of host and pressed drinks on everyone. He offered Théo soft drinks only but without making a performance of it. Henri's wife, Precious Jade, was not the aloof beauty I had expected but a small, comfortably round woman. Her hair, which was completely white, was dressed in an untidy French pleat from which long wisps were constantly escaping. She proved to be a favourite with all the grandchildren and joined in their games with as much enthusiasm as they did.

The talented Marie-Claire proved very much less formidable than I thought she would be. She was a beauty with long blond hair curling about her face and large bright blue eyes. Unfortunately, the effect was spoiled by the sulky expression of her mouth and the rather gangling way she walked.

Aunt Claire was a big bulky woman with an almost permanent expression of hostility. As I watched her, I could see that she certainly had her cross to bear. Her body was riddled with arthritis, making every movement painful. The disease had attacked knees and ankles reducing walking to a hobble. Secondary sites in arms and shoulders made use of a stick or even human help to rise or sit impossible, because any pressure on the joints caused more pain. The skin over her distorted fingers was white and shiny and doubtless yet another source of discomfort. Away from her mother Marie-Claire was good company. When the two of them were together for any length of time they quarrelled frequently, which led to long pointed silences that were uncomfortable for everyone else.

Marie-Clare varied in her attention to her mother from fawning, almost lover-like absorption to complete indifference. Not easy companions, certainly, yet given the older woman's problems she was surely allowed some discontent.

Albert, Henri's oldest son, was a younger version of his father. He had the same large frame and an equally open and outgoing manner. Théo whispered to me that he had a very fashionable gynaecology practice in Paris. Looking at him I could understand why women would feel comfortable with him. His wife, Paule, was tall, slim, elegant and appeared very reserved. More sotto voce revelations told me she had been his nurse and receptionist before they were married. She had provided the push that had gained him his current lucrative partnership, and she was very conscious of her present position in Parisian society. They had four children: Benoit, Josse, Simeon, and finally the much longed for daughter, Pascale.

The second son, Maurice took after his mother. He was shorter, slighter and had a definite oriental cast to his features. Perhaps because of this he had chosen a Eurasian wife, Fleur. The couple had met when they were both at university. Fleur specialised in company law and still worked part time as an advocate. Despite or perhaps because of her extremely challenging speciality, Fleur was not in the least pompous and was full of restless energy. She was very good company as she had a fund of funny stories from the world of big business. They had three children: Corentin, Delphine and Mei-Lin – the two girls had been named after their respective great-grandmothers.

The only people still to arrive were Christophe, Henri's youngest son and his wife Helene. The young captain had caught a late duty and was not able to travel north until the next day.

In the old calendar, the Advent fast was not broken until after midnight on Christmas Eve. Madame had prepared the traditional Christmas Eve meatless supper – though her 'Le Gros Souper' could by no stretch of the imagination be called penitential.

We had celery with an anchovy sauce, followed by little fingers of fried salt cod with a 'Raito' sauce – a spicy tomato sauce with olives and capers. The main dish was eel with artichokes, and it was followed by the famous thirteen deserts. I was somewhat concerned at this but it turned out to be bowls of fresh and dried fruit with plates of little cakes; everyone helped themselves to what they wanted. In fact, the whole meal was much lighter and easier on the digestion than I had first imagined, especially as almost everyone trooped off to midnight mass half way through. Only Aunt Claire remained behind to watch the sleeping babies.

My bed was in the old holiday home I had lived in when I first came to France. I was sharing with Aunt Claire and Marie-Claire plus the missing Captain and his wife. The others were spread between Mme Colbert's house and Théo's cottage in La Calotterie.

Despite the fact that it was past two in the morning, I had some difficulty getting to sleep. Eventually I got up to make myself a cup of camomile tea. Within a few minutes I was joined by Marie-Claire. I whispered my apologies for disturbing her.

"My dear girl," she said loudly into the night, "once Maman has taken her sleeping pills it would take an earthquake to shift her. In Paris we wouldn't think this was at all late." Marie-Clare took the mug of herb tea I had made and sipped at it gingerly. I started on a second cup for myself.

"I thought I would take this opportunity to ask why you have been privileged to join the sacred Christmas family gathering. Boyfriends and girlfriends aren't usually welcome."

"I don't know." I said mendaciously. I think Madame Colbert just felt sorry for me. I'm Théo's business partner. Perhaps that counts in her eyes."

"Ah, dear Théo, the family down and out whom everyone has to tip-toe around," Marie-Claire said with an edge to her voice.

I immediately felt such a rush of rage that I could have happily poured her scalding cup of tea over her head. Instead, I said quite mildly, "That was a bit uncalled for wasn't it?"

"You haven't fallen for the myth of the poor jilted boy, consoling himself with a wine bottle have you?" Marie-Claire looked rather amused. "The truth is rather different. Young Théo was already drinking pretty heavily before he started going out with Brigitte. She was the prettiest of the gang of girls who used to hang around the football team. When the lads started to pair up, she and Théo got together, more fool her. She spent more time on her own than romancing with Théo. He was always training with the team or messing around at the gun club or going to night school. Although I believe he only went to college so that he could go drinking with the lads after class.

"Finally the wretched girl saw sense. He hadn't given up a thing for her. Married life would be more of the same but with housework and a couple of kids thrown in for good measure. Fortunately she had the chance of a job in Paris and she grabbed at it with both hands. Seeing how Théo ended up, it was the best day's work she ever did," Marie-Claire finished with a smirk.

"What about the other boy, the one she was going to marry instead?"

"Oh Brigitte didn't have anyone else – at least not then. I think she said it just to turn the screw a little."

I did some mental calculations. Madame had told me that Théo and Marie-Claire had been brought up together. I wondered if the so fortuitous job in Paris had been found by a certain young student at the Sorbonne. It was also possible that the result of her meddling had not been quite what she anticipated. The story painted quite another picture of Théo to the one I had been building up.

Suddenly I was so tired I could hardly stand. I excused myself and stumbled off to bed where the black clouds of sleep engulfed my weary brain.

2

Next day the family gathered again at Mme. Colbert's house. There seemed to be an endless supply of coffee, croissants and homemade jam for the late risers. Captain Christophe and Helene finally arrived towards noon. The lady was wearing a very new maternity smock over what was to-date a very small bump. The announcement seemed to give everyone a great deal of pleasure.

Théo made time to wish me "Joyeux Noel" in French and "A very merry Christmas" in heavily accented English. My body warmed to him as it always had. My mind, however, sent out screaming messages that this was a reformed drunk on whom it would not be a good idea to base my emotional and economic future.

When the religious stalwarts of the family returned from Morning Service, the grand present opening ceremony was performed. I was amazed at the stack of gifts which were piled in front of my chair. Silk scarves, perfume, high quality tights and a range of the latest English bestsellers in paperback showed the consideration and good taste of Théo's family. I hadn't realised that Théo would be opening my gift in front of an audience.

Contacts from my days in the engineering industry had helped me find the latest piece of computer software to help control business finances. Fortunately, one bit of computer software looks very much like another and the moment passed without too many inquisitive remarks from the family.

I had to be taken outside to see Théo's gift to me. Inside a large box under a light packing of straw were a dozen sets of spiky twigs, all carefully wrapped in sacking. It didn't look much, but they were old fashioned English Roses, obtained from a first class specialist nursery in Kent. Théo said that they were to be the basis of my new garden at La Cloche Blanche. His thoughtfulness touched and pleased me. I expected barbed comments from Marie-Claire, but she seemed as delighted as everyone else. Our conversation of the previous night had apparently cleared the air – at least for her.

The main meal of the day was to be at four o'clock. Not too early for the adults or too late for the children who had all had a snack of milk and cake at midday. Henri was just beginning to fuss with aperitifs when we had an unexpected caller, M. Delavoie. He stood at the Madame

Colbert's front door looking his usual grim self and demanded my presence.

"Bonne Fête, Mademoiselle," he said stiffly. Then he looked at the interested faces crowd that was growing in the hallway. "Please will you accompany me to my car? Perhaps what we have to say should not be heard by half of Equires."

"I will come with you," Théo said promptly.

"No, you will not Colbert. I want to speak to the organ grinder not the monkey." M. Delavoie turned on his heel and walked towards his car. I gave Théo's hand one quick squeeze and followed the Inspector. In the end I was glad I was alone because the interview was not a very pleasant one.

"We have checked on the family staying in your hostel. The girls are not the one's being sought by the police," M Delavoie said formally.

I tried to say something, perhaps that I was glad or sorry, I don't really know, but it did not matter because the mechanical voice simply rode over mine.

"You are not to think, Mademoiselle that you can do the job of the Police all by yourself, however you might congratulate yourself and that oaf Colbert on finding your missing guest."

I opened my mouth then closed it again without saying anything.

"I think I should further caution you that if you don't take greater care about the sort of characters you invite into your establishment you will be getting rather more visits from the police than you might care for. And those visits will be very much less pleasant than this one.

"Monsieur, you are being less than fair," I spluttered. It did not matter. M. Delavoie had got out of the car and was walking round to open the passenger door for me to leave.

I made my way back to Mme. Colbert's house with as much dignity as I could manage. My scarlet face must have told the family that something was very wrong. I thought it best just to tell then straight out what had happened. The amount of indignation on my behalf and the degree of support they showed for me was quite heart warming. After a few moments I cut their protests short by saying I must telephone Rosine to assure myself all was well.

Rosine had no real problems to report. The woman and the boyfriend had gone out on Christmas Eve and not come back until the early hours. They had got up late and consumed such a quantity of bread at breakfast that she was sure they had been taking provision for lunch as well. The two little girls had been pleased with their gifts and had said their thanks very prettily. Even the woman has shown some gratitude. That had earned her a sharp push and some sarcastic comments from 'Gypsy Pete'.

"Is the lout giving you any trouble, Rosine?" I asked.

"No, none at all Madam, but I am glad that Eric is here with me. My brother does not like le salaud, and he makes it very clear."

"What are you doing for Christmas dinner?"

"I am going over to the Hotel Napoleon. Chef has invited me to eat with the staff once the guests are at the coffee and brandy stage. You would like it Madame, we are having roast beef and plum pudding."

We exchanged greetings, and then I rang off. I returned to the party with just enough time to have a glass of Muscat and a small plate of canapés that Théo had secured for me before we were called in to the feast.

"Up to a few years ago, Chérie, we always had the same traditional menu: fresh oysters, roast turkey and Bûche de Noel, a chocolate log. It was good but predictable. Then Tante Precious Jade, with great daring, made a small innovation by offering cooked oysters made with a recipe she learned from her own grandmother. Since then the ladies have felt liberated and are now gently vying with one another to produce the most delicious menu, trés bon!" he said, patting his middle.

"It does not always result in success," Théo continued. "A couple of years ago Helene, as a new bride, tried out a different recipe for oysters. It had been given to her by the wife of an American Officer who was in France on some sort of exchange visit. Something went wrong, and the little shellfish were so tough you could bounce them off walls – which I regret some of the children actually did. It ended up with poor Helene completely heartbroken in the kitchen. The fact that the rest of the meal was absolutely superb was no comfort to her. Maman told me later that the wretched American wife had been following a 'tradition' of her own. One that said when you give some other woman a recipe you always leave something out or alter it in some way so your rival's cooking does not compare well with your own."

"What a rotten trick!" I exclaimed.

"I don't know if Christophe helped fate along," Théo whispered, "but the American Major and his family were returned to the States early and under something of a cloud."

I looked over at Christophe, his arm around his wife's shoulder telling some long and involved story to his parents. It went through my mind that, yes, there was indeed steel under all that bonhomie. There was some of that in all of them – including Théo, as I had seen for myself. What had gone wrong all those years ago? Further speculations were ended by the entrance of the first course: hot oysters with a spinach cream sauce. Just half a dozen and I could have eaten the delicate little mouthfuls all over again.

The main course was spectacular. Three great pumpkins were brought to table, each containing five or six individual stuffed fillets of turkey in a wine sauce. Bowls of pureed pumpkin accompanied the meat, together with a garnish of salad leaves. The dish was greeted with a well deserved round of applause. The cheese board came next. It was loaded with bewildering variety. There were minuscule cream cheeses topped with candied fruits to please the youngest children, right up to well aged Roquefort to tempt more sophisticated palates. There was even a round of Blue Stilton, in honour of myself. How could I tell Madame it was not one of my favourites? I need not have worried, as all the men wanted to try a slice and I got way with just a sliver, which I could manage.

I was amazed by how well even the tiny children coped with the long meal. Certainly the parents did not ignore them. They were asked how they enjoyed each dish, and friendly hands gave discreet help with things like cutting up, naturally and without fuss. Portions were child-friendly. No little one was given a daunting plateful to deal with, and there were no recriminations if food was left. In fact, leftovers were quickly snaffled by a greedier neighbour, so there was an incentive to eat up.

The final course was, of course, Bûche de Noel. On this occasion the chocolate cake was soaked in rum, covered with a cream of *marrons glacés* and decorated with light and dark chocolate leaves. The pastry chef at the Hotel Napoleon could not have done better. After the meal, Madame served tiny cups of strong coffee, and Henri promoted Madam's liqueurs and fruits preserved in spirit.

Eventually, there were games for the children organised by the men, and it seemed hours of washing up for the ladies. When the last dish was dry and stacked away, it was a real relief to sit and watch an old film on television.

"What would you do if you were asked to give this dinner?" Théo murmured into my ear. The question so mirrored my own thoughts that I replied without consideration. "I would cheat! Young Edouard would find himself in charge of my domestic as well as my public kitchen."

It was only when I saw the beard twitch that I realised that I had been led by Madame's good food and wine into disclosing far more than I intended.

CHAPTER TWELVE

1

It seemed as if I had hardly got to sleep before I was wakened by a light hammering on the chalet door. I rolled out of bed, thrust my arms into the unwilling sleeves of my dressing gown and padded downstairs to see what could possibly be the matter. It was young Simeon, one of Albert's sons.

"You are wanted on the telephone, Madame," he said, self importantly. "Mamie says you must come at once."

That chased the sleep from my brain. Without even returning for my slippers I raced to the house over the frosty grass in my bare feet to find out what new disaster had struck.

My caller was Rosine. Our unwanted guests had done a moonlight flit. She sounded really upset, so I told her I would return as soon as I was dressed. Madame, also in her dressing gown, appeared from the kitchen to put a steaming mug of coffee in my hand.

The journey back to the chalet was cold and rough on my poor feet. I got washed, dressed and brushed my hair within fifteen minutes. Even so, Théo was waiting for me with the van's engine running when I emerged.

Rosine's face was swollen from weeping. I could not comprehend why she was so distressed. The money we had lost was negligible, especially if it meant that the appalling family had been taken off our hands. Wordlessly, Rosine led the way to the first floor rooms. The absconders had left, yes, but not empty handed: they had stolen towels, sheets, and a blanket off a bed. In one corner was a mess of empty tins and food debris from the remains of a scratch meal. Rosine opened the connecting door to the room that had been occupied by the children. The smell hit us as if it were a physical thing, before the realisation of what had been done. Every wall was smeared with excrement, every surface covered.

Quite calmly, I wondered aloud what sort of mentality could do such a thing, then I found myself running for the toilet to bring up my coffee and bitter bile. When I returned I had control of myself once more. I sent Rosine and Eric home, despite the young woman's protests. She had put up with enough. When she had gone I asked myself where on earth I should start.

Théo was speaking rapidly into his mobile phone; he finished his conversation and then looked at me.

"Chérie, go and report this to M. l'Inspecteur. Hopefully it will ruin his breakfast as much as it has ruined ours. I have called up the gang – they will be over in half an hour."

"No!" I protested.

"Yes, Chérie, there is a time for independence and a time to enlist help. You will have plenty of opportunities to repay the favours, I promise."

I gave in; it was not much of a struggle. My telephone call to the Sous-Préfecture revealed to my infinite relief that Inspecteur Delavoie was, for once, not on duty. A sergeant and a female uniformed officer were dispatched to visit the scene of the disaster, take my statement and sympathise with my plight. They held out very little hope of the culprits being caught, or even of anything very terrible happening to them if they were. My anger soured into depression.

As the officers were leaving, I spotted Rosine's mother Mme. Bonneau walking briskly towards the hostel with Eric trailing behind her. However, instead of giving me the justified dressing-down I dreaded, the fierce little woman had come to help.

"Madame, I am most grateful, but I can't ask more of your family."

"My dear Madame," she scolded, pushing past me. "Here you are with no mother of your own to help you and my dozy pair of good-for-nothings letting such things happen as soon as your back is turned. Never worry; we will soon have things back to rights."

She ran up to the stricken chambers and began to organise a grand clean-up. Within minutes she was joined by Théo's construction gang. At first it seemed as if everyone was milling about, getting in each other's way. Mme. Bonneau soon had things flowing smoothly. The rooms were stripped of everything moveable. Eric carried downstairs chests of drawers and armoires, and stacked them in the narrow yard. There they were scrubbed down, carefully dried and re-polished. Mattresses, carpets, curtains and the remaining bedding were all removed for laundry or sent to the tip if beyond even Madame's cleaning skills.

Théo's team washed down ceilings, walls, floors, and applied fresh coats of paint and wallpaper. I asked in amazement where they had obtained the rather pretty rose-patterned rolls on Boxing Day. All he would say however was 'trade'. At midday Théo's cousin Christophe arrived with baskets of food for the workers.

"Mademoiselle, at Christmas everyone provides enough food for an army. It was no trouble to put up a few sandwiches."

There was rather more than that in the hampers, but very little was returned to the Colbert's house.

Eventually there was nothing more to do, and people began to drift off back to their own homes. Mme. Bonneau and Eric were the last to leave. As I began to repeat my thanks she dismissed them with a wave of her hand.

"It was nothing, my dear Madame. These men, they just need a little organising. It has been many years since I had so much fun. Now you yourself must leave. Return; spend the evening with good Madame Colbert. Forget this little unpleasantness." She hurried back down the street, Eric following like a liner behind a tug boat.

"Her intentions are of the best," soothed Théo.

"If one more person gives me an order, I swear I'll tell them what to do with their good intentions complete with holly and Christmas wrapping." I stopped, realising how unjust were my words, and felt the prickle of tears behind my eyes. Théo stood quiet and unmoving until I taken control of myself.

"What do you want to do, Chérie?"

The answer to that was easy. "I want to get the smell of paint and disinfectant out of my lungs."

"Come, Chérie, there is an hour or so before dark. Let us go to the Cloche Blanche. You can plan your garden; we will walk, smell the wood smoke from our neighbours Yule logs, and talk of roses and summer."

It was so completely right. I simply nodded my head and let Théo wrap me in my coat like a child. We locked up and walked out of the empty, quiet town.

2

The faint mistiness, which had been in the atmosphere all day, had thickened by the time we reached the old house. Our feet scrunched on the path as we strolled round towards the lawn. Some clearing had already been done but there was still a melancholy and neglected air about the place. On a grey December day, the ruin of what must have been a magnificent garden seemed only too complete. We stood looking at it, our breath steaming slightly on the frosty air.

"The easiest and probably the best answer, Chérie, is to grub the lot, bring in a rotovator, and dig in a couple of tons of good, fresh soil," Théo said thoughtfully. "I have a copain who will probably let us have a good deal..." He got no further because the old man we had seen before suddenly appeared from round the corner of the building and rushed at us, his stick raised. We both instinctively retreated a few steps: in sheer surprise, not fear, for he would have been no match for Théo. But we shouldn't have bothered moving, for the old guy stopped as suddenly as he had appeared, and stood in the middle of the garden near the remains of the old roses. The fight seemed to have gone out of him. He lowered the stick and leaned on it heavily. To our amazement we saw tears steaming down his lined face.

I felt the weight of his misery, and looked away. When I turned back he had gone. It was as he had never been there, except for the slight lingering odour of pipe tobacco.

"Where did he go?" I asked Théo.

"I don't know – it was impossible to keep staring at him when he was weeping like that. I had to look away."

"Me too," I confessed.

"The poor chap is obviously getting worse. Let's go and talk to Maman. If anyone knows who the guy belongs to, she will. I think it is time we spoke to his relatives, for his own sake as much as ours. If he starts waving his stick at some of the gang they might just start to retaliate, old as he is."

We walked into the darkening afternoon. Théo took my hand and shoved it into the pocket of his greatcoat along with his own. I could feel the nest of a crumpled handkerchief and the scratch of old toffee papers. It was as intimate as making love.

3

Mme. Colbert welcomed us as if we were refugees from a major disaster. We were ushered into her kitchen and fed mugs of steaming soup. Cold and weary as we were, it was wonderful. When life had finally returned to fingers and toes, Théo asked his mother about the mysterious old man. We could both see by her reaction that she comprehended exactly who we meant.

Madame walked across the room and closed the door against the rest of the family. Then she took up her coffee cup and came to join us at the table.

"You are describing Monsieur Fourcroy, the former owned of La Cloche Blanche who died in the retirement home. He was always an 'original'. Even as a young man he was obsessed by one scheme or another. During the years after he inherited the old Cloche Blanche from his parents he spent most of his time growing roses for show.

"He won prizes everywhere for his blooms; one year he was awarded a Gold Medal in Paris. I think he was trying to develop a new variety, but unfortunately the ultimate accolade eluded him."

"Yes, Maman," Théo asked gently, "but who do you think we have been seeing these last few weeks?"

"Robert Fourcroy, who else? Have you not been listening, my son?

"Maman! M. Fourcroy has been dead and planted in the cemetery for months now."

"Yes, my love," the old lady agreed. She got up and began to potter nervously around her kitchen.

"For heaven's sake?" exploded Théo, quite baffled.

Madame remained with her back towards us.

"It is said, by people who believe in these things, that some great passion, be it hatred or love, will call back the spirits of those who should be safe in the arms of the Lord Jesus. Robert loved nothing and no one as much as he loved his roses. The very last of them are now dying slowly in the ruin of his once lovely gardens. Perhaps, indeed, he watches over the Fourcroy roses to which he devoted so many years of his life. He protects them as he would his lover or his child."

"What can we do, Madame?" I said. "It seems so very sad."

"I believe you do not need to do anything, not now. From what you say, I think he has given up. I doubt you will see him again."

"We can save his wretched roses," said Théo.

That was the point where I started to learn more about the cultivation of roses than I really wanted to know. My education commenced as Madame began to prepare her St. Etienne dinner. It continued through the meal, and advice followed me as I finally escaped to the guest chalet around midnight.

The next day, all that information was put into practical effect as the three of us – Madame, Théo and myself – crammed ourselves into Théo's van with half a garden centre in the way of tools, bales of straw and sacks of soil, compost and fertiliser.

The new site for the rose was chosen, then prepared with meticulous attention to detail. Huge holes were dug, sour soil carted away, fresh materials carefully layered, and finally the precious plants were disentangled, lifted on forks, and transplanted in their new home. Almost as an afterthought my Christmas gift roses were heeled in to await their turn another day.

We never saw M. Fourcroy again – if that's who it was – but sometimes during the years I lived at the Cloche Blanche, when I went to gather the beautiful white roses just touched with gold, I would catch a whiff of extra strong pipe tobacco.

Some weeks later, when we were sorting through the attics, I found application forms for the registration of a new variety of rose. They had been made just before the stroke that had landed M. Fourcroy in the nursing home, and had been cleared away by his relatives as being of little importance. It was for that same gold-tinged white rose that scented my garden from early June to late September. To my surprise it was not to be called Fourcroy but Blanche Douce. Not astonishing, given the name of the house, but I recalled that Mme. Colbert's baptismal name is Blanche...

4

I returned to my hostel. The family party was breaking up and it was time for me to go home. Oddly enough I was quite sad to say 'good-bye' to the family that had made me so welcome. I was especially touched when both Claire and Marie-Claire sought me out and asked me to be sure to come to the party at their flat in Paris the following year.

Once back in the Rue du Château, however, it was very pleasant to relax amongst my own familiar surroundings and deal in a leisurely manner with the few outstanding tasks from the Boxing Day disaster. I was also delighted to see a heavy delivery of mail bringing bookings for my hostel. Most were for the first half term of the year or Easter, but there was a significant minority from people who, for reasons known to themselves , wanted to visit the Pas-de-Calais in inhospitable January and February.

Théo had not mentioned what we were to do on New Year's Eve. I knew that some special surprise was being planned. It was the form the party would take that I chose not to guess. The cold weather was keeping Colbert Construction busy with bursts and repairs to ancient central heating systems. Even so, just after dusk the old van would clatter along my street and I would rush downstairs to greet Théo with increasingly passionate kisses. I was surprised how important those evening visits had become to me, and how much I looked forward to them.

The night before Réveillon, I waited until Théo was ensconced in his usual armchair then asked him what he had in mind for the following evening.

He studied his finger tips with elaborate concentration.

"I thought, Chérie, that you might have had enough of parties. Perhaps we could stay here and toast the New Year with a bottle of Bollinger as a special treat."

Oh yes?

"That's a good idea, love. In that case, there is no real need to get dressed up. A jumper and jeans will be perfectly adequate, won't they?" It was unworthy of me but I still enjoyed Théo's reaction. He nearly choked on his glass of Suze, blushed and then went pale. *If this is how you keep secrets from me, my dear, we will have few problems*, I thought.

There was a certain amount of glass twirling whilst some furious thinking went on.

"I don't know about that," he said at length. "It might be nice to get dressed up a bit, even if it is just to be the two of us."

"You're right," I solemnly agreed.

Truth to tell I did not have a real party dress. Of course I had some good clothes, which I had worn at Madame Colbert's house at Christmas. Formal suits from my days in Industry teamed with a really nice silk or satin blouse sufficed for most occasions. I tossed the problem around in my mind for the rest of the evening.

Early the following morning I got out my car and drove into Le Touquet. Behind the empty seafront the town was thronged with people mostly concerned with last minute shopping for New Year's Eve parties. Women, and men too, passed me with baskets piled high with fresh vegetables, and the elaborate parcels supplied by the butcher, fishmonger, *charcutier* and *patissier*.

Caught by the atmosphere, I went from shop to shop looking for a suitable outfit for the evening. Nothing attracted me. The sales seem to have started early and the boutiques were full of end-of-line styles in either tiny or extra large sizes, together with a few optimistic and inappropriate early spring fashions. The sky darkened, and the wind from the sea became bitter, and I was disappointed, dispirited and cold to the bone. An especially strong blast of icy wind drove me into Madame Sophie's. The window display was no different to a dozen others I had seen on my expedition. Madame – tiny, stocky and vivacious – bustled forward to ask what I wanted. I explained briefly about the surprise New Year Party. A dress was selected almost at random from the racks.

"Try this on," was the command. 'This' was a pale cream drapery that I felt would not suit me or the time of year. I protested, but even so found myself being hustled into the fitting room; I submitted willingly – after all, a few minutes of warmth in the shop would be quite welcome. I had only just removed my coat and scarf when Madame invaded my cubicle.

"This has come from our Paris shop today. You might like it."

It was faintly Greek in design, pleated black silk hung from two gold brooches on the shoulders in a deep V back and front. It was caught at the waist with another gold medallion, and two gold embroidered black chiffon scarves floated from the waist to the hem. It was wonderful! When I put it on I felt like Helen of Troy. I said I would have it even before I looked at the price tag. It was not cheap, but it would not break the bank. I emerged from the shop not long after, feeling extremely satisfied. The unsuitable pale cream confection had never even left its hanger.

I matched my beautiful dress with a pair of amber earrings and patent leather strap sandals with a gold mesh butterfly perched just above the toes. Superb! That night, and for several years after, it was my special outfit, and I felt as if it added its own happy magic whenever I wore it.

CHAPTER THIRTEEN

1

Théo called for me at half past seven. He was dressed in a formal diner jacket, pleated white dress shirt, and a red velvet bow tie. Although his unruly hair and beard were, for once, carefully barbered, he still looked like a pirate – just a very sophisticated one. He was also wearing a touch of expensive cologne; ten out of ten for effort.

He held me at arms length. "You look magnifique, Chérie. You are truly beautiful. Before we go to the not so surprise party, I need a moment or two just for us."

We went up to my flat in silence, and when the door had closed behind us he took me in his arms, enfolding me with the gentleness enforced by his superior strength. I felt secure, protected.

"There is not much about me that you do not now know, my Genèvieve. There is no easy explanation as to why I crossed the line from being one of the boys to being a serious drunk. Neither are there any promises I can give you that mean more than the breath of their utterance, that those days are gone and will not return. You know that I have loved you from the moment I approached you in the square. I told you my feelings on Christmas Eve.

"Tonight, my dearest love, I ask you to be my wife. I offer all that it is in my power to give you. I ask for your support as my wife which you have already given so freely to one who was a stranger to you."

He dropped to one knee and covered my hands with kisses. Gently, I released my hands from his and placed them alongside his cheekbones. I turned his face up to mine.

"Yes, my love, I will marry you. I will try to make you happy, as you have brought happiness to me."

The next few minutes were very private and personal. They ended with Théo producing from his pocket an engagement ring. It was an enormous sea green solitaire on a plain gold band. It was gorgeous, and suited me perfectly. Even the fit was right.

"Darling, how did you manage to know the size I take in rings?"

"Easy, Chérie – after a while you get used to gauging pipe fittings with your fingers."

I aimed a swipe at his now rather mussed hair, which he avoided with ease.

2

Eventually, we put ourselves to rights, and walked over to the Chez Henri. That generous-hearted man had put his restaurant at the disposal of Rosine and Edouard. It was transformed. I could recognise the nimble fingered work of Rosine and Marie-Liesse.

Half the business community of Montreuil were there, dressed in their best and determined on an uninhibited good time as sometimes I think only the French can enjoy.

I felt myself regarding the proceedings on two levels. Primarily as a guest and reveller, sipping the mulled wine 'welcome', exploring the buffet, visiting the well run bar, and taking part in the singing, quizzes and dancing. I especially appreciated the midnight toast to the New Year with Théo and myself pouring a fountain of champagne into skilfully stacked glasses.

With a completely different section of my mind, I appreciated the food. It started with tasty little nibbles as guests were arriving, before moving onto more substantial hot dishes later in the evening. This was then cleared away without fuss to be replaced with cheeses and sweet dishes. It was never too much, always enough, and just right for the tastes and appetites of the guests. I noted how the entertainments were staged to keep the party atmosphere going but not get too hectic.

Our engagement was announced, and Edouard pushed into the room an elaborate cake, not accompanied on this occasion by a brandy sauce. There were more toasts and shouts of joy as we were swamped with the most sincere congratulations. It left me breathless with happiness and exhilaration.

My internal observer did ask what Edouard would have done with his splendid cake if I had not said 'yes' to Théo. Probably applied a little judicious editing on the icing and used it for his own engagement party.

The celebrations did not begin to break up until three in the morning. Rosine and Edouard had more than made their point. Nevertheless, it was definitely not the time to commence hard headed business discussions. I sought them out, thanked and congratulated them on their success, and suggested a meeting in a few days' time.

3

For me, New Year's morning started with coffee and croissants.

Fortunately champagne does not leave much of a hangover, and Théo was fine having had only a small glass of bubbles at the midnight hour. It was important for us to go and see Mme. Colbert as soon as possible. Even so, she had heard the rumours by the time we made it round to her house.

"Your engagement gives me nothing but pleasure, my son," she declared, kissing him fondly. ", I have suspected my Théo's intentions for many months now. I can only wonder why it took him so long to ask you." She kissed me too

She continued. "I do have a concern, my children. I do hope you are not considering getting married in Lent. It is an old superstition and one not much regarded now, but it would please me if you waited until Easter. I would not like you to tempt providence."

I had not thought much about a wedding day. Lent was too soon, even if I had wished to risk offending Mme. Colbert, which I did not. Easter was difficult because I had a lot of bookings for my hostel. By late spring or early summer we had hoped to open La Cloche Blanche. I had the sudden vision of one of those old fashioned engagements that go on and on for years, the principals dwindling into old age and still no wedding in sight.

"There is no problem, Maman," Théo said positively. Easter is early this year. We have a window between the end of Easter holidays and the start of the May Day holiday. We shall manage very nicely."

All of a sudden it seemed far too close. Still, arrangements always take the time allocated to them whether long or short, and Mme. Colbert would surely help me. Then I remembered the martial Mme. Bonneau and suspected I might have another ally.

There was clearly something else on Mm. Colbert's mind. She got up several times to rearrange cushions or magazines, offered us more coffee, until with characteristic gentleness, Théo rose and, taking his mother's hand, drew her down onto the settee beside us.

"Maman," he said, "whatever it is, just tell us. You are worried that is obvious, all this fussing is not like you."

"It's about the missing children. No, not the ones belonging to that dreadful family that caused so much trouble at Christmas and made M. Delavoie speak so rudely to you. It's the real ones, the ones on the posters in Le Touquet."

"What about those children, Maman?"

"They are staying next door in the holiday home owned by Mme. Rolland. It was the woman who first made contact by telephone. There was a story of a domestic disaster followed by the illness of the relatives who said they were going to take them in. With hindsight, she gave far too much information. She did not have to justify why she wanted to hire a holiday home – it's advertised as available the whole year round."

"The woman turned up when she said she would, and paid in advance – cash. Lucie has seen almost nothing of the family until last night. The parents went out about 10 o'clock. It was only natural to wonder if the children were all right. Lucie went round just to make sure. The girls were still up, playing cards at the kitchen table. Lucie says they were the ones – the ones in the picture." Mme. Colbert was twisting her handkerchief in her hands.

"Why has Mme. Rolland not contacted the police herself if she is so sure?" I asked.

"She told me when she came in for coffee this morning. She said it was a shame, but it was as well not to get involved with the police. Once they got you on their computer they had their claws into you forever."

My heart sank. After all the trouble of the past couple of weeks, the very last thing I wanted was another confrontation with M. Delavoie. It was not my holiday home or even my neighbour, so this was one I could walk away from. Théo, however, was blandly telling his mother that she could safely leave it to us! Young Théophile might not live to see his wedding day – if M. Delavoie did not kill him, I just might.

"What we must do," Théo declared, "is go straight round there, bang on their front door and demand proof of identity." He looked as if he was prepared to attack the holiday home immediately.

"Théo, my son, the police can do that sort of thing – but you could get into all sorts of trouble if you try it as a private citizen. Mme. Rolland could have, should have made such enquiries when the woman made her first approaches to rent the Gîte. Unfortunately, money in advance answers a lot of potentially awkward questions."

"What we should do now is telephone the Sous-Préfecture and let them deal with our suspicions." Even as I said the words I knew that another interview with M. Delavoie after a second misidentification was more than I wished to contemplate.

"Let us wait until dark and see if we recognise those girls ourselves," said Mme. Colbert. "We do not want to put our heads into the lion's mouth unnecessarily."

This was wise advice, so we agreed to reassemble in Mme Colbert's kitchen at 5 o'clock.

4

By 5 o'clock it was black night and a thin mizzle of small frozen rain was falling. Théo had dressed in black polo neck jumper, balaclava and black jeans. I believe he thought he looked like a member of the SAS, whose adventures in translation formed his favourite leisure time reading.

Madame and I forbore to tell him how he would show up against the frozen landscape. The plan was that Madame and I would knock boldly on the front door and invite the family to the Epiphany celebration service at the local church. There was, as it happened, going to be such a service at St. Corentin's, including a special children's choir. Mme. Colbert told me a much-loved former priest was to come out of retirement to preach the sermon, and there would be hot drinks and English mince pies in the parish house for everyone afterwards.

The young woman who answered the door looked a bit nervous at first but relaxed as Madame got into her stride on the delights in store at St. Corentin's. Suddenly, there was a scream from inside the Gîte. The voices of young girls shouted that there was a black man peering in at the kitchen window. At that point all hell broke loose. A bloke who looked like he topped seven foot came hurtling out of the kitchen pushing us roughly aside and advising us in heavily accented French to make ourselves safe inside.

Théo, realising he had been spotted, was trying to make his escape over the garden fence, but got himself entangled in the 'Mile a Minute' vine that covered it. Théo said after that he did no more than push the man who was ineffectually grabbing at his jumper. Unfortunately, his antagonist went somersaulting backward onto the wet grass.

The two girls started to scream 'Murderer', then darted out of the back door and began to attack Théo in real earnest. As everything began to get seriously out of hand, Madame Colbert, in a voice that would have halted London's traffic, called "Stop!"

It gave enough of a pause for her to order everyone back into the holiday home with the promise that we would sort this out like Christians. To this day I don't know which Christians she meant, but I suspect the list might be headed by Torquemada rather than St. Francis.

Madame made everyone sit round the kitchen table.

"I know you are the runaway family sought by the police," she declared. "I will give you ten minutes to explain yourselves before I bring in the Inspecteur de Police to arrest you all."

It was a bold stroke which shouldn't have worked as well as it did.

I looked at the family. They were a very different proposition to the vindictive gypsies who had revenged themselves so effectively on me. The woman was blond, with short, well cut hair and a good quality dark wool suit. Her right arm was round the shoulders of her elder daughter, whilst her left stretched out to hold the hand of her lover. He had the younger girl on his knee, cradling her with his arm. He was very tall, though not as tall as he had seemed at first. He was perhaps six foot four and as thin as a rail. Sparse, light blond hair was slicked over his scalp and his ears rivalled those of Prince Charles. A very small pair of round glasses magnified weak, pale blue eyes. He had the most beautiful hands I think I have ever seen; long elegant fingers that he used to express himself when he spoke.

It was the woman, however, who addressed us first.

"I was indeed Mme. Van der Zwaluw, the most wanted woman in France – or so it seemed. If you are prepared to listen, then I am willing to tell you our story, although it might take longer than ten minutes."

"Madame," I interrupted. "In justice to yourself and your children, would you permit them to tell their story to Mme. Colbert without you or your partner present, whilst you talk to Théo and myself? It would help enormously."

"Help whom?" she replied, smiling rather bitterly.

"Right now we believe that these children have been snatched away from loving grandparents by a woman who is barely sane and her abusive lover. We descended on you tonight to rescue these little ones, return them to safety and to turn you two over to the authorities." I could see my words adding to the burdens already on her shoulders and her body bending under their weight.

"Except," I added more briskly, "I feel we have already acted like a bunch of prats rather than commendable upholders of the law. Before we make further fools of ourselves, it might be a good idea to get your version of the story. If you can trust Mme. Colbert to interview your daughters without you, we could perhaps justify our giving you some assistance."

The woman gently pushed her daughters toward the living room door.

"Naomi, Rachel, go with this lady and tell her truthfully anything she wants to know. If you are frightened, call out and I will come to you."

The two girls looked apprehensive but did as they were told.

The story ran as follows. Juliette Tourret met and married Ari Van der Zwaluw when he was working in northern France as head of sales for a small but very prestigious instrument company who had its headquarters just outside Amsterdam. After a few years Ari received promotion to Sales Director and the family had moved back to Holland.

All went well until the loss of one of the company's major customers coincided with a general downturn in the economy. Ari began to work longer and longer hours, spending more and more time away from home. When Ari did return to the matrimonial home he began to use Juliette as a punch bag to relieve his anger and frustration. During one particularly violent episode he knocked her down the stairs and she broke her collar bone.

She had been taken to hospital and Ari began to chide her gently in front of the nurses for being so clumsy and worrying them all so badly. It was then that she realised that he could have broken her neck – and not only would he have got away with it, he would not have cared that he had killed her. She began to fear for her life.

When Juliette got out of hospital she took her daughters to her mother's house in Dunkirk, and sued for divorce. It was then she began to understand the strength of the networking amongst the male business community to which Ari belonged.

The divorce was contested, judgement given to Ari on the grounds of mental cruelty. He was also given custody of the children. She received no financial settlement. Although it was allowed that she was entitled to a proportion of the value of their house, she could not claim it until both children were no longer in need of a parental home.

Social workers took the girls away, and, due to Ari's work commitments, they went to live with their paternal grandparents. The couple, both of whom were in their seventies, were puritanical and very strict. They insisted on a regime for the girls that consisted of school, homework and church. Non-academic school activities were discouraged, as were friendships with other pupils.

Unfortunately – despite or perhaps because of the new regime – the girls' school performance deteriorated. Their physical health also began to break down. They grew pale, thin and subject to every infection going the rounds. This was not noticed as soon as it should have been, because the move to the paternal grandparents' home also necessitated a change of school.

Eventually, the teachers did become concerned, especially Jean Van Eerde, who taught mathematics and physics. Two polite but useless home visits to the Van der Zwaluw household made him worried enough to locate and consult with the mother. Mutual concern about the children blossomed into something closer and deeper between divorcee Juliette and bachelor Jean.

Recourse to the courts did not seem a viable option, given the tenuous nature of their evidence. Instead, the family decided on an illegal move to England. They all spoke a reasonable standard of English, and science teachers were still very much in demand, despite the British government's cutbacks. They had planned to lay a false trail of the girls being taken into France by their mother.

Jean had given his notice to the school in a perfectly proper and normal way. There was very little reason for the casual observer to connect this event with the disappearance of the two girls. The new family intended to slip across the Channel to new lives in England.

What they had not allowed for, however, was the speed and

effectiveness of the search instigated in Holland. Nor the delays the Christmas holidays would entail in Juliette obtaining her new documentation. Juliette Van der Zwaluw was now Mme. Van Eerde. Unfortunately, the new passport was taking some time to come through. All they needed was a few more days of quiet living and then they would disappear forever.

Théo said nothing whilst the sorry tale was unfolding. When it was over he asked a sudden question.

"If you two are going to be such perfect parents, how come you left your children alone on New Year's Eve whilst you went out?"

Jean and Juliette looked a bit sheepish. Jean however eventually answered. "You will understand that we have not been able to do much shopping with the place being plastered with photos of the girls. We had nothing in to toast the New Year. It seemed such a shame as it was our very first together. So we went out to get some wine and soft drinks for the girls from a bar."

"Why did the two of you go?" Théo persisted.

Jean blushed furiously. "This is a very small holiday home, with little chance for privacy. I wanted a few minutes alone with my new bride."

"Where did you go for the wine?" asked Théo.

"The Coq d'Or, just off the town square."

Théo dug out his cell phone and dialled. There was the usual exchange of greetings and then Théo asked about outdoor sales the previous evening. There was a long pause but eventually some answers were given and Théo signed off. He wrote furiously in his note book and asked me to pass the paper to Madame Colbert with the girls. Apparently the answers tallied. Half a bottle of Champagne and a six pack of colas had been sold to a thin guy with a pretty blonde just after ten o'clock. The girls confirmed Maman and Monsieur Jean had returned just before eleven. They had turned on the television, but the programme they wanted to see had not yet started.

Théo got up. "We need to consult. But do not worry; we will do nothing without informing you. I truly believe you have nothing more to fear from our amateur detective work." He led the way out of the door. I followed with Mme. Colbert on my heels. Just as we were going through the door, the youngest girl shyly touched Madame's arm.

"Can we still come to the Epiphany service, Madame?"

"Bien sur," who would have had the heart to refuse them?

Back in Mme. Colbert's house, Madame poured drinks for us all – Pineau de Charent for us and Suze for Théo. After a few minutes of silence, whilst she fussed with biscuits and crisps, she asked the question we were all thinking: "What do we do now?"

"Maman, tell us what the children told you."

Madame fished out her glasses, a notebook and a pen from her handbag. "My memory was never anything much," she explained, "and recently it has got worse than ever."

The stories were essentially the same. "Daddy had to spend a lot of time away on business. Mummy and Daddy were not good friends any more. Daddy had bought then both new bicycles after Mummy fell down stairs."

Mme. Colbert looked up from her notes. "They both maintain that Mummy fell down the stairs, but they blush and wriggle when they say it, then want to talk about something else. They speak with great pleasure about their time with the older Mme Tourret. Their mother was a teacher before her marriage, a Professeur not an Assistante they claim with some degree of pride. Juliette taught them at home after she had taken them away from school.

"They spoke with affection of the dog that had had puppies, and the old cat who liked best to sleep on Mamie's lap in the evening. They spoke of M. and Mme. Van der Zwaluw more formally as Grand'mère and Grand'père."

Madame put her notebook to one side. "There is one more story worth retelling," she said. "I gather that there was to be an examination on the use of the French language for which there was to be some minor school prize. The older girl Naomi had been put in for it, even though the test was most usually aimed at girls in the senior class. The grandparents had been coaching her for weeks. The night before the exam she was compelled to study into the early hours of the morning. According to Naomi her brain felt like cotton wool. She did not do well in the test, forgetting some of the most basic rules of grammar. The day after the results were announced both girls had to take their bicycles to a charity shop supporting under-privileged children..." Madame made no further comment on the incident, but her rigid posture and strictly neutral tones said volumes.

"They seem to like Monsieur Jean. When they get to England they want to see the Queen and go a place called the Cavern Club, in some town in the North of England whose name I could not catch. They are also to have a puppy and a kitten each. I just hope this school where Jean has got a job has a tolerant attitude to pets."

"Why should the school's policy on pets matter?" asked Théo.

"Because he has got a place in a private boarding school, and a house goes with the job. The girls were willing to chatter on but suddenly I thought it was politic not to ask any more questions."

There was no decision to be made. Théo, thoughtful as ever went straight across to tell the family Van Eerde that we were sorry we had bothered them and anything we had learned we would keep to ourselves. Madame promised she would speak to Lucie Rolland and confirm that the Van Eerdes were not the family sought by the police. This was the spirit of the truth, though not its literal interpretation.

For the curious, the posters were soon replaced with others featuring an identikit picture of a guy who was wanted for passing counterfeit cheques. The fugitive girls were forgotten – if they had in fact even been very much considered. Certainly no report ever appeared in the local papers following up the story.

On 6th January two closely bonneted girls with ugly old fashioned spectacles attended the Epiphany service at St. Corentin's with Mme. Colbert. They were introduced as the daughters of one of her niece's friends. Many months later Madame received a postcard of 'The Fab Four' postmarked 'Liverpool' bearing the legend 'Love from N&R'.

Despite careful explanation I think Mme. Colbert was still at something of a loss.

CHAPTER FOURTEEN

1

The events since New Year's Day had not given me much opportunity for my own concerns. However, the interview with Rosine and Edouard could not be postponed any longer. We met in my flat at 2pm. The young people looked more relaxed and confident than I had ever seen them before.

"Once more, I would like to give you my congratulations on the New Year's Eve party. It was a wonderful success. I would, however, like to ask you if you had any problem with the costs?"

"No, Madame. Part of the exercise was to show we could run a commercial enterprise. The event was ticketed, and the bar actually did better than our calculations. Even with a generous present to M. Henri for loaning us his establishment, there's been a substantial addition to my 'dot'." Rosine was justifiably proud, but I had another question.

"A modern young woman like you is still saving up for a dowry?" I was surprised.

"But of course! Today more than ever, especially in a profession such as ours where, more often than not, we live on the employer's premises. A sum of money safely banked is essential to ensure that whatever disasters may strike there are funds for accommodation and food for a reasonable period of time until we can get on our feet again."

There was no answer to this except to admire the young woman's prudence. I reverted to business.

"I have great pleasure in offering Edouard and yourself the positions of head chef and assistant manager at the Cloche Blanche. We hope to open the hotel on 14th July with a grand party. If, of course, there are any alterations to this date due to unforeseen circumstances, we shall consult with you both."

If Rosine was disappointed with status of Assistant Manager she did not show it. The offer was both generous and appropriate and we both knew that. However, I suspected that Rosine's ambitions would not be half satisfied until she was a manager – if not owner of her own hotel.

We discussed terms and conditions, and agreed it would be sensible to have the local Notaire draw up a legal contract that both parties would sign. It would be part of the agreement that Edouard would make himself available for consultations as to the fitting out of the kitchen to full professional standard.

The next bit was tricky and needed to be put in just the right way. Théo and I would be married in April. We intended to move into a specially refurbished apartment in one of the towers of La Cloche Blanche. This would mean that not only the manager's apartment at my hostel was vacant but the job of Hostel manager also needed to be filled.

I tried to explain delicately but found both Rosine and Edouard looking at me without comprehension. Ah well, time to call the agricultural digging implement a shovel.

"Would you and Edouard like to live here at the flat in the Hostel?" I asked. "It would give you a degree of privacy and a break from the Hotel. We could arrange an amicable monthly rental; taking into consideration you might be occasionally disturbed in the night. I would also be interested to know if your mother, Mme. Bonneau, could be persuaded to consider the post of manager here in the hostel. I would continue to be the owner and do all the relevant paperwork. Madame would just be required to oversee the place, make sure all ran smoothly and cope with any emergencies such as our stranded veterans. Marie-Liesse could take on your role, Rosine, as senior assistant, and I would leave it to your mother to engage whatever other occasional help she needed."

I could see by their faces that the proposal was very acceptable. However, they solemnly stated that they would give the matter some thought for themselves, and consult Mme. Bonneau about the position of manageress.

"If Madame is interested, ask her to call on me at her convenience."

2

At ten o'clock next morning Mme. Bonneau, her black hat decorated with two artificial red roses, asked to see me.

I welcomed her and poured coffee for us both. I restated the offer I had outlined to Rosine and Edouard. She went over very carefully just what her responsibilities would be and those that would continue to rest with me. I respected and commended her caution.

"You understand, Madame," she said at length, "that for many years I have been responsible only for my own home and family as a good mother should. Perhaps I took on a little housekeeping now and then for families in the town when times were hard, but nothing more."

"My dear Madame, your family are now beginning to start independent lives. Perhaps you should think of this as little more than an extension of your previous domestic duties. Certainly on the day of my disaster you showed excellent management qualities."

She inclined her head, taking tribute were it was merited. Then almost immediately she became concerned again.

"My son, Eric, will not in the immediate future be able to take up an independent life."

"I do not have a position at the moment I could offer your son," I said firmly. "However he is very welcome to keep you company here when he does not have duties elsewhere. Obviously any work he does, either for the Hostel or at La Cloche Blanch, can be recompensed on a day-work basis." With this, she was content.

3

The engagement party for Rosine and Edouard was held in the Hotel Napoleon. The management had most generously provided the food and given them the use of one of the smaller conference rooms. It was quite a substantial contribution from an establishment that could and did charge a hundred Euros a head without wine for one of their gourmet evenings.

Rosine, tiny as a ten year old, and her fiancé Edouard Vincent, who was not much taller and equally slight in build, were both dressed in formal evening clothes. They looked for all the world like two children who had borrowed their parents' clothes to play dress up.

There had been rambling speeches of good wishes mixed with embarrassing reminiscences of childish indiscretions from boozy uncles on both sides of the family, as both of the young people had lost their fathers tragically early. Women, of course, were not expected to or even allowed to speak on their own behalf at these occasions.

Rosine seemed happy to take the traditional silent role. When it was time for Edouard to do his party piece, he looked as if he too would have preferred to sit quietly and look decorative. When he did get to his feet he made the conventional speech well enough. There was a long list of people he felt he ought to thank. He offered compliments to all of Rosine's relatives and finally a tribute to the bride-to-be. To my ears this was the only part of the monologue that sounded genuine.

Edouard then added an acknowledgement to Théo and myself. I was touched and pleased. Edouard's appointment and his acceptance had been an act of faith on both sides. For Edouard it meant leaving a prestigious establishment with a management whose talent was nationally acclaimed. He would then join a completely new and untried venture; with owners whose experience of the catering trade were a couple of years running what in truth was little more than a bed and breakfast boarding house.

We, on the other hand, were trusting the entire catering operation of our new hotel to a diffident young man without head chef experience. We had all calculated the risks and found them acceptable.

Edouard finished at last and, dropping down onto one knee, took a white leather box from his trouser pocket and presented Rosine with her ring to a torrent of applause.

I saw Rosine's expression when the ring was produced. There was love and pleasure in her face, but also a good measure of surprise. Later, I joined the group of matrons all crowding round admiring the ring and wanting to try it on. This latter was a custom I have never understood. I felt that so important, so precious a token, shouldn't be handed round like a box of sweets.

It was not difficult, however, to see the cause of Rosine's surprise. The ring was remarkably handsome and looked very valuable. It was a half hoop of five diamonds. The very substantial stones flashed and glittered in a way that left very little doubt that there gems were of high quality. How had a young man in his early twenties, in a job that was notoriously ill paid, saved up the money to pay for such a treasure? I hoped he had not put himself into debt when a far simpler ring would have done the task just as well.

One of the pushier aunts, with more nosiness and less tact than the rest of us, asked the question outright. Edouard replied with more good humour than I could have managed, that the stones – flawless yellow diamonds, according to the jeweller he had taken it to – were far out of his price range. He had simply paid for the cleaning and refurbishment of the shank which had worn thin. It had been his aunt's engagement ring. The aunt had given it to Edouard's mother before she died, and he had inherited it from his mother when she passed on.

From that moment the party atmosphere disintegrated. Various family factions stood in little groups talking earnestly. If anyone else approached they would instantly fall silent. At a remarkably early hour guests started to drift away. Surprising, as there was still plenty of food and wine left. One didn't need the second sight to know that something was radically wrong.

Théo and I sat with a small group of friends who, like us, were not relatives. Whilst Rosine was helping one of the older aunts to her taxi I took the opportunity to ask about the history of the ring.

Edouard was open and cheerful as he recounted the story. His father had been the fifth of six brothers. The oldest, Frédéric, had done part of his military service in what was then French Indo-China. Family legend said that Frédéric had obtained a bag full of gems for just a couple of knapsacks of army rations.

"I always thought that the story was just a tale for children on Christmas Eve, because my aunt and uncle never had any money," Edouard said ruefully. "My mother always believed her brother-in-law had brought the stones for the ring back from his army service. There was also a beautiful jade cat which my aunt gave to my cousin, Simone, when she was just a little girl."

"To your cousin?" I queried. "What about her own offspring?"

"No, Uncle Frédéric and Aunt Elizabeth had no children of their own. My uncle did not marry until his late thirties. My Aunt Elizabeth was a gentle, modest woman from Dieppe. They met at her local church when Frédéric was doing military training there. He took up his long distance courtship again after he was demobbed from the army when the French left Indo-China in 1954. It was then, I suppose, that he had his diamonds made into this splendid ring. A further seven years passed before the couple actually married. Aunt Elizabeth always said she felt like poor old Rachel in the Bible story. Family legend said they always wanted children, but couples intent on producing a quiverful, rarely have engagements of such protracted length."

"Aunt Elizabeth was lovely." Edouard's face brightened at the thought of the old lady. "She kept open house, and there was always someone calling in and being invited to stay for lunch, dinner or both.

"Eighteen months later, my parents married. My mother was Alice Hahn. Despite the large age gap, the two sisters-in-law took to one another immediately and remained close for the rest of their lives. I know my mother's most frequent visitor and only friend was my Aunt Elizabeth.

"I loved my mother very much, but she was not always an easy person to get along with. She was very shy and always ready to take offence. She kept her distance from the rest of the family and ensured my father did too. A few years after their marriage they only met up with the rest of the tribe at weddings and funerals."

He sighed and then continued: "I suppose I can understand it in a way. Grandfather Hahn had been Jewish, although the family hadn't been religious for a couple of generations before that. Grandmother Hahn was widowed quite young and ended up living for a time with a man who was married to someone else. Maman always thought that the Vincent family held her background against her. Whilst I know that Grand'père's family were all devout Catholics, it's ten to one they never thought twice about Alice's relatives. When you know the family history the Vincent's weren't all that pure either."

"So what happened?" I asked.

My uncle died in 1996. He did not leave a will, but on the other hand it did not matter very much as they lived in a rented house and had very little in the way of savings. My aunt moved to sheltered accommodation. I do know that more than one member of the family went round regularly to relieve her of pieces of furniture, books, my uncle's tools, lots of things my relatives assured her would not fit into her new home or for which they were sure she would have no further use. They very kindly suggested they would be prepared to take them off her hands," he said with slight bitterness.

"Aunt Elizabeth confessed to my mother that she was not at all sure she wanted such radical services, but was too embarrassed to refuse her late husband's relatives. It was dreadful and pathetic at the same time. I was only a schoolboy back then, but I remember my mother being offered some things and declaring with much offended virtue that she would take nothing. I think it was partly in revenge for all these petty depredations that when my aunt made her own will she left everything she had to her only brother, Joseph, rather than to any of her husband's relatives."

He continued: "My father had a stroke and died suddenly about two years later. My mother and Aunt Elizabeth became even closer. They went on holiday together; they even lived together for a short period when my aunt's flat was being renovated. My Aunt had her first stroke in 2001. She was in hospital for about six weeks, but eventually did manage to return home. I know it was then my aunt pressed my mother to accept her ring, her silver backed hair brushes and her fur coat. My mother refused them at first but must have eventually been persuaded because I know she eventually owned both the coat and the ring. I don't think my mother ever fancied the hair brushes."

Edouard finished the sorry tale quickly.

"Shortly after my aunt returned home she suffered a fall and broke her hip. The end was inevitable. Aunt Elizabeth died of pneumonia in the Maison de Retraite, the old folk's home up near St Saulve's. At that point I suspect my aunt was glad to go. This was around Easter 2002. Not long after my mother's house was burgled. It was thought she must have come across the robbery in progress, because she received a blow to her head. Maman recovered, but was never quite the same afterwards. She died quietly in her sleep about a year after her beloved sister in law."

"How come the burglars did not get the ring?" I queried.

"Maman had already given it to me. Her fingers had become very swollen with arthritis and she could no longer get her rings over her knuckles. In a fit of temper and shame she gathered them all together and swore she would throw them away. I asked if I might look at them. Typical Maman, she asked what use women's rings would be to me. I said I might just have a girlfriend one day. I already liked Rosine very much. She said I could have them if I wanted them. To tell you the truth I did not like the thought of giving Aunt Elizabeth's ring to the church jumble sale and Maman was angry enough with her twisted fingers to do just that."

Edouard sighed and glanced round the room. "Now it looks as if family greed is going to rear its head once more. We might as well pack up here and go home."

Théo suddenly laughed. "This is too good an opportunity to miss. You have got rid of the stuffed shirts; you have food and opened bottles of wine, which will surely not keep. Ask a few real friends round, young people, to help you celebrate properly." Théo offered his mobile phone. "Tell them to come just as they are. If you think the hotel will be a bit toffee nosed about them tramping through their grand entrance hall, direct them to come via the kitchen door."

Rosine returned to find bow ties and jackets being removed and glasses being refilled. The rejuvenated party was still going strong when Théo and I discreetly made our departure in the early hours of the morning.

CHAPTER FIFTEEN

1

I was wakened next morning at nine o'clock by a thumping on my front door. I was not best pleased to see Inspector Delavoie. I opened the door to him dressed in a towelling robe and a headache. Nevertheless, I invited him politely into the breakfast room and asked what I could do for him.

"I wish to see Mademoiselle Bonneau," Monsieur L'Inspecteur said coldly.

I reflected crossly that I hadn't exchanged one pleasant word with Onesime Delavoie since I had arrived in Montreuil. Obnoxious as the man was, I had not previously had cause to doubt his detective skills. Staring at him in astonishment I responded, "neither Rosine nor her sister are here. My hostel is closed for another couple of weeks before our new season starts. My staff, like myself, are on holiday."

"I am perfectly aware of this, Mademoiselle Sinclair," he replied pompously. "When, however, I called at Rosine's home her mother told me she was spending the night here. Supposedly the modest young woman had not wanted to cross the town in the early hours of the morning following the bacchanalia held to celebrate her so-called 'engagement' to that rather self-important washer-up at the Hotel Napoleon."

I could feel my temper rising and a suitable retort formed itself in my mind. But I suddenly began to laugh when I realised that I was falling for the oldest trick in the policeman's handbook: get your suspect angry and off guard and indiscrete statements may follow. The only mystery was why he should be practising these techniques on me, other than he detested my fiancé Théo for reasons which should have been forgotten years ago.

"M. Delavoie, may I offer you a cup of coffee?" I said. M. L'Inspecteur looked a somewhat disconcerted.

"Please Monsieur, take a seat, we will share a little late breakfast and you can tell me what this is all about without tricks. Be assured I will help you if I can."

To my surprise M. Delavoie sat heavily in one of the breakfast chairs near the window and said "Very well Mademoiselle, but I would prefer chocolate if you would be so kind. I drink far too much coffee these days."

When I returned from the kitchen, the low winter sunlight was streaming in through the window. Under the golden beams the policeman's face looked tired; lines were beginning to etch themselves around his mouth and eyes. There was a fuzz of beard on his chin which spoke of extended night duty without the opportunity to go home to wash and change.

Fortunately, even when my hostel is closed I still placed a substantial order with Mme. Couroyer at the bakery for croissants and other breakfast rolls to cover unexpected visits from Théo and his ever growing team, who always made a point of calling if they were in the area.

Happy inspiration made me take out my fine china and put butter, honey and Mme. Bonneau's homemade plum jam in handsome little dishes whilst the chocolate heated. The unexpected kindness seemed to relax the man. He protested that he wished for nothing to eat but his hands automatically reached for a croissant as he began to tell me the story.

"Mademoiselle, you must understand that rumours of local events come to the notice of the police station along with the regular reports on regional crime. My officers have been aware of the arrangements for a party to celebrate Rosine's engagement for some time. Some off duty officers were actually invited to attend. The Bonneaus are well liked in this town, they are decent, hardworking and honest, despite Eric's little bit of trouble. They have not had the best of luck, but they never complain nor try to sponge off the community. My people could have arranged to be elsewhere when the guests at the Hotel Napoleon, having wined and dined well, started to go home in their cars."

I nodded, although I knew not where this was heading.

"What we had not expected was a stream of respectable middle-aged citizens visiting the police station claiming that Rosine's brand new engagement ring really belonged to them."

"First there was M. Bertrand, brother of the late Elizabeth Vincent, brandishing a copy of his sister's will and protesting that the ring was his. He was followed by a couple of the Vincent sister-in-law shouting that the ring had been promised to them before Elizabeth died. Finally we had M. Le Francois the Notaire who insisted the ring belonged to Charles Vincent, the youngest of the Vincent brothers who is also a personal friend of our Xavier."

"Monsieur!" I protested. Why didn't all these people come forward when the old lady died? Why wait till now?"

"A good question, with no very good answer, Mademoiselle Sinclair!" M. Delavoie rubbed his hand over this face. "All the relatives had apparently been convinced that the ring had been lost or stolen when the old woman went into hospital. They had more or less resigned themselves to its disappearance. What has upset them all so much is that

Alice Vincent had managed to secure it. The woman must have worked really hard at annoying her relatives," M. Delavoie finished explosively, licking jam off his fingers with energy.

"What sort of value are we talking about here?" I asked.

"The jeweller who did the cleaning and refurbishing said he made slightly more of it than was justified. The young man obviously did not wish to sell the stones, he just wanted to present his fiancé with the family treasure, so it was perhaps overvalued, a harmless fiction. In reality he estimated it at €7600 new, say €6300 without tax and take off another 10% because of the refurbishment. Say approximately €5500. These are of course selling prices; the buying price would be a great deal less. We are not talking about a vast fortune here."

"How can anything be proved one way or another after all this time with so many of the people originally involved now dead?" I queried.

"Right now, I really don't know," confessed the detective. "Whatever solution we come up with there is going to be a rift in the family. This, of course, does not worry the police, but I personally would not like to see Rosine Bonneau's married life start off under a cloud."

Suddenly M. Delavoie got up, as though embarrassed at showing such a sentimental side to his nature.

"Until the provenance can be shown without dispute, I am authorised to take the ring into official custody. When the young woman does emerge from whatever love nest she and young Edouard have found for themselves, please inform her that she is required to present herself and the disputed piece of jewellery at the Sous-Préfecture. If she has not been to visit us in the next twenty four hours we will come and look for her. You can assure your waitress that she will not find that amusing, au revoir, Mademoiselle Sinclair."

With that M. Delavoie departed, and I was left to make of it what I could. As I cleared away I noticed there was hardly a crumb left on what had been a well loaded breakfast tray.

2

Rosine appeared pale and tearful just before lunch time having heard on the rumour-mongering Telephone arabe that she and her ring were wanted by the police. I could give her little comfort except to offer to go with her to the Sous-Préfecture and promise vaguely that it would all be sorted out eventually. Once the dreadful visit had been made and a receipt issued for the disputed ring, Rosine was only too glad to return to her mother's house. I went with her to reassure Mme. Bonneau as best I could.

I wandered home through the damp grey streets feeling very low.

Suddenly I heard the unmistakable rattle of Théo's van. It screeched to a halt beside me, Théo jumped out and I was enfolded gently in a massive pair of hairy arms. For a moment we exchanged kisses which had nothing to do with polite greetings. I extricated myself, chiding him gently.

"Théo! Every lace curtain on the street must be twitching. Don't you have any work to do?"

"For once, Chérie, I am happy to say that I have. However it is not as important as ensuring that you have escaped unharmed from the clutches of M. Delavoie."

"I am perfectly safe. In the end he was even civil, so there was no need to ride to my rescue like St. George! But as you are here do you want to come in for a coffee?"

I felt I should shoo him away. He was undoubtedly busy. I knew this seemingly casual visit would have to be made up with unpaid overtime on whatever chantier he was working, but Théo's large presence was comforting.

He gave me his slow, wicked smile. "Chérie, I would beg you for a little *quelque chose* – just to keep me from the brink of starvation."

We went into my kitchen. I made Théo's favourite potato omelette whilst he sliced uneven chunks from a baguette and poured dressing on a salad of curly endive leaves.

"Delavoie is right," Théo said as I finished the history of the morning. "Unless the mystery is solved, the allegations will hang like an unpleasant smell over Rosine's marriage. We must help them. Even if they were not friends, we would not want any hint of scandal to affect our joint business venture."

"What do you propose, M. Maigret?" I asked with a touch of asperity.

"Let us start with the simple questions," Théo said. "Who knew about the ring?"

"Théo!" I exclaimed, "Elizabeth Vincent lived here in Montreuil for nearly fifty years. The whole town must have seen her ring at some time."

"They may have seen the ring, Chérie, but that is not the same as knowing about its romantic origins or supposed value. When Edouard took it to the jeweller it needed cleaning. The fire we saw in the stones last night may have been dulled for many years under a layer of household grease and the remains of pastry dough."

I shuddered at the thought and resolved to keep my own ring in its box when cooking and cleaning.

"I don't call cheating some starving Vietnamese villager out of valuable jewels with stolen Army stores particularly romantic," I said stiffly. "According to young Edouard, it was a well known story in the family so I suppose that all the brothers, sisters-in-law and cousins would have heard it."

"So why wasn't there a greater fuss when the ring supposedly went missing whilst Elizabeth was in hospital?" Théo looked at me with his head on one side.

I joined Théo at the kitchen table and started to nibble at a piece of bread. The crisp crust and savoury smell tempted my appetite and I took a more substantial bite. Through the crumbs I replied, "It was believed that it had been taken by one of the hospital staff, but as there was no proof it was not worth pursuing?"

"Come now, Chérie! We have here a ring worth thousands of Euros – or rather Francs at the time. It goes missing, but no-one says a word – why?"

"I give up!" I replied, scooping up a morsel of Théo's omelette on my bread. Théo generously pushed his plate into the centre of the table.

"The family knew the ring was destined for the unpopular Alice. They did not care what happened to it. Edouard himself says that his mother was nervous and shy. None of the Vincents would have been surprised that, lonely and unsupported as she was, Alice did not stand up for her rights."

"So why are they all claiming the ring now?" I asked.

"Greed, Chérie, greed!" Théo said, scooping the last of the omelette from under my wavering hand.

"Seriously, Chérie, it is the story of the burglary that worries me. It strikes me that perhaps someone knew the ring was in the old lady's possession and tried to secure an inheritance to which they were not entitled."

"Then why didn't Alice accuse her attacker?"

"If she saw her assailant at all, the blow to the head could have very well caused a degree of amnesia. I fear, however, that the potential robber might have more on his or her conscience that attempted theft. If Alice died less than a year after the attack, the charge could be murder."

CHAPTER SIXTEEN

1

Théo gave a last wipe of bread over what was by now an almost polished plate. "Here you can help, Chérie. I must now go back to work, but will you find Edouard and ask him if he knows anything else about the wretched ring? I will come tonight and we will form a plan of action.

Oh, by the way, Maman says M. Binet at the Charcuterie has an excellent *Daube provencale* today if you don't fancy cooking." With a wave of his fingers he was gone.

I put on my coat and walked round to the Hotel Napoleon's kitchen entrance. Edouard was chopping salad vegetables in the preparation room and looking quite miserable. I wished him 'bonjour' and seated myself on a stool in the corner of the room.

"I saw Théo this morning," I began. "He is determined to get to the bottom of this mystery and I am going to help him."

"Thank you, Mademoiselle Sinclair, but what can either of you do? It was all so long ago. I have spoken to my aunts. I offered to sell the ring and share the proceeds with everyone who thinks they have a claim."

That was greater generosity than I had anticipated or quite frankly seemed sensible.

"What was their reaction?" I asked gently.

"Each person I approached threatened never to speak to either of us again if anyone else touched a centime of the money."

It was about what I expected.

"Is there anything else you can tell me about the history of the ring?" I asked. "The box you produced last night was bright and new. Do you, by any chance, have the original box?

"Yes, it's in my room here at the Napoleon."

"Can I see it?"

Edouard rinsed his hands and left the kitchen. He was back in less than five minutes with a small blue ring box. He thrust it at me then after washing his hands once more returned to his duties.

The little box looked very battered. I pressed the small metal catch and the lid sprang open to reveal a white velvet cushion and a white silk lining both now much discoloured by time. On the silk in ornate printing was the name and address of the jeweller: 'M. A. Gonthier, rue d'Ecosse, Dieppe'.

"May I borrow this?" I asked.

"Why not? There is no longer a ring to put in it..." was the dispirited reply.

"One more question, mon cher Edouard," I ventured. "Who do you think has the best claim, after yourself, I mean?"

"Maman was honest to a fault. She was the sort of person who would take a ten Euro note she found in the street to the police station. She would never have kept anything that was not hers. If the ring was truly not Maman's to keep or to give away, then I suppose M. Bertrand is the logical heir.

"My Uncle Joseph is a wealthy man; he had a very successful chain of butcher's shops in Dieppe. He sold them when he retired and came to live here in Montreuil to be near his sister. From all I have heard he invested the money well and has continued to prosper. I have never known him to be mean or grasping. Mme. Bertrand – his wife, my Aunt Viviane – has not been well for some time." Edouard returned to his work and refused to say any more.

2

That evening, as Théo was carving faces into his piece of Camembert – a practice I suspected he would not have attempted in his mother's house – he said, "I think we should visit Dieppe and see if the successors to M. Gonthier still have a jewellery shop in the rue d'Eccose."

"We could do that by telephone. It'll take all day to go to Dieppe."

"Correct, Chérie, but two immovable people in your shop are less easy to put off than a caller on the telephone. Besides, I have not had a true sole Dieppoise for some time."

"Your mother is an excellent cook," I exclaimed.

"Yes, but she rarely cooks it just for the two of us – too fiddly."

I made a few more token protests, but the following Saturday saw us on the road to Dieppe. We hopped onto the motorway just south of Montreuil, and the journey took us far less time than I calculated and certainly was quicker than it would have been for poor Frédéric way back in the days when he was courting Elizabeth Bertrand.

Once in Dieppe, we parked on the Esplanade. Like many French seaside towns, the long line of hotels overlooking the sea seemed bleak and unwelcoming out of season. The sky was grey, and the wind whipped the leaden waters of the Channel into long, white capped rollers. Behind the grim façade, however, was a bustling town. I was amazed to find that there was still a very prestigious jeweller on the rue d'Ecosse rejoicing in the name Gonthier et Fils.

We had dressed in our best clothes in order to look like potential customers. As we pressed the bell at the side of the security locked door, I doubted we would fool the sophisticated assistants for five minutes.

Théo, blithely oblivious to the assessing glances of the staff marched up to the nearest counter and demanded to see M. Gonthier.

"Père or Fils?" was the sharp retort.

"Father." If anyone would know about our long ago transaction it would be the older generation. The senior man would also have the authority to allow us to look at any records that survived.

"I'm afraid M. Gonthier is out." There was a glitter of triumph in the assistant's eyes

"Then we'll see the son," I countered.

"But I thought it was M. Gonthier senior you wanted to see?" The Assistant was having fun at our expense.

"Mademoiselle Martel, I will attend to these customers, and I would like a word with you in my office later this afternoon." A young man in his early twenties and very formally dressed grinned at us. "How can I help? I am, Philippe Gonthier, the youngest of the illustrious line."

"The matter is quite delicate," said Théo. "Is there somewhere we can speak privately?"

"I'm intrigued. We have a private viewing room that is empty at the moment – please come with me." He led the way to a discreet door at the back of the show room. He gestured us to seats in front of a leather topped table.

"Some of our staff can pretend to be above themselves. My grandfather always used to tell us children that the biggest sale he ever made was to a farmer who still had manure on his boots." Suddenly realising what he had said, the young man blushed scarlet and muttered something about it not applying to present company as he seated himself opposite us.

Théo produced the little blue box. "Is this one of yours?"

The young man took it and examined it.

"Yes, most certainly, but it is very old we have not used boxes like this for over thirty years."

"We have reason to believe the box is more like fifty years old."

"How can we possibly help?" Philippe was still smiling but beginning to show some concern.

Théo repeated the story of the old engagement ring and its disputed provenance, and then asked: "Do you still have records from, say, 1954?"

"My grandfather was in charge of the shop at that time. He passed away five years ago. There might be records somewhere, but I don't know where, and finding one transaction amongst the hundreds we do every year would be a mammoth task."

"Is there anyone from the older generation who might remember such an unusual transaction?"

"No, my grandfather was the only one of his family to survive the war. Only Grand'Mere is left of that generation and she is not at all well. No, I don't think we can help you, but it's a fascinating story. Now, whilst you're here, I see Madame is wearing a very fine engagement ring. Can I show you some wedding rings? We have a range of ladies' and gentlemen's matching rings with quite distinctive designs – very modern but of traditional quality."

We barely got out with Théo's wallet intact. The rings were very handsome, at an equally handsome price, and not at all suitable for a man who did building restoration work. I wanted Théo to have a wedding ring even if he could not wear it all the time. I was, however, not all that fussed about matching rings, and for myself liked the ones with an excised design rather than a plain band.

As we walked down the street I tucked my arm into Théo's. "I suppose the trail ends here?"

"Not necessarily. There is still Grand'Mere."

"We can't go bursting in on a frail old lady! Besides, we have no idea where she lives."

"I planned a courteous approach rather than, as you delicately put it, 'bursting in on' her. As to where she lives, I have an idea."

We continued walking. "Where would the family of the most prestigious jeweller in the town go to church?" Théo mused.

I could see the way his mind was working. "Obviously she worshipped at the largest church in the town, especially if it was only a few hundred yards from her shop." We returned into Puits-Sale square and found the ancient church of St. Jacques. We entered through the fourteenth century doorway into the gloomy interior. There were several people in the chancel and some older ladies were arranging flowers by the pulpit.

"Go say a prayer, Chérie. Leave this to me." Théo straightened his jacket, smoothed his hair, and approached the most formidable of the group – a round faced woman whose distant relatives probably knitted at the side of the guillotine.

I did as I was bid and went into the Sacred Heart Chapel and lit a couple of candles, one for Rosine and Edouard and one for Théo and myself. I had plenty of time both to say my prayers and to contemplate the Life of the Virgin carved into the consoles of the centre chapel before Théo returned to me. I could see by the smile on his face that he had obtained what he was after.

"Let us go for lunch, Chérie. There is nothing more we can do for an hour or so. I would be most discourteous to arrive with Madame's soup – and besides, I am hungry."

Containing my curiosity, we left the church, rounded a corner and walked straight into the Marmite Dieppoise. There Théo introduced me to the joys of sole dieppois. I could understand why Madame Colbert did not choose to cook it very often. As well as a fine fat sole baked in a wine and cream sauce, the dish is decorated with freshly cooked prawns and mussels. It was delicious.

3

It was nearly three o'clock before we left the restaurant. Whilst we had been eating, Théo had explained that he believed that a woman like Madame Gonthier would most likely be a pillar of the local community. Amongst all the social benefits it would also be good for business. The most likely church would have been the grandest within reasonable reach of her home, ergo the visit to St. Jacques. The flower arrangers had indeed known Mme. Gonthier. She was, however, no longer active in the church, as age and illness had confined her to her own home.

"However, Chérie, they did know where that home was, and it only took a little masculine charm to draw out of those rat trap mouths the address we need. Now lunch is over, and well bred ladies are thinking about tea, we are going to visit."

I looked at those kind eyes, with their soft curling lashes and decided that the ladies of St. Jacques had not stood a chance.

As we did not know Dieppe very well, we took a taxi to the address Théo had been given. The driver stopped in front of a very fine house on the outskirts of the town. Wrought iron gates led up to a typical French villa complete with Gothic turrets and a Greek portico.

A uniformed maid answered our ring and explained that Madame was ill and did not see visitors.

Théo produced the antique box and asked that it be taken to the mistress. We were invited into the hall and left to admire ourselves in the Venetian glass mirrors. We must have stood for more than half an hour before the woman came back down the stairs and said that Madame would see us.

"Mme. Gonthier is very weak," she hissed. "Please do nothing to upset her."

I feared that would be impossible.

We were shown into an overheated room. By the fire a white haired woman dressed in formal black sat in a winged armchair. Even seated she gave the impression of being tall, and she certainly was very thin. Deep lines were etched in her face, but she sat perfectly upright.

"You have come about the Vincent Diamonds, have you not?"

"Yes, Madame," Théo replied.

"I hoped this day would never come, but perhaps it is as well that I sort things out before I go. Le bon Dieu knows best. Please seat yourselves and prepare to listen. We do not have long. The Nurse will even now be calling my son. When he arrives, all conversation will be at an end." She wheezed and coughed into a lace handkerchief.

"Do you know what it was like for jewellers during the war? No, don't bother to reply, you can't possibly imagine. There were times I envied our Jewish competitors – the far sighted ones got themselves and their stock into Switzerland before the borders closed. There were those who were not so pre-cognisant, but that is all ancient history now."

The old woman seemed to permit herself a smile before carrying on. It made me shiver.

"Who wants to buy jewellery during a war? The Boches would come in for trinkets, but they demanded such presents and discounts that we were virtually giving stuff away. When peace was declared we were almost ruined."

I wondered where all this was leading. Théo, sensing my impatience, laid two fingers on my arm. I understood. The story had to come at her own pace. Interruptions would only result in further delays.

"Eight years after the defeat of Nazi Germany we were still struggling. All we were doing was some pawnbroking and selling sterling sliver christening cups and diamond chip engagement rings to stupid shop girls. It was back street trader stuff. Yet we were the Gonthiers, once the premier diamond house of Northern France. To get back into that market we had to have collateral.

"Then Frederic Vincent turned up with his little wash leather pouch of uncut diamonds. The fool had no idea of what he owned. He wanted an engagement ring for some working class girl eking out a living as a tailoress.

"My husband did not set out to cheat him. They worked out that our cutter would dress the stones, set them in a ring and the fee would be taken from the other uncut gems. The ring was made. The man deigned to say he was pleased with a ring that could have graced the finger of a princess. It was not until the lout left the shop that my husband realised that he had gone off without picking up the pouch with the rest of the diamonds.

"The man did not live in Dieppe. We did not know how to contact him or his fiancé. We waited a month, two, but he did not return to collect his property. It was then I persuaded my husband to use the diamonds to borrow money to get our business back on track."

"You sold them?" I gasped

"No, you silly girl! It was enough that we *had* them. The rich prefer to lend to the rich. All we had to do was show that we did not need the money and credit came flowing in. It bothered my husband, Alphonse. He made me give my solemn word that I would never sell the gems and would give then back if anyone with just title came looking for them. No one has – till now. Do you have title to the stones?" Madame looked up at Théo.

"No, Madame, I do not. The ring your husband had made all those years ago is in dispute – more treasure on top of that makes the whole thing even more complicated," Théo replied.

"Bon," she said with a wicked smile. The old lady turned to a carved wooden box on a side table by her elbow. "Here are the diamonds left with us in 1954. I charge you with returning them to their rightful owner. They are now off my conscience and firmly on yours – I wish you joy of them." She coughed and dabbed her lips again.

"Wilfred, my son, and my grandson Philippe know nothing of this, not a thing. Alphonse and I were hardly proud of what we had done. If you try to implicate any of my kin I swear I'll haunt you from my grave."

She thrust a dry and cracked little pouch at Théo. "Take it, take it!" she cried urgently. We could hear footsteps on the stair. Théo shoved the pouch into his pocket.

"I wish you a good death, Madame." He stooped to kiss her cheek but she turned away, starting to cough and wheeze in good earnest. The next moment a shorter, stouter replica of the young man we had seen that morning, thrust himself into his mother's room. He insisted at the top of his voice that we leave instantly. We did without any attempt at explanation.

We had to walk back into Dieppe. We were cold, wet and exhausted by the time we returned to the van.

As we drove out of the town following the signs for the motorway Théo said, "This makes everything that much more difficult."

Théo passed the ancient pouch to me. I carefully opened it. Inside was a crumbling piece of paper covered in some sort of oriental script and half a dozen lumps of what might have been mistaken as amber toffee.

"We need to get that paper translated. M. Chang at the Golden Dragon in Etaples is a customer of mine and I am sure he will help if he can," Théo commented.

I was sure too – especially for a discount on the repair of his guttering!

"If those dull lumps of rock are indeed uncut diamonds, they are probably worth a fortune. They must be the property of M. Bertrand. The inheritance goes from Frederic to his wife Elizabeth then to her brother. What it does not do is throw more light on who is the legal owner of the ring."

"All we can do is follow the clues that we are given. Surely the truth must eventually emerge," Théo mused.

I was not at all sure this was necessarily true. "So what do you suggest we do?"

"Something tells me we should not try to move too fast with this, Chérie. Going straight to M. Bertrand or even our friend Onesime may very well be a mistake. Let us get the paper translated and then decide on our next step."

"What about Mme. Gonthier? If she tells the story to her son, he might accuse us of theft?"

"I don't think Madame would do that. I truly believe she kept the secret of the diamonds from her children. It would not surprise me if in a very few days, Mme. Gonthier will not be able to tell anyone anything."

I took Théo's meaning. Looking down at my hands I saw the stone on my own beautiful ring catch a stray beam of the remaining light.

Without thinking, I said out loud: "I must be sure there are no misunderstandings when it comes to passing on my own ring."

"You should make a new will when we marry, Chérie. Just add a paragraph leaving it to our eldest daughter."

I could not have been more shocked if Théo had slapped me. Did he want, expect, a family? I would not see forty again, he knew that. I was too old, it was too late. I suddenly had the feeling that I had made the biggest mistake of my life and I could not see what to do about it.

I hardly said another word for the rest of the journey back to Montreuil. Théo seemed blissfully unaware of the bombshell he had dropped. When we stopped in front of my hostel I jumped out of the van, made some excuse and sent Théo off without even a goodbye kiss, then I hurried inside alone.

CHAPTER SEVENTEEN

1

That night I was unable to settle or rest. I walked from room to room, turning the problem over in my mind. How badly did Théo want children? Did I want a child at all?

Could I still carry a child to term? I was healthy, vigorous even, with none of the symptoms of the onset of the change of life. On the other hand, I could not deny that the time had passed when I could have expected a delivery without danger either to myself or the new baby. Did I want to take such risks for either of us?

Could I even conceive if I wanted to?

Sharply, I told myself to get matters in perspective. To find the answers to the physical questions, I needed professional advice; the others could follow once I knew where I stood. I would make an appointment with Mme. Deroussent, *medecin gynecologie et maladies feminines*.

Decision made, I went to bed. Even so I did not sleep well. Despite my good intentions, the same questions circulated in my brain. When I did finally fall asleep my dreams were troubled with vague impressions of ghostly children.

2

Next morning I waited until I could be sure the Doctor was in her office and then I made my way to the Place de Gaulle with every intention of making an appointment. I reached the ornate door with its brass plaques stating the specialties of the three partners who shared the premises – and walked right past. I lingered for a few moments outside the shop that sold fine wines and rare gourmet foods, then steeled myself, turned – and passed the door again and walked across the square to the Salon de Thé.

Coward!

I ordered a pot of camomile and a couple of sables – plain sugar biscuits. They came promptly. I stared into the pale golden liquid in my cup and tried to get my ragged breathing under control. I had not felt like this since Maman and I had visited the consultant together back in Scotland. What was the terrible news I could not face this time?

Two of the local gossips came in. I studied my tea with renewed concentration, determined not to catch their eye. They settled themselves at my table anyway.

"My dear Mademoiselle Sinclair,' cooed Mme. Rolland. "Have you heard the news?"

"Brazen, quite brazen in my opinion," said Veuve Delcroix with a look of satisfaction.

I put my cup down. "I've no idea what you are talking about."

"You know the new hotel, the one next to the Chapelle de l'Hotel-Dieu?" Chirped Madame Roland!

"Sacrilege, Sacrilege!" This from Veuve Delcroix.

"Le Couvent?" I asked. "Wasn't it converted from the old hospital building?" I asked.

"Yes, that's the one – all swank and no substance, if you ask me," Veuve Delcroix again, although I did not disagree with her.

"So what has happened?" I asked.

"Not what – who? Brigitte Gobert has come back from Paris and taken on the job of hotel manager."

I began to comprehend the excitement. "*Théo's* Brigitte?" I asked.

"Yes, the hussy! And you'll never guess who she has with her."

I went very cold inside. "Who, you'll have to tell me."

"Her *daughter*!"

No. this was not possible. I couldn't let myself believe it.

"The little basket is calling herself Stéphanie Gobert – but we all know who the father must be." Veuve Delcroix spoke between thinned lips.

Madame! Mme. Rolland and I said in harmony.

"Perhaps I shouldn't have said that, but it is what most people will think." Veuve Delcroix seemed unrepentant.

I put a ten Euro note on the table and staggered out into the square. I very nearly ran home. Once there, I locked and bolted the door behind me in an effort to shut out the world. I also locked the door to my own apartments before I flung myself onto my bed and cried as I had not since my father's funeral.

3

I think I must have slept eventually, for I surfaced briefly when I heard the telephone ring. I let it ring on – it was not for me, there was no one I wished to speak to. Perhaps the front door rattled or perhaps it did not... nothing seemed very real.

Perhaps, I thought, I would get up at some time in the not too distant future, and get on with my life, even though it was a life for which

I had no further enthusiasm. But then again, perhaps I would not, perhaps I would just stay safe in bed, in the dark and dream I was someone else; someone happier, someone with a real life not one built on quicksand.

Then there were strong arms around me, and kisses on my mouth, and tears that were not my own trickling down my cheeks.

"I locked the doors," I said stupidly when I could speak.

"I am a builder – locked doors mean very little to me. You, on the other hand, are my life! I would not have you shed one tear for me, let alone the floods I have caused you."

"You want a daughter, you have a daughter, and she is nothing to do with me. I wish to die," I moaned.

"Chérie! I love you and want to spend my life with you and only you. Can we start from there and try to pick up the pieces?"

"Is Stéphanie Gobert your daughter?" I demanded.

"I do not know. Brigitte and I we never... we just didn't. This is an old fashioned place; there were too many prying eyes, too great an expectation of good behaviour. Couples then were content to wait, at least most were. Some always slipped up, probably always have. My only worry, Chérie, is that we are talking about a time when there are gaps in my memory, when I cannot swear to all I did.

"I ask myself why Brigitte would go away saying she found someone else if she was carrying my child. I would have married her just as soon as the banns could be called, no question."

"Is this the child of the unknown lover?" I asked hopefully.

"I don't know, Chérie. There is only one way to find out, we must ask her."

"We can't do that!" The very idea seemed shocking to me.

"I don't see why not. Brigitte has made the first move by coming back. Le Couvent is a three star hotel, but it is not the only one in France. If she had wanted to avoid speculation then she might have gone anywhere. I will telephone the hotel, book a private room and ask her to join us for dinner, without her daughter I think. There may be things she does not want to discuss in front of a girl just seventeen."

"Us, Théo?" I asked.

"Yes, it must be both of us. You would never be sure unless you heard whatever she has to say for yourself."

Théo mopped at my face with his rather grubby handkerchief.

"Now, Chérie, what is all this nonsense about me wanting a daughter, or a child of whatever gender?"

"You said so yourself, on the way back from Dieppe. You said I must will my engagement ring to my eldest daughter."

"I did?" Théo sounded unsure. "If you say so, I must have done, but it is one of those things people say, I'm not actively knitting afternoon jackets."

"Afternoon jackets?"

"You know, those little cardigan things that babies wear."

"Ah, matinee coats."

The thought of Théo's great hands knitting a layette made me smile for the first time in twenty-four hours.

"Chérie," Théo said seriously. "When two people get married, or just become sexual partners, they put themselves into the hands of God. How frequently do you hear of babies coming into this world despite pills, condoms and diaphragms? Equally you hear of couples who spend everything they have – and sometimes what they do not have – on every kind of fertility treatment, and still there is no baby. I am content to be married to you and leave babies to the Lord."

Théo hugged me and planted a kiss on my mouth.

"That is not to say that I will not perform my manly duty with enthusiasm when called upon to do so. I also regret to tell you it will not prevent my mother lighting candles to The Holy Virgin, St Rita and St. Anne. I trust, however, those kindly saints will do their best for all four of us."

"Four?"

"Yes, you, me, my mother, and whoever might or might not come to join us, that is unless you have a history of twins in your family."

I aimed a swat at his massive shoulder and felt my cares drain away.

4

The interview with Brigitte Gobert took place two days later. I confess I went to the *salon de beauté* that afternoon and had my hair styled. I then let Mademoiselle Ophelie give me a makeover and manicure. Perfumed and pampered, I left the shop rather stunned by the cost of my transformation.

I dressed carefully in a formal suit and silk blouse. I felt as if I was going for a job interview. Brigitte met us in the foyer. She was not that formidable: she was below average height and slightly plump, as if she had sampled hotel cooking a little too well over the years. The long blond hair of her teenage years was now carefully cut and styled, but black roots showed it needed a little help these days. She was wearing her corporate suit, although she must have been off-duty for this private dinner. Perhaps it was the best outfit she had? Her make-up was a little overdone – but who was I to talk?

We were shown up to the first floor and ushered into a small private room. The menu was rather uninspired given the prices, but there was enough choice to ensure that there was something to everyone's taste.

Brigitte talked with ease about neutral subjects until the fuss of ordering, tasting the wine and spreading of napkins had been accomplished.

"I am delighted to see you Théo, and you Mademoiselle Sinclair, but I am at a loss to know why you need to have this private tête-à-tête."

Either the woman was as thick as the hotel's vegetable soup or there was something wrong. I could tell that Théo had picked it up as well.

"We were an item in the past, Brigitte," Théo said carefully. "The town has not changed that much since you went away. Your return has given the gossips a great deal of food for their speculations."

"I don't see that at all," she declared stoutly. "Marie-Claire said you were a successful business man and about to get engaged – congratulations, by the way. She said no one would think twice about an old girlfriend turning up nearly twenty years on."

Marie-Claire, Théo's spiky cousin. A name to conjure with!

"I didn't know you were that friendly with my cousin," Théo said.

"We didn't pall about or anything. We didn't have a lot in common with her going to the Sorbonne and me not even doing all that well at the Lycée. But she was very kind to me that last year in Montreuil, and we have kept in touch ever since."

"Brigitte, if you can bear to do so, will you tell me about that time, and why you went away?"

Suddenly Brigitte looked a lot more like the trainee hairdresser she had been, rather than the sophisticated Hotel Manager she had become.

"Is it necessary Théo? It's all a long time ago and I didn't treat you all that well when I left."

Blow that for a game of soldiers, I thought. She very nearly ruined his life! I felt like upending the water jug over her carefully groomed hair. I stayed my hand when I realised that aggression would not get us the information we sought.

"Please, Brigitte, it could be very important." Théo gave her the full power of his beautiful violet eyes, and she melted just as she must have done all those years ago.

"When we started to go out, I was really pleased. You were doing well at college, there was a rumour that there might be some Colbert money left to inherit, and you were quite tasty looking then."

The little cat!

"After a while it got a bit... Boring! Sorry, Théo. There was your college course, and homework – you were so conscientious about doing your homework, it was a pain. When you weren't doing overtime for your boss, it was either football practice or the gun club. Believe me there is no fun in watching football on a cold wet afternoon and ball trap is not a spectator sport."

No mention of excessive drinking at this time though. Marie-Claire is not a woman to be trusted.

"That summer, the summer I went away, Marie-Claire came to have her hair done at the salon where I was working. I was moaning about how little you and I were together. She asked me to have a coffee with her on my half day. I thought I would, there was little enough else for me to do.

"She bought a whole pot of coffee and a plate of cakes and we talked about all sorts of things, but mainly about you and me. Marie-Claire said I could do so much better for myself than a rundown hairdresser's salon in this one-horse town. She said she could get me a great job in Paris, she even knew of a place where I could stay – no big deal, but fine whist I was getting on my feet. It sounded wonderful. Paris! The nightlife, the shops, the boys I could meet. Suddenly I couldn't wait."

"What about the other man, the one you said you were going away with?" Théo asked mystified.

"You are such a silly Théo!"

Well, yes he was, for considering this fool for more than two minutes together.

"There was no other man, or at least not then. It was Marie-Claire who said I should pay you back for all the time I spent waiting around for you. So we made up that letter between us."

Brigitte suddenly looked uncomfortable. "I didn't mean to cause you all the grief that I think I did, Théo. It seemed just like a prank then. We were only kids. Afterwards, I had my own troubles and I didn't have much time for thinking about anyone else. Sorry, Théo."

I didn't know what Théo might say to this, so I hurried on with: "You say you had your own troubles. What happened?"

"Well, when I got to Paris, Marie Claire was ever so kind at first. Made sure I was settled, took me around a bit. Then suddenly she was not there for me anymore. She had classes to attend, more flipping homework. I knew that song and it was already old. Her friends didn't take to me very much. What did I know about Albert Camus and Jean-Paul Sartre?

"Suddenly I was on my own and lonelier than I had ever been in my life. I didn't know many places to go. I had no money for the few places I did know. You wouldn't believe how expensive Paris can be."

Wait for it, here comes the bloke, I thought.

"There was this guy where I worked."

Told you!

"He was the only one who was nice to me. He would treat me to a walk along the Seine and buy me some hot chestnuts or a coffee at a stall."

Cheapskate!

"Well, one night I let him... Well, you know."

One night and the rest.

"The next thing you know the rotter had gone off to the Midi, with no forwarding address – and I was having a baby."

I could have written the script myself, but I must admit that I was curious about how she had got back on her feet, so I asked: "What happened?"

"Well, it was a blessing in disguise. I could not keep on at the hair salon. They were very swish, and a pregnant shampoo girl did nothing for their image. That meant I could not afford my room even if they had been willing to let me stay."

"Couldn't you have come back here?" I asked.

"Not really." Brigitte looked awkward and I did not press her.

"So what did you do?" I asked again.

"I got a job in a big hotel. It provided me with accommodation, and the other girls were really good at looking after Stéphanie when it was my shift. I found I liked the life, and I was good at it. I went from sort of under chamber maid to assistant manager quite quickly. That's were I stuck, though. The manager was a distant cousin of the owner and not much older than me."

And there are no other hotels in France? I wondered, but asked: "So what brought you back to Montreuil?" This was the crunch question.

"Marie-Claire came to see me at the Hotel in Paris. She told me about Le Couvent and how it was going to rival the Hotel Napoleon one day. She said that the company who owned the chain were looking for a manager but hadn't advertised yet. If I applied she would put a word in for me. Well, I asked how it would look if I came back to Montreuil. Marie-Claire said she doubted anyone would notice. That's when she told me how well you had done for yourself, Théo. I'm glad, I'm truly glad."

Théo and Brigitte talked about mutual acquaintances over coffee and petits-fours. I think we were all relieved when we put an end to the meal and wished each other goodbye. Brigitte did not come with us down to reception but disappeared into the bowels of the hotel. As Théo paid the bill I took the opportunity to look carefully at Stéphanie Gobert. She was even smaller than her mother and built on more delicate lines. She had dark eyes, Asian cheekbones and long, black and very straight hair. I might not trust everything Brigitte said about her life but one thing was sure, Théo was not the father of her daughter. The one thing two blue eyed parents cannot do is have a black eyed child.

I determined that I would frequent the Salon de Thé for the next few days until I met up with Veuve Delcroix. I would then tell Madame a great deal in the strictest confidence. That should ensure that every adult in a twenty mile radius would know Brigitte Gobert's secret within twenty-four hours.

I also promised myself that if I could do Marie-Claire Bigot a bad turn I would jump at the opportunity.

As we crossed the town back towards my hostel I tucked my arm into Théo's. "That must have been rough for you, my love. Has it brought back a great deal of hurt?"

"No, not hurt, but I cringe when I think I was engaged to that woman. On balance, I think it might have been worth all the trauma, the descent into drink and madness, losing almost everything, just to be rid of her." Théo stopped suddenly and turned to me. "There is something I must ask you, Chérie, and it is very important that you tell me the truth."

I wondered what was coming next.

"Do you think I am no longer tasty?"

Poor Théo looked so mournful I could have laughed. Instead I pulled his head down do mine and licked his nose. "You are *very* tasty, mon ami."

CHAPTER EIGHTEEN

1

The January holiday I had allowed myself was coming to an end. It was time to get on with some work. I visited the Tourist Office. The staff there are not overwhelmed with callers in the early months of the year and they were most helpful about providing names and contact details of the companies who ran organised trips into Northern France.

I composed a presentation about the hotel and what it could offer that was different to those already on their books. I had thought long and hard about this. La Cloche Blanche was a handsome building but not historically important. Every restaurant in the town, including the Salon de Thé, offered some kind of regional specialities on their menu. It was the guided tours and history lectures that would make the difference for Calamier Tours.

I recruited M. Errard at the bookshop to do the historical background. He also agreed to be my senior lecturer on the history of Montreuil. I had originally considered some big name from Paris. I began to doubt that however much an academic might shine in university circles they would not bring much kudos to my popular tours. Not only did M. Errard know his stuff but he also had the happy knack of bringing the past to life. You would swear he had known personally the novelist Victor Hugo and Sébastien le Pretre de Vauban, military engineer to King Louis XIV. There was the added incentive that interested clients could be persuaded to buy books on the area from his shop.

Once the literature was ready, I tailored it specifically to each of the four enterprises I had chosen from my list. I wanted middle-ranking businesses that had not been doing package deal holidays for too long. They had to have sufficient funds and prestige but not be too tied to their current client list. I spent hours on the Internet checking facts. Finally I did what was, for me, the most difficult part – I rang up each firm and spoke to the Business Manager personally.

As with so much of what one dreads, it all went relatively easily. Only one company turned me down flat. I simply replaced the near sighted stick-in-the-muds with another company from my list. Once the initial contact had been formed, I then made up a business package. I was quite proud of myself. I had been out of the commercial world for more than two years but I thought I had retained my skills quite well. I sealed and addressed the envelopes and decided to walk them over to the Post Office straight away.

As I crossed the double squares I saw workmen putting up brightly coloured posters. On my way back I slowed to read one: it proudly proclaimed that the Cirque Maxime was coming to town. The poster showed a huge-maned lion roaring, an African elephant with enormous tusks, and a couple of clown faces. I strongly suspected that lions and elephants would not be part of the show, but I had to admit that the poster was eye catching. I wondered if Théo would like to go. It might be fun. I had not been to a circus since I was a child; and on that occasion I had been scared silly by an extremely sinister pair of clowns.

"Disgraceful, disgraceful!" I jumped slightly at the sound of the voice as I had not realised that there was anyone behind me. It was Madame Rolland, Madame's neighbour from Equires. "Gypsies and vagabonds!" she continued. "There won't be a hen or line of washing safe whilst they're here. No decent girl will be able to go out alone, and there will be fights every night. I don't know what M. Delcroix was thinking about when he gave them permission to come. Not after last time. I'm sure Madame la Veuve will have something to say about it." Madame Rolland clasped her handbag to her chest as if the clowns in the poster would snatch it from her.

I wished Madame a good afternoon and made my way home. Whilst I don't think of myself as a gossip, I have as much natural curiosity as the next woman, so that night I asked Théo about the circus.

"Le Cirque Maxime usually visits at this time of year before going south to celebrate Mardi Gras," he told me.

"They haven't been here during my time," I protested.

"There was a bit of trouble two or three years ago, and I think the proprietor thought that he might try Hesdin or Samer for a change. Unfortunately those towns don't have a big catchment area, and I suppose the takings were not so hot."

"So what happened?" I prompted, intrigued.

"Some local yobs did a bit of heckling at the shows. Certainly some of the girls in the town thought the circus lads were worth checking out, which did nothing to help keep the peace. There was a bit of a roughhouse in the Place de Gaulle."

"A bit of a roughhouse, what happened?"

"It might have ended with just a bit of pushing and shoving, but that fool Delavoie was too heavy handed as usual and it turned rather nasty. A number of people including a couple of policemen were quite badly hurt

"So why are they being allowed to come back?"

"Three reasons. First, it wasn't all the fault of the circus folk. Second, in the current political climate it is good to be seen to be offering accommodation to the tziganes." There Théo stopped.

"And the third?" I urged.

"The good President of the Council, M. Delcroix, dearly loves a circus. He will be there every night making a welcome speech at the start of the performance, then sitting in the best seat in the house through the show and chatting up the tightrope walker after."

"What about his mother?"

"I think she prefers the acrobats."

"Théo!"

"No, Chérie, it is true. I think Monsieur would even defy his mother if he had to, but Madame La Verve is as keen on circus folk as her son. Now, Chérie have you prepared anything special for dinner tonight?"

I hadn't prepared anything as I had been too engrossed in my plans for La Cloche Blanche to think about food. I muttered that I had been busy.

"Bon, Chérie. Then let us go together to the Golden Dragon in Etaples. We can order their plat du jour and then get M. Chang to translate the words on that scrap of paper whilst we eat. They are never very busy on a Monday evening and we are being very dilatory detectives."

Chinese food sounded like a good idea. I grabbed my coat and we headed for Etaples.

2

After parking the van we walked down the main street to the Golden Dragon. The gold and red decor and bright lights stood out against the grey streets. There were only two or three other couples dining, and M. Chang greeted us enthusiastically. Confronted by a menu of over one hundred dishes we silently agreed on the two person special: very tasty it was too.

We did not see M. Chang again until we had consumed our lychees and it was time for coffee. I opted for jasmine tea, for in my experience Chinese restaurants don't often do coffee well.

"M. Chang, can you spare us a moment?" Théo asked. The Chinaman looked surprised but continued to smile. Théo brought out a photocopy of the old paper. "Can you tell us what this says, please?"

The round faced Asian manager put on his spectacles and looked at the paper for a moment.

"I'm sorry, Monsieur Théo, This is Vietnamese and I was born in Hong Kong. It is akin to me asking you to translate Greek or Russian – possible but not probable."

Théo looked as if someone had stolen his teddy bear. "I'm sorry, M. Chang," he said dolefully. "I'm afraid I did not think things through."

"Do not be so sad, my friend. I will ask my staff. There may be someone who can help you." He ambled off, only to come back within a minute or so – which, to my mind, was suspiciously quickly.

"Alas, there is no one in the kitchen who reads Vietnamese. I am so sorry." M. Chang continued to smile, but his eyes were never still. He seemed very anxious to get us out of the restaurant.

We thanked him politely, paid and departed, but we did not go far.

"There's something very odd there," Théo said. "I've never seen the guy so nervous or on edge."

"I think I might know what it is," I replied. "That business about going into the kitchen, I suspect he might have some people there who do not have the right papers. To be specific, someone Vietnamese he does not want seen."

"That's silly. I want a little note translated, not to snoop into his employment records. Even if I knew someone was here illegally – and how would I know that? – I am not likely to go telling on him to the authorities."

"When you have something on your conscience, everyone is a potential threat."

"So, what should we do?"

"One of three things, go to one of the bigger towns and find a proper Vietnamese restaurant and see if they will do us a favour. Give the note to M. Delavoie and let him use police sources, if he feels it's worth it. Or nip round the back and see who comes out of the kitchen for a cigarette break and offer €10 for a word with the Vietnamese guy and €20 for a quick translation."

Without another word we both came to the conclusion that the third option was the preferred one, so we turned into the next side street and made our way to the back door of the Golden Dragon.

It took a little bit of patience, but eventually a man came out. In the end it cost us €40, because the man could not speak much French and we needed a translator. A three-way conversation revealed that what we had was a receipt from a shop called the Golden Buddha for twelve uncut diamonds for the princely sum of ten million Dong.

"How could a simple soldier get hold of that kind of money?" I gasped. The nightmare was getting worse.

"Easily, Chérie, do not fret over the reputation of this long departed military man. That's only about €500. Edouard's Uncle Frédéric was out in the Far East for a couple of years. He was a religious man who did not smoke, drink or go with women. I would also bet he did not like the local food. He was a bachelor with no dependants, so no deductions from his pay. He ate in the mess, went to church and saved up his francs. Just before he came home he bought the uncut stones. Perhaps one of his church group might have advised him on what to do.

"Where did the story of the army rations come in?" I asked.

"That we will never know, but I could hazard a guess."

"Guess away," I urged.

"Frédéric Vincent was a bit of a joker and also something of a story teller. He was a regular speaker at the fraternity of St. Joseph's meetings held at St. Saulve's. He also ran a Church children's group that I attended for a while as a boy. He had a fund of tales and parables to illustrate his homilies. I think he made the knapsack story up – it sounds more daring than spending time in French Indochina attending socials at the local Catholic church."

"So what do we do now?" I asked.

"Visit M. Joseph Bertrand, we have held onto his property longer than we should. Perhaps the sudden inheritance of six uncut diamonds will sweeten him into relinquishing claim on Rosine's engagement ring."

Théo did not sound too hopeful. I had to remember that in a small community he must know all these people and be able to assess how they might react. I hoped he was wrong this time, but I said nothing.

3

Joseph Bertrand and his wife lived in Neuville-sous-Montreuil across the river Canche from the high town. They had a modern bungalow not far from the centre of the village. We called just after 2pm, hoping that Madame might be taking a nap and we could speak to Monsieur alone. It took him some time to answer our ring. When he did come to the door he was wearing rubber gloves and a pretty flowered pinafore. It was obviously clean-up time. He threw his accessories into a corner when he saw who his visitors were and rather reluctantly invited us into his lounge.

The room was cold, and I had the impression it was not used very often. The furniture was heavy and appeared to be expensive. There was a large flat screen TV and a top quality tower unit, but no books or magazines nor any sign of CDs or videos, although they may have been concealed in one of the matching cabinets.

He waved us to be seated then, before we could state our business, he made his own position clear. "It's no use you trying to browbeat me, Théophile Colbert. I have no wish to hurt young Vincent and his fiancée, but what is right is right."

"Edouard told me he had offered to give the ring back," I countered.

"No, mademoiselle, he proposed to share it. I was offered an equal amount with the four remaining members of the Vincent clan. That is theft."

M. Bertrand's voice was rising. We heard a low muttering from the bedroom. Joseph got up and closed the door. In a much softer tone he said. "My wife is not well. I'd appreciate it if you keep your voices down."

We nodded our agreement.

In little more than a whisper Théo said: "We have found that Frédéric Vincent bought more diamonds than went into the ring." He held out the little leather bag. "There are six uncut stones in here, a receipt from a Vietnamese gem merchant to show how many stones were bought and that they were a legitimate purchase, despite family legend. They are quite large pieces and must be worth a fortune. They most definitely belong to you. In the light of this windfall could you not be generous about the disputed ring?"

In an equally subdued tone I said: "Edouard is certain that Elizabeth gave her ring to Alice. They were very good friends. Alice might have been difficult but she was known to be an honest woman."

"My sister Elizabeth was good to everyone with whom she came into contact. You would be more accurate in saying she let that wretched Alice Hahn impose on her. That woman was no better than she ought to be. Her mother was a disgrace to the community. She drank like a fish, and there more than one so called 'lodger' did not sleep in the spare bed."

"Monsieur!" Théo protested. "Whatever Madame Hahn senior may or may not have done, there was never anything said about Madame Alice! She was rigidly correct."

"Either that or she was better at hiding it," M. Bertrand snarled.

Suddenly, a very old woman staggered into the room. She was wearing a cotton nightdress that hung off one bony shoulder. Her grey hair fell in rats' tails down either side of her head, and there was the distinct odour of incontinence.

"Alice stole my ring," she cackled. "But I showed her. I made sure she would never steal from anyone else."

M. Bertrand jumped up. "Sweetheart, you have been dreaming. Go back to bed let me put you to rights, then we will have a nice cup of coffee."

"I don't want coffee – I want champagne! You never let me have champagne now. You drink it all yourself. You're mean to me."

"Now, Vivienne, you know the doctor said it isn't good for you. It doesn't go with your tablets."

"Alice would not give me the ring. She kept waving a bit of paper at me, saying Elizabeth wanted her to have the ring. I hit her, I hit her over the head with my stick, you should do that when someone tell you lies."

The hag leered at us. "I want a glass of champagne! I want it now! You always used to give me Champagne when we were courting. You don't love me any more." She started to cry. I felt mortified. I glanced at Théo who looked furious.

"Come back to bed, my dear, and if you are good, perhaps we'll have a small glass with our dinner," coaxed M. Bertrand.

Eventually, he managed to calm the woman down and lead her away. It was some time before he returned. Théo and I sat in silence.

M. Bertrand poured three glasses of brandy without asking. He downed his own in a couple of swallows and poured himself another.

"Vivienne was the most beautiful woman I had ever seen. She was witty, intelligent, well read. I could not believe my luck when she agreed to be my wife. We have two wonderful children who have done well at university and gone on to good careers. I thought I was the happiest of men. Then five years ago, Vivienne started to say and do some strange things. I consulted a doctor, then a couple of specialists. There is nothing that can be done. She can only get worse." I could see tears in the man's eyes.

"You knew what she had done to Alice though, didn't you?" Théo sounded cold and stern.

"I didn't know, not for sure," M. Bertrand protested.

Théo let the silence lengthen.

"Look," said M. Bertrand at last, "What good would it do to prosecute her? The doctors say she does not have... very long now. She probably would not even know she was dying in an institution, but I would. I'll make it up to young Edouard."

"How?" asked Théo.

"They can have the diamonds – the uncut ones, I mean." M. Bertrand said hurriedly.

"It is the ring that was the source of the trouble, and will remain so unless something is done," I contributed.

"The letter from Elizabeth to Alice must have been destroyed..." M. Bertrand hesitated, then finished lamely, "...years ago."

"You know that, we now know that, and in her rational moments even Madame Vivienne knows that. But what was destroyed could be resurrected," said Théo.

So that is how we became forgers.

4

M. Bertrand searched in his files and found a blank piece of paper that looked old and was rather crumpled. With an old fashioned nibbed pen and a bottle of liquid ink, he wrote a letter addressed to Alice Hahn which stated that the ring and the bag of uncut stones were for her and her son Edouard when she was gone.

The handwriting did not matter, as there were no letters still in existence in the hand of Elizabeth Vincent née Bertrand, but he disguised as best he could in case someone who knew his writing saw the letter.

After the actual forgery was completed, we folded the letter and baked it very gently in the oven for five minutes. It looked perfect.

M. Bertrand promised he would hand over the gems and the letter to M. Delavoie in a couple of days. He would claim that he had been going through old documents because of the disputed ring and had found the booty in a secret drawer of a bureau that had belonged to his sister. The story was thin but should hold.

We shook hands and we saw ourselves out. The brandy in our glasses was untouched but M. Bertrand was pouring himself another generous helping as we left.

As we drove home I asked Théo, "Do you not feel sorry for the man?"

"No, I don't think I do. All he had to do at the engagement party was say he knew that Elizabeth had given the ring to Alice and there would have been no more trouble. There was the desire to protect his wife, yes, but there was greed there as well."

"On the other hand, without the false accusations Edouard and Rosine would not now have a very substantial stake for their future, although they don't know it yet. We may have lost our partners. On the strength of the money from the diamonds they may decide to go it alone."

"Do you really think so, Chérie? Moi, I think not, but time will tell."

CHAPTER NINETEEN

1

About a week after our interview with Joseph Bertrand, Inspecteur Delavoie made one of his usual dawn raids. The hostel was now open and we had one or two of our early birds eating breakfast. The man seemed almost disconcerted to see someone up and working as early in the morning as he did.

"I would like a private word with Mademoiselle Bonneau," he said politely enough.

I called Rosine and asked her to take Monsieur le Inspecteur to my private sitting room. I would cope alone in the breakfast parlour. They were up there for far longer than I had anticipated.

When Rosine finally came downstairs it was obvious she had been weeping for some time, and had a man's handkerchief pressed to her face.

"Madame, Madame," she mumbled into the cloth before rushing out the front door.

M. Delavoie came down a few minutes later. I stood blocking the way out and stared silently at the man.

"I assure you, Mademoiselle, that I have not been bullying your waitress. I am not sure what has caused all those tears, but it was not the heavy hand of the law. In fact, I thought the news I brought her might give her some pleasure."

I believed him.

"I would appreciate a few moments of your time," M. Delavoie continued.

"Monsieur, may I offer you a cup of chocolate?"

The detective hesitated. I acted. I went into the little kitchen and put together a simple petit dejeuner. By the time I had returned M. Delavoie was seated by the window. The other guests had departed to their business appointments or their explorations. The Parlour was empty apart from us.

"I called today to return to Mademoiselle Bonneau her engagement ring," Delavoie explained. "M. Bertrand visited the Sous-Préfecture a few days ago with a letter purportedly written by his late sister and a most remarkable leather pouch. Do you know what was in that pouch, Mademoiselle Sinclair?"

"There is no way I could know, Monsieur Delavoie."

"Stop playing with me, Mademoiselle. I can detect the hands of you and that oaf Colbert all over this business. I want you to tell me what has really been going on," he said, glaring at me.

I set out a selection of breakfast breads and conserves and then paused, the pot of steaming chocolate in my hands.

"M. Delavoie, let us be clear on one point. You will refer to my fiancé as Théophile or M. Colbert. If you call him 'that oaf' just once more, the next pot of boiling chocolate I make for you will be poured all over your trousers – and I am prepared to take the consequences."

M. Delavoie eyed the chocolate pot and said, "I believe we can compromise on that point, Mademoiselle." I filled his cup.

"The pouch contained six uncut diamonds. We had them evaluated by an expert. They are large, of the finest quality, and should cut well. They are worth a fortune."

"How very surprising, and what good luck for Rosine and Edouard," I said calmly.

"You could try for a little more reaction than that, Mademoiselle. You are hearing this for the first time, are you not?"

"I can do hysterics. Quite well, Monsieur, would you be impressed?"

"Perhaps not," was there a hint of a smile on that grim face?

"I had fingerprint tests done on the letter and the leather pouch. I found M. Bertrand's and Colbert's on the pouch and the diamonds, together with those of an unknown individual. I found those same unknown prints on the letter." M. Delavoie was watching me carefully.

"You undoubtedly think you want to know many things," I said. "I wonder though, as an officer of the law, would you prefer to remain if not ignorant at least innocent of some of them? The problem, if we can even refer to it as a problem, has its roots more than sixty years ago. Many of those involved are now dead, and those that still remain are old and so sick that it will not be long before they go to face the greatest judge of all."

M. Delavoie nodded his agreement.

I continued: "Rosine is completely guilt free. Even the much disputed ring came as a surprise to her on the evening of her engagement party. Edouard Vincent was right in assuming that the ring legally belonged to his mother and she was free to give him the jewels as her sole heir. Do you really need to dig any further below the surface?"

"How did you find out? Why did you, as you put it, dig below the surface?"

"We wanted to help Rosine and Edouard and we had some luck." I said simply.

"I shall be watching you, Mademoiselle Sinclair. You and that..." he looked at the chocolate pot, "...Théophile. If you put a foot wrong I shall have no hesitation in bringing the full force of the law down on your heads."

"I would expect no less Monsieur," I replied.

I ushered the detective to the door and watched him stride down the street. Despite all the friction between us, there was something basically decent, honourable and perhaps even likeable in the man. He was also so patently lonely. That, however, was no business of mine.

2

It was gone noon before I saw Rosine again. She came back to the hostel with Edouard in tow.

"We would like a word with you, Madame," she said formally, even though she was visibly shaking with the weight of her news.

"Would it be better if we postponed this interview so that M. Colbert can be here also?"

"I must tell you now, I must or I will burst," Rosine declared in a more natural voice.

I regarded the pair. I knew at least the substance of what they had to tell me. Yet I had no real idea of what decisions they would make about the money they now had at their disposal. I thought of Théo's calm confidence. Then I looked again at Rosine and Edouard, neither of whom seemed to have any regrets or reservations in their demeanour.

Perhaps our agreement had not meant very much to either of them. Had we just been stepping stones to the future they envisioned? Were we to be discarded now something better offered? I thought that there had been friendship as well as a practical business arrangement. Perhaps I had been wrong.

"Do not look so sad, Madame," Edouard said gently. "We have nothing but the best of good news."

We went up to my sitting-room and whist I made coffee I put a call through to Théo's mobile. All I got was the answer phone, but I left a message saying Rosine and Edouard were at the hostel and to contact me when he could. Finally we were seated and Rosine started her tale.

"Madame, M. Delavoie had the most amazing news," she began. I heard again the story of the surprise discovery of the letter from Aunt Elizabeth confirming that the unlucky engagement ring did belong to Edouard.

"Dear Uncle Joseph has visited all the members of the Vincent family and convinced them that the ring really is mine. I am so happy!" Rosine clasped Edouard's arm.

I thought better of M. Bertrand: he had kept not only to the letter but to the spirit of the agreement to make things up to young Edouard.

"But Madame, Madame!" Rosine was now literally bouncing with excitement. "That is not the best of the good news. Uncle Frédéric had brought more stones back from the Far East. He and Aunt Elizabeth never did anything with them, but at the end when Elizabeth was giving her things away, she sent them to Madame Alice Vincent with a note saying they should eventually go to Edouard. Oh, Madame, Madame, they are larger and even more valuable diamonds than the ones for the ring. The Police have had them valued by an expert. They are worth at least a million Euros! Think of what we can do with that amount of money!"

"Congratulations," I said dryly.

"You do not seem too pleased, Madame. Think! We can build an extension to La Cloche Blanche and offer accommodation for more guests. We can build a pool and Jacuzzi in the basement. We have the basis for a Michelin star hotel!" Rosine's face was alight with the prospect.

"There will be funds for a wine cellar of distinction – a point that has always worried me," Edouard added gravely.

I held up my hand. "My friends, we need to go through this carefully, so I understand everything. You do know that you have enough capital with this inheritance of diamonds to start your own hotel completely independent of anyone?"

Edouard smiled, and putting a restraining hand on Rosine's arm, he said: "Madame, we want very much to continue with the agreement to which we have already put our names. Les Advocates can deal with the legal aspects, because we will have to have a new document drawn up, but that is not difficult. Now I hope we will be financial partners as well as business colleagues – and, of course, friends. Your ideas for La Cloche Blanche are excellent, just what we would do independently. Let us put our resources together and within two years we will rival the Hotel Napoleon."

"Quite so," I said weakly. Then an inner voice screamed at me that any that lack of enthusiasm now might damage my relations with my young partners for years to come. I really did not want that. "This is wonderful, wonderful," I exclaimed. "But it is so sudden I can hardly take it in. Let us leave financial deals and business plans until another day when such dry topics might have more attraction. Today, let us toast the new Cloche Blanche."

I got up and took a bottle of champagne out of the wine cooler and three glasses from the cabinet.

Some very innovative plans were proposed that afternoon, not all of them were completely practical.

It was to be my week for visitors. Next day Mme. Colbert arrived just as we were putting the last of the breakfast dishes away. She accepted coffee and then asked if she could speak to me privately. I suspected I knew what she was going to say. And say it she did, immediately we were alone.

"You have been engaged for over a month now. My impulsive son has stated you want an April wedding. What plans have you made?"

"I have been giving it some thought," I said feebly.

"Thought is all very well, but with two months rather than two years to complete your preparations, a little *action* is also necessary." Madame looked at me quite sternly. "With all your thinking have you even settled on an actual date?"

Feeling like a schoolgirl, I looked at my feet and actually blushed.

"You know at this late stage you will probably not get a Saturday?"

"I thought we might have just a very quiet affair."

"Affairs have nothing to do with weddings: weddings are for show and tradition!" Madame said firmly. "Now where do you want to be married? At Théo's church in Equires?" There was a look of hope in Madame's eyes.

Despite what I had told Madame, I had not thought about my wedding at all. Suddenly, however, I knew exactly what I wanted.

"No, Madame, my mother married my father in the church of St. Saulve. I would like to be married there, too."

"Bien," disappointed, but not too much, "you must call the rectory."

"Should Théo not be involved in these decisions, Madame?"

"Yes," she said. "We will tell him what we have decided and he will agree. Now here is the number."

As Madame had predicted, there were very few slots left in April. The parish secretary was helpful and finally consulting with Madame Colbert we booked Friday 22nd April at noon, then confirmed the same date and matching time with the Mairie for the legal ceremony.

"Next, the reception," Madame was implacable. "How many people are you catering for – both for the wedding breakfast and for the evening entertainment?"

"Madame, I don't know. I have no close relatives; I have lost contact with most of my friends and work colleagues in Scotland... Put me down for the entire Bonneau family, M. Olivier and Valerie from Chez Henri, and say two couples from Scotland for the Bride's side. Who do you wish to invite?"

Madame Colbert looked slightly disconcerted. "My poor

Geneviève, I hadn't realised you were so isolated. This is something of a problem. We have a big family, and there are a certain number we cannot leave out without giving offence. More importantly, who is to give you away?"

"My dear Madame, don't you think I'm a little old to be 'given away'?"

"This is not about women's liberation. Here in France women have been the head of the household for generations. It's about show and tradition. What do you think about your solicitor M. Le Francois?"

"Do you really wish to know, Madame Colbert?" I countered coldly.

"I suppose not." Mme. Colbert was not offended but not distracted either. "I know! M. Delcroix, perfect, he is President of the council, and you have not quarrelled with him, not even when the fire brigade hosed down your cake. Bon!" And in her mind it was settled – and I suppose it was.

I brought us back to our plans for the guest list. "I suppose we could start with those who came to the Christmas festivities. Also, are there any of M. Colbert's relatives still living?"

"They were a line already beginning to die out when Benoit and I first married. There is one old uncle still left, whom we must invite, but he is now too ill to come. We must also invite my eldest brother and sister. Father Simeon will not leave his monastery but Sister Emmanuelle might very well get dispensation to travel. I would very much like to see her again."

"Don't forget members of the Gun Club, and Théo may have business acquaintances it would be politic to invite."

"Yes, true, but those would be evening guests. Let us agree a number for the wedding and reception, then I can weed out the fringes of the family."

Where should we hold the reception? I had an idea. "Madame Colbert, there is something I really need to talk over with Théo. I am not trying to procrastinate, honestly."

I got a very old-fashioned look, but Madame thawed a bit when I suggested we went together to consult the florist and the photographer that morning. Both establishments were conveniently situated in the main square.

"Before we go to the florist, my dear, you must think about your attendants?" Madame held up her hand. "I know your first reaction is to say you don't want any, but remember – show and tradition. Now what about Théo's Cousin Marie-Claire?"

I swallowed the desire to tell Blanche Colbert that I did not want that woman in the same town as me, let alone as an attendant at my wedding. Then I thought of putting her in some frilly pink frock that would make her look hideous. My face must have shown my anger, for I saw Madame Colbert's kind, violet eyes take on a look of concern. I recognised Théo in her every feature and suddenly I was not angry any more.

"I would like Rosine as my witness," I said, "But what about your brother's little granddaughters as flower girls?"

"All three of them?"

I could see the calculations in her eyes. She would certainly sacrifice Marie-Claire if she could get the three little ones centre stage. I searched for their names, finally finding them: Delphine, Pascale and Mei-Lin. Precious Jade's younger granddaughter was not really quite old enough to be a flower girl, but she was incredibly cute which would more than make up for it.

"That would be very nice," said Madame weakly, "now what about your dress?"

"I shall go to Madame Sophie's in Le Touquet," I said firmly. I had seen the meringue skirts and all revealing bustiers in the dress shop in Montreuil and I wanted nothing to do with them. What did a bride over forty wear? A neat suit and a modest corsage? No, thank you! What did Madame say? 'Show and tradition'! I might be short of ideas, but I would bet Rosine's diamonds that Madame Sophie would have enough for both of us.

4

We visited the photographers and florist and eventually Madame Colbert went home, I returned to my flat and collapsed gratefully into my armchair, wishing desperately that Théo and I could pop into the Mairie, grab a couple of witnesses off the street, and then tell everyone the deed was done.

Théo was late coming round that night. He looked as if he had been put through a wringer.

"Would you like a coffee?" I asked.

"No, Chérie, Thank you, I am awash with coffee."

"What's the matter? Is one of your chantiers going badly?"

"No, I am glad to say that things are going well at the moment on the work front." He reached out and touched the wooden table. "I have just spent the last two hours with my mother talking over wedding plans."

"Did she mention 'show and tradition' by any chance?"

He put his head in his hands.

"It is probably more than you want to think of at the moment, but there are certain things I need to know."

"Certainement, Chérie, but do you think I could have at least a small kiss first, just to remind me why I am putting myself through this?"

That was no problem. Eventually, I asked: "How many people do you think the main dining room at La Cloche Blanche will hold?

"Fifty," Théo said without compromise. "I have measured it out and done the maths."

"Could the dining room be ready for 22nd April?"

"I think I see where you are going with this. It would be a sort of preview, an advertisement for La Cloche Blanche, and we could use the stills and perhaps a video for publicity – good thinking, but Chérie, what about the people who will come in the evening?"

"You remember the lovely porte-fenêtre that leads out into the garden? We could open the French-window and add on a marquee. It should not be too chilly at the end of April but we can put in some space heaters just in case. We will have to have caterers, so the kitchen just has to be functional and hygienic not fully equipped."

Théo took a pen out of his pocket and raised his sleeved to doodle on his shirt cuff. I gave a little scream of horror and provided a notepad.

He scribbled furiously for a few minutes. "Bon, Chérie, it will work. We can put garlands as barriers to the upper floors because the bedrooms will not be fully finished, but if anyone does go up it will not be dangerous. The cloakrooms and bathrooms on the ground floor will all be complete. When do Rosine and Edouard plan to get married?"

My stomach fluttered for a moment. Surely he was not going to suggest a double wedding? Every bride wants to be the star of her own show.

"I think they plan to wait until the autumn," I said casually.

"Even better," Théo rubbed his hands. "That will give us a second round of publicity when we are fully operational. Now, Chérie come, sit on my knee and we will discuss our honeymoon plans, in detail."

CHAPTER TWENTY

1

The circus came to town in style with a big parade though the main streets before the raising of the big top on the municipal camp site. Speaker vans had been blaring out the news for a couple of days previously. I had not been particularly interested, but Rosine had begged and badgered until I agreed to go and see the parade with her. As it turned out, it was indeed very well worth seeing. The parade was led by the ringmaster, resplendent in a scarlet and gold uniform and carrying a whip and baton, followed by the band on an open lorry playing 'Entry of the Gladiators' – badly.

A team of acrobats in pale blue silk tights with sparkling silver tops formed human towers then tumbled once more to the roadway. They were followed by a sort of imitation sled on wheels pulled by a team of huskies. The young woman driving the sled had make-believe Inuit furs that started where her bosom finished and finished where her legs started. However she had a very nice fur hood to keep her warm.

The next lorry had two young men in leopard skin tights and a ballerina in white waving languidly at the watchers. The legend on the vehicle said they were the 'Tolstoy Brothers – Trapeze Artists' and 'Cosette – Tightrope Walker'.

Then came a third vehicle bedecked with gold spangled voile curtains. It was supposedly a harem scene. An enormously fat man sat on a papier-mâché throne flanked by two bruisers with serious muscles. Three or four young women with diaphanous trousers and beaded bras lolled about on oriental rugs. However, every eye was taken by the woman in the centre of the group who was doing a sensuous belly-dance. Her honey coloured flesh shimmied and roiled as if it had a life of its own. It was so overtly sexy I could not watch and looked away.

My gaze fell on M. Delavoie, who was positioned by the town fountain with a couple of uniformed officers. He was standing quite still, his eyes riveted on the passing cavalcade, and the expression on his face was that of a man who has just seen the Holy Grail.

Last of all came the horses. Handsome dappled greys, three riders in cowboy gear each controlling two mounts. The beasts looked magnificent and gleamed with health, but I could see why they brought up the rear – the municipal cleansing department would have their work cut out later on. A diminutive girl in a Native American costume postured and gestured in front of the group with a sign that said 'The Boot Hill Gang' in English. It certainly seemed as if the Circus would put on a good show. Théo had booked us tickets for the Saturday night. I was now looking forward to it.

I turned again to look at M. Delavoie. He was taking no interest in the rest of the procession whatsoever, but continued to stare after the harem lorry. Was Monsieur Granite susceptible after all, or did he just suspect the enactment of some unnamed crime?

2

The next day I set out for Le Touquet. I did not relish the trip much, but I had promised Madame that I would get things moving, and we could not order the bridesmaid's dresses until I had at least some idea of what I wanted for myself.

Madame Sophie sat like a benign toad amongst her racks of clothes. I plastered a smile on my face and explained why I had come.

"Madame, I have nothing in my shop that will suit you."

I was shocked. I had really expected the old Jewess to solve all my problems for me. I remembered the perfect New Year's outfit. Surely I was not so difficult a subject?

"The designers think all brides are eighteen and want dresses that wrap their non-existent bosoms like a bandage, with a sprinkle of sequins to make it fancy. It is not fashion, it is packaging." Madame made a disgusted gesture. "I am now going to give you some advice that goes against my own business. My niece studies design in Paris. She is talented, that one. In time she will be one of the forces to be reckoned with in the world of Haute Couture. But for now she is a young student without a name. Telephone my Rebecca and you will have a dress that is magnificent."

I found myself on the street clutching a business card and no further forward. I wandered from shop to shop. Madame might have exaggerated, but in essence she was right. The off-the-peg wedding dresses were aimed at the very young bride and were all froth and twinkle. Beautiful creations, yes, but they were not for me.

I drove home, slowly, and once there I telephoned the number on the card. The phone was answered on the second ring, but there was a lot of noise in the background. Rebecca Suss sounded even younger than I had imagined. When I explained about her aunt Sophie and the wedding dress project she became very animated. She asked me to hold on whilst she moved away from the source of noise. Now she was all business.

"A wedding dress, oui, how many attendants?"

"One adult and three small children," I replied.

"You are an older bride and want something striking, but not twenty metres of white net. Oui?"

"Absolutely correct."

"I must see you. Can you travel to Paris? It is difficult for me to come to you."

"I can visit once or twice but I have my own business to run so I can't make unlimited trips to Paris," I countered.

"Once I have the ideas we can work through my Aunt Sophie. I will attend you for the final fittings, but I must see you to get the initial concept."

I had come so far I could invest in a journey to Paris. We agreed to meet two days later at her college.

"If you do not like my ideas, there is no obligation and no cost to you beyond your train fare to the city. However, I think, Madame, we will work well together," Rebé Suss promised me.

3

I took the early morning train from Etaples and was in Paris by eleven o'clock. I took a taxi to the college. Paris traffic is ferocious, and it was all I could do to prevent myself from hiding my face in my hands as cars and commercial vehicles seemed to head straight for us. We missed collisions by bare centimetres.

Rebecca Suss was small, olive skinned, with a thick plait of black hair hanging down her spine. She wore a black skinny jumper over jeans. Her hand when we shook was cold with a birdlike fragility. She led the way to an empty classroom.

"My supervisor says we can use this room. It's free for the next couple of hours," she said.

"That's very generous," I replied neutrally.

"I've told my supervisor that we are working together on the wedding section for my end of term show. My Aunt Sophie is always complaining that there is nothing for the mature bride. I thought this could help us both, if you chose to commission my design, that is."

"I think perhaps you are going too far too fast." My voice was harsh.

"You are right, but I felt I had to explain that if you do commission me to design your dress I'd want permission to use it in my final year show."

I examined this thought and found I was comfortable with it.

"I agree, but you must also consent that your dress being used in the publicity material for my new hotel without further charges. Copyright or whatever will remain with you but I have full rights also."

"That seems a bit complicated but should not be a problem, I will consult," she countered.

"So what do we do now?" I asked.

"Please take off your coat and jumper. Would you walk up and down, sit, stand and just move about as naturally as you can? I would also like you to talk to me, about yourself, your wedding and your fiancé. I'll do some preliminary sketches and we can move on from there."

Thinking that as I had come all the way from Montreuil I might as well cooperate, I did as she asked. As might be expected, I moved awkwardly, feeling those large dark eyes taking in all my figure faults and clumsy gestures. However, I seemed to get used to it after a while. Rebé sat cross legged on a desk, sketching furiously with charcoal and chalks. Some pages she put to one side carefully, others she hurled into a wastepaper basket.

Finally she said simply, "Come and look."

The design was based on a dress that might have been worn in the late middle-ages. Figure hugging top and sleeves with a wide fur collar that plunged from shoulder to waist. A triangle of contrasting fabric in the vee preserved modesty. There was a wide sash of similar fabric round the high waist from which dropped a full skirt that flowed into a train at the back. The edge of the skirt was trimmed with the same white fur as the collar.

"I thought deep royal blue velvet for the gown, white faux-fur for the trimming and perhaps a touch of white lace just at the edges of the sleeve and say a deep rose pink for the silk in the bodice and sash."

I had never seen anything so lovely in my life. Then her skilful fingers were at work again.

"If you have a pearl necklace and earrings, then I could finish the outfit off with a little cap sewn with pearls and very light veil that would fall from the cap as far as your hips. Your attendants could wear a similar design, without the train and veil, perhaps in white silk with blue ribbon. You are Scottish, Madame, so perhaps your flowers could be a blue and white St. Andrews cross? If Monsieur would wear a dark blue velvet dinner jacket with bow tie to match your sash, we would have something to make the world sit up and take notice."

I continued to look at the sketch, my mouth slightly open saying nothing.

"If you don't like rose satin, then white or silver lace could be used." Rebé was beginning to be concerned. "You do like it, Madame?" Then she looked at me properly. Tears were streaming down my face, and

I could not have said a word if I could have thought of one to say.

"Bon," she said with satisfaction. "I will make up three little dolls with contrasting trimming. I think, however, you will like the rose, old rose, nothing garish. I will send them to my aunt and she will take your measurements. As the outfits will be used at my show, I will charge you only for fabric and a little something for my time."

"When your show is over you will return the garments to me?"

"Specialist cleaned and ready to wear again – if you so wish," she said with amusement in her voice.

I might not wear the dress again but I might very well use it in the publicity for La Cloche Blanche or even put it on display in one of the reception rooms. If the Queen could do that so could I!

"Shall we say a deposit of €500 and a further €1000 after the garments are made and accepted to your satisfaction?"

"This would consist of... what, exactly?"

"Your wedding dress, sash, cap and veil, one adult dress with cap, three children's dresses with caps all in artificial silk and ribbon. I would even throw in a bow tie in rose silk for monsieur."

Without hesitation I reached for my handbag and cheque book, asking, "Will you do me a sketch of the bridesmaid's dresses so that I can show Rosine and the children's grandmother?"

"Certainly," Rebé took up her pad once more.

On the train all the way back to the coast I dreamed of walking up the aisle of old St. Saulve dressed like a queen, in particular Charlotte of Savoie, queen of Louis XI. It seemed appropriate, as the old church had been built during her reign.

On my return home there was business to be dealt with. Of the four companies I had approached concerning a travel and stay partnership, one declined, one accepted and sent a contract for Théo and me to sign, one asked for further details and one requested a meeting at their offices in London, a bore but doable.

I sent a letter of acknowledgement to the decliners thanking them for their time and saying in effect the door was open if they ever wanted to change their minds. I answered the questions of the ditherers as fully and comprehensively as I could. Made an appointment to see M. Le Francois to discuss the contract and telephoned the last company concerning and appointment in London. Despite the fact it was they who wished for the interview, the secretary I spoke to huffed and puffed as if it were the greatest imposition in the world. We finally agreed on a late afternoon appointment some three weeks hence. That night I asked Théo if he would like to come with me.

"What could I do, Chérie? I would just stand about looking stupid whilst you nattered on in English."

"If you don't fancy coming to the business meeting you could go and see some of the sights in London. We could perhaps do a little shopping; have an English meal for once before coming home. I must admit it would be good to have company on the journey."

"In that case, Chérie, I say yes – but remember, just a little shopping?"

"It's a deal." But as I said it my mind strayed to a blue velvet dinner jacket...

4

It seemed as if half of Montreuil was turning out for the circus on Saturday night. People were streaming towards the brightly lit Big Top. I saw many of my neighbours and fellow business people. There were also quite a few young men I did not know. Some wore hoodies, while others wore biker's leathers. I had a very uncomfortable feeling that trouble might be brewing.

The shouting, however, started before the show even began: racial slurs against gypsies and explicit comments on the female performers.

The clowns were sent out to try to defuse the situation. That worked to a certain extent, but the barracking did not totally die down until the police started to march up and down the aisles. Even I found them intimidating, with their big guns in leather holsters.

The show started promptly, the organisers did not want to do anything to re-antagonise the hecklers. Within minutes the uneasy peace had become riveted fascination. It was a wonderful show. I do not have much experience of circuses, but to my eyes the tricks and showmanship were superb. I wondered vaguely what such a class performance was dong wandering about the little towns of northern France.

The star turn was undoubtedly Zeinab and her Turkish harem. It was a combination of a strongman act, dance and acrobatics, very well done. Even the band, which had its limitations, seemed to pull out all the stops. Whilst the performers were taking a bow, I happened to glance around. M. Delavoie was leaning on a tent support near one of the exits. Leaning but certainly not lounging. Every line of his thin body was tense. His eyes riveted on the figure of Zeinab spotlighted in the centre of the stage. I nudged Théo, but before I had attracted his attention, Delavoie had slipped back into the night.

After the show Théo asked: "What would you like to do now? We have not eaten yet. Would you like go up to chez Henri and have some supper?"

I must admit I just wanted to go home, but my fridge and larder only contained basics and Henri always had something good on his 'specials' board.

"That would be nice, thank you Théo," I replied.

As we walked to the top square we could hear the wail of police cars – the local force must have thought they needed reinforcements. I shuddered as we entered the familiar restaurant; this was not like the Montreuil I had come to love. Chez Henri was nearly empty. M. Olivier was polishing glasses behind the bar and looked worried.

"Mademoiselle Genèvieve, Théo!" He greeted us pleasantly enough, but his gaze more on the door to the street than his customers.

We ordered and were served with brisk efficiency. Long before we had finished, Henri was putting chairs on tables to signify the end of service.

As Théo went to the bar to pay I heard him mutter to Henri: "What is the matter old friend? You're as jumpy as a crab on a griddle."

"There is nothing, nothing at all Théo just a slow night, even I get them occasionally."

"Henri this is me you are talking to! If I can help I will."

Henri paused for a moment then said "It's just that I've seen some faces from the old days. Types that I thought I'd never see again. They did not come in, just leered through the window pretending to read the menu. I'm going to put the shutters up as soon as you've gone. Just make sure you walk Mademoiselle right to her door tonight." Henri did not say any more and Théo did not press him.

Théo wanted to stay the night but I demurred. One of the bedrooms was free but I did not want to give the gossips any fuel for their speculations.

I was especially careful about locking up after Théo had gone. When I went to bed I did not sleep well as my mind was bothered by fears as real as they were unformed.

I drifted off eventually, only to be woken by a terrific banging at my front door. I grabbed a gown and my slippers then flew down stairs before all my guests were disturbed.

The blue light of a police car flashed lurid through the window into the breakfast parlour. Théo! Had something happened to Théo? I fumbled at the chains and locks on the door, panic making me clumsy.

Onesime Delavoie stood there dirty, dishevelled and soaked in water from head to foot. In his arms he carried a large blanket wrapped bundle.

He crashed the door open, pushed past me and strode rapidly up the stairs to my private sitting room calling over his shoulder, "Come on you useless woman, can't you see I need help!"

I was too shocked even to object to his rudeness but the bundle murmured 'Onesime'. I scampered up the stairs in his wake and was in time to see the detective lay his burden tenderly on my sofa.

"See to her and treat her well or there will be an accounting between you and I, Mademoiselle Sinclair." Then he rushed back out of the house and the police car screeched away.

"Inspecteur Delavoie lacks people skills I'm afraid." The voice was low, sweet and with just a tinge of accent. I turned and looked at the woman on my couch. She was as dirty and wet as the Inspecteur had been. As the blanket fell away I could see the remains of a spangled costume and some bright pink areas on her flesh that looked like burns. It was the harem dancer from the circus.

"You should go to the hospital!" I exclaimed.

"I can't. There are reasons." She started to cough with, I assumed, probably smoke inhalation. It also prevented unwanted conversation. Explanations could wait.

CHAPTER TWENTY ONE

1

An hour later, the woman, Zeinab, was back on my couch in one of my cotton nightdresses and wrapped in my thick winter robe. Even so, she managed to look exotically beautiful. We had cut off the remains of her costume, before I helped her into a tepid bath and then applied the burn salve from my kitchen's First Aid box. True to my Scottish roots, I had persuaded the woman to drink some hot sweet tea. She was not enjoying it much, but she drank it anyway. All I had learned so far was her name, or at least the name she currently used and the fact she was part of the circus – things I had worked out for myself.

I sat in the armchair with my own mug of tea. I reckoned I had been as shocked as anyone that night. I watched her over the rim of my cup.

"What happened tonight?" I asked. "Why did Inspecteur Delavoie bring you to me?"

"Do you think I owe you an explanation?" she said in a mocking tone.

"No," I replied calmly. "You owe me nothing, I was glad to help. I confess to being curious, and if I know a little more perhaps I can be of further assistance."

She acknowledged the riposte with a nod of her handsome head.

"You know there was trouble at the circus tonight, though I suppose it must be last night now."

"Yes, we were there, but it seemed to calm down."

"There was more trouble later. We usually let people walk about the camp site afterwards – pet the horses, visit the fortune teller, that sort of thing. I told Raoul it was not wise with the louts being so edgy earlier on, but Raoul is not a man who changes his mind easily. He gets donations to cover the care of the animals, and of course his sister is the fortune teller."

"And Raoul is?"

"He is the Ring Master and owner of our little menagerie."

I remembered the man in the scarlet uniform who had led the parade. "I thought the Circus was Maxim's?"

"That was Raoul's father. Eventually, we got all the punters off the ground and went to do the usual clearing up. A few of us were too keyed up to sleep so we joined up in Raoul's van to talk over our plans and play a few hands of cards. It must have been after one o'clock when we heard the horses start making a fuss. We scrambled out of the van and ran across the camp site. We could smell smoke and Raoul telephoned for the fire brigade whilst the rest of us went into the stables to lead the horses and dogs to safety. We found that at least three separate fires had been started, one at the back of the tent, one right by the huskies' shed and one in the big top itself. We got the animals out and made sure our people were safe, but all that straw and hay!

"The kennels and stables went up like Roman Candles. It spread to the nearest vans. Mine was right next to one of the fires. There was no chance to save anything."

Zeinab looked grim, then tears formed in her eyes, but she dashed them away impatiently.

"Eventually the police and fire brigade turned up. It felt like they had taken hours but it must have been just a few minutes in reality. Monsieur Le Gallant wrapped me in a blanket and brought me here."

There was a lot I was not being told. For instance, why was Monsieur Delavoie – who was not exactly known for his chivalry, why was he carrying this lush creature around the countryside? Why had he been so fascinated with her both on the day of the parade and during the show? Why could Zeinab not go to the hospital to have her injuries tended but have to rely on my less than expert care? It was suddenly all too much, and I longed just to go to bed and shut out all the problems.

"I obviously can't force you to tell me anything you don't want to, but please don't insult my intelligence," I said wearily. "There is a room here you can use. It's en suite so you won't have to meet any of the other guests. I'll bring your breakfast up myself in the morning. I don't have any sleeping tablets but I have aspirin or paracetamol if you need them." I opened the door and took her to the room.

"I'm sorry and I truly am grateful," she whispered as she went into the bedroom and pulled the door closed behind her.

2

Théo was at my door at first light. I don't think I had had more than two hours sleep and was not at my best. Living in La Calotterie as he did, he had only just heard of the fire. He looked worried.

"This is not hazing by the local louts. It's serious trouble."

I told Théo about my midnight visitors.

"I don't like this, Chérie. Get rid of her as soon as you can. I don't think it's safe to have her here. If Delavoie insists she stays another night, I am going to sleep here too and the grannies can think what they like." I did not try to dissuade him.

"I have to go now, Chérie. I have a lot on today, but if you are worried give me a bell on my mobile, I'll be round with the heavy brigade."

"The Heavy Brigade?" I queried.

"Read your British History. They are the ones who won!" he laughed.

I promised I would, and sent him on his way with a kiss.

I let Zeinab sleep on into the morning: after all, she had endured a far worse night than I had. It was past 10 o'clock when I began to prepare a breakfast tray. But then there came a fierce hammering at the front door. It was the fusillade that I had come to learn was M. Delavoie's trademark knock. I opened the door and he once more pushed past me. He looked round the breakfast parlour and whirled round to face me.

"Where is she? What have you done? If any harm has come to her through your negligence I'll have you deported back to England quicker than you can whistle Rule Britannia."

It was enough and more than enough. I slapped him, hard. I have never seen a man looked so shocked.

"You arrogant pig!" I shouted. "What gives you the impression that my hostel is an extension of the Gendarmerie? If this is how you treat your friends it is no wonder you have so few. You will speak to me with decent manners or by the Blessed Virgin I'll ensure your underpants fly from St. Saulve's weather vane again. And it's Scotland I come from – Scotland! Your geography is as pathetic as everything else about you."

Delavoie's expression went from shock to white hot anger. I truly don't know what would have happened next if a husky voice had not drawled, "Underpants from the weather vane? That sounds like a tale worth knowing."

Zeinab was standing at the foot of the stairs. She looked sexy and gorgeous with my old robe worn slightly off the shoulder and her black hair curling round her face. I was instantly dismissed from Delavoie's mind. He moved to her side as if attracted by a magnet, and his hands went gently to her face and his whole world was in those dark eyes.

"How are you? Are you in pain? Were you disturbed in the night?"

The detective's long thin hands moved down to her waist, and he pulled her closer to him.

"I'm fine, Onesime. Do not worry, we gypsies we are tough," she reassured him. They had both completely forgotten about me. "Did you get the Nurali brothers? Did you find the goods?"

"Les salauds were long gone. We could not miss the stuff – it was in the horses' feed. A couple of the Sapeurs-Pompiers got a lungful and had to be taken to hospital. I was so worried about you, but I dared not contact you for fear that you were under observation."

At that most interesting moment the coffee machine gave its usual woof of protest at the end of its cycle and Delavoie remembered me once more.

"Go and do some shopping, Mademoiselle, and don't come back for an hour!" he said abruptly.

I went. That did not mean I could not try for information. I walked to the camp site. Yellow marker tape was strung between the trees; grim looking officers from police and fire brigade stood around enforcing those 'keep out notices." In the air was an odour I remembered from my student days – marijuana. The 'stuff in the horses' feed' – words I had heard from M. Delavoie. From the stink in the air this was more than a couple of surreptitious roll-ups hidden from the authorities: this must have been serious smuggling.

I wandered back to town, and when I found a secluded spot on the ramparts I phoned Théo on my cell phone. He answered at the second ring. I told him about the weed. He already knew. The news was all over town.

"They smuggled the stuff in by hiding it in the horses' hay, quite a scam!" was his comment. "A circus is always travelling, never in the same town for more than a couple of weeks and sometimes much less, no time for the cops to get suspicious. The suppliers just add their own couple of bales to the order of regular feed – cool."

"You sound like you admire them!" I felt myself growing hot.

"No, Chérie, I despise them. Too many youngsters who think it's macho to blow a little smoke end up dead, addicted to substances far stronger. Go back home now. That petit flic can't make your kitchen into his office then turn you out into the street." I could hear Théo getting angry. "Do you want me with you?"

At that moment it was the last thing I wanted. It would not do for the pair of us to be walloping Onesime Delavoie. He was not exactly the most patient of men. "No Théo, there is no need, honestly." I agreed that Théo would come for diner and rang off.

Théo having diner meant I had to go shopping in real earnest and I headed for the charcuterie. When I finally returned home I expected M. Delavoie would have already taken his leave. I was surprised to see him still there, sitting opposite Zeinab in the breakfast parlour and talking earnestly. They became silent as I entered. The policemen stood gave me a curt nod and left without another word.

"Would you like to get dressed?" I asked Zeinab. "I have some clothes that would fit you at a pinch."

"That would be most kind, Mademoiselle. I feel like a slut slopping about in a dressing gown. All I had went up with my caravan."

"What about money, credit cards, your passport?" I asked.

"Fortunately, I had very little actual cash in the van. Caravans are too easily broken into. I have already contacted my security service and they are organising replacements for all my documentation. Onesime loaned me his mobile to make the calls. I regret my costumes, they were specially made for me, Still, with no big top to perform in I suppose that is not so important. I had insurance and clothes can be replaced."

I looked carefully at the woman. She was not as young as I had first assumed. In addition to the exotic looks and perfect body there was... well, not exactly a hardness about her, more a toughness – competency. Apart from a couple of quickly dried tears she had taken all the horrible happenings in her stride. I thought too about the reaction of Onesime Delavoie. There was certainly the man/woman thing between them, but was there something more?

I led the way to my own rooms and found her knickers, socks, a track suit and tee shirt. My bras would be no use to her whatsoever. I offered to lend her some money so she could buy something to fit. Again 'dear' Onesime had been there before me.

I left her to wash and dress in peace with some more burn salve I had obtained from the pharmacy.

Half an hour later she joined me in the kitchen. In her borrowed clothes and with her hair in a simple pony tail she looked less like an exotic dancer and more like what I suspected she was.

"You are a police officer!" I said.

"How did you know?" She seemed weary rather than surprised.

"Little tells, but that's not an issue. What is important is how we can help you."

"And who are 'we'?

"My fiancé, Théo and myself."

"Not the town drunk?"

"Drunk no longer! And if you plan a future with Monsieur Delavoie you really do need to take certain of his statements with a pinch of salt."

This time I really had surprised her.

"We are just colleagues, nothing more!" she said stiffly.

Yes, right! Still, her emotional life was none of my business. In fact, the whole sorry show should have been none of my business, but they had made it so when Monsieur Le Detective had hammered on my door.

"You must have had some confidence in me to come to my hostel when you did. Please trust me a little further and tell me what it is you fear.

I already know about the circus being used for distributing drugs"

"Onesime said you were loyal, intelligent and brave. That's why he brought me here."

I could not have been more surprised if she had said he had been elected Pope. To cover my confusion I moved to make some coffee. Besides, it sounded as if it was going to be a long story.

"My grandparents were Algerian," she began. "They came to France in the early 60's just before all the troubles. They had a small import-export business – exotic rugs, fabrics, nick-knacks, you know the sort of thing. They never made a fortune but they got by. Mama was convent educated and met my father at their local church. He was studying law and eventually qualified as an advocate.

"There were four of us children, my three brothers and myself. Life was all very normal except we could all speak Arabic and I had a Grand'Mere who had tattoos on her face who secretly taught me belly dancing at night. That all changed during the 1991 riots. Grand'père had passed away by that time, my oldest brother was married, and my twin brother and I were away at school. In the lovely flat over my father's offices my parents lived with Mamie who was very frail by this time and my youngest brother who had some kind of autism and needed a lot of care.

"Between the police, the rioters, panicking locals and the fire, I lost them all. I wanted to kill someone, anyone, everyone. Somebody was to blame and I was going to have justice for my murdered family. There was enough money even when divided between the three of us to finish my education and support me till I could earn my own living.

"I switched from fine arts to the law and tried to find those responsible. As you can imagine, I did not do too well at my studies. It took me a lot longer to graduate and pass my bar exams than it should have done.

"To supplement my income I taught dance at a shady bar in Montmartre. Eventually I grew up. I realised that everyone and no one was to blame for the destruction of my family. The rioters had real grievances and no way to get them redressed. The police were just doing their job and finished up fighting for their lives. Our neighbours were all concerned about saving their own families and had no thought to spare for ours.

"If I wanted to help, if I wanted to save other families from suffering as ours had done, I needed not just to dispense justice after crimes were committed – I should try to prevent them before they happened. I joined the police force. I was a bit late in starting a career, but my degree in law, my race and my established credentials in the underworld through the dance club, made up for a great many hours on traffic duty."

"What happened to your brothers?" I asked. "The ones who survived, I mean."

"Avram tried to revive Papa's law practice. It was hopeless. Too many records had gone up in flames. There was no computer back up in those days. Eventually, he moved his family to the Dordogne and joined an existing practice as a junior partner. He says he is contented enough drawing up wills and contracts for land deals. His house is locked and barred like a fortress, even in that rural spot, and he worries every minute his wife and children are out of his sight. If Rachel, his wife did not have the patience of her biblical counterpart, the marriage would have failed years ago.

"My twin, Jacob, died of a drug overdose about the time I joined the police. The authorities had the compassion to rule that it was accidental, but it was not."

"So how did you come to join the circus, and where does M. Delavoie fit in?" I asked.

"Many leads come to us through statistics. That might not sound very exciting or romantic, but those of us in the field have a lot of time for the backroom boys. In certain areas of France the price of weed had dropped by something like fifty percent. There was a lot more stuff about, and the quality, whilst not the best, was very acceptable. It was clear that there was a new supplier on the scene working to the best supermarket principles: quality, price and availability. There was one puzzling factor – the source seemed to be always on the move. It took longer than it should to make the connection.

"We held a seminar in Paris about a year ago. We brought in hundreds of local Inspectors, split them up into groups and gave each one the same problem. It was Onesime who came up with the possible solution. Like all good answers it was simple once you knew. As I have told you, I have had a second life as an exotic dancer since before I joined the force. I was the obvious choice to go underground. Examination of the pattern of distribution with the timetable of the travelling circuses highlighted Maxime's."

"Wouldn't a simple raid on the circus have given you all the evidence you needed?" I queried.

"Yes, but it would not give us the supply chain nor the brains behind the scam. It's certainly not Raoul. His failing family operation was suddenly boosted by bigger audiences and injections of money from a financier. In truth it did not take much capital for the circus to start making money in its own right again. His was a case of tunnel vision rather than a blind eye."

"So what was your role, exactly?" I urged

"To be eyes and ears, to find out how the scam worked and to find some lead to the next level of administration."

"What did you discover?"

"It was all very straight forward, as all the best plans are. The horses come from the Carmargue. Their trainer says they are sensitive and must have special feed to enable them to perform well. This may be true of racehorses but this lot are about as sensitive as a hammer. Nevertheless, bales of their own special feed come up from the Camargue and are delivered to the next town on our route. In it are one or two packages of a very different kind of grass. Who is going to check bundles of hay?"

"The material is mostly grown down in the Bouches-du-Rhone with perhaps some supplements delivered by boat from Algeria on a bit of deserted coast between Sète and Aigues-Mortes. The two strong men sell it to clients who wander round after the shows. But the really clever bit is the money. That is where so many scams come undone. Raoul goes to the bank the morning after every show, ostensibly to deposit the previous night's takings. What he is depositing is the drug money. He keeps the circus money in an elaborate safe in his caravan. All the circus expenses, vets' fees, wages, ground hire, maintenance and the rest he pays in cash, then similar sums are taken from the bank account. Raoul has cheque stubs and receipted bills to prove his expenditure and the money is clean."

"Crafty, very crafty! But where did all this trouble come from?"

"Probably a rival organisation, the black market is swimming in money, enough to satisfy everyone, but not one of the big bosses is willing to share. They do a better job of destroying each other than the law does in catching them. It is significant that no one local recognised the louts who disrupted the show. That means the mob was from Lille rather than the Le Touquet set. That makes sense, because whilst Le Touquet has its rough element they target the casinos and tourist scams rather the drug trade. They buy in the cocaine and amphetamines they need to facilitate their clients."

"So what happens now?" I asked.

"Retribution, whoever is running this particular racket is going to look for someone to blame. Onesime believes there is a leak in the local Policier. That is why he wished me on you."

"You are in danger?"

"Yes, I think so, but I will be able to disappear very soon now. A new female Inspecteur will be transferred to Cassis or Bandol in the South of France for a while. Eventually, I suspect she will be recalled to Paris. Unfortunately this trouble came out of the blue. We need just a couple of days whilst the necessary arrangements are made."

Why me? I agonised. Could they not hide this woman in a safe house or even a convent? 'Not in my back yard' I chided myself. The old Amnesty International slogan came to mind. 'All it needs for evil to flourish is for good men to do nothing'. I would give what help I could.

"Now tell me..." Zeinab said, "...what is all this about underpants on the weather vane?"

I told her!

CHAPTER TWENTY TWO

1

Despite his bold words about sorting Inspecteur Delavoie out, Théo crept into the hostel by the back door. The three of us dined together on Crab cocktail and steak au poivre – I felt we all deserved a treat.

We were enjoying coffee, and Zeinab was telling us some story about her club in Montmartre, when her mobile shrilled. She looked at the number display and answered immediately. Théo and I watched her as she said 'yes', 'no' and 'continue' to the voice on the other end of the line. Eventually the call finished.

Zeinab returned to her seat looking worried. "That was from the Sous-Préfecture. It was supposed to be a message from Onesime asking me to meet him at the Camping Ground."

"Supposed to be?" I queried.

"Yes, but it did not include the code word we had prepared for such an eventuality. If les salauds have found out who I am, I could be in danger. Without my evidence the case we are building up is not very strong. I think I am being lured into a trap."

Zeinab began to speed dial on her mobile. First one contact then another, but she was obviously having no luck. Eventually she stood up.

"I can't contact Onesime. It might mean he is actually on his way to the meeting place. I can't let him down. I'll have to take a chance and go."

"That's madness! You yourself told me that that there is a... mole or whatever in the Policier," I protested.

"Yes, but don't you see that if this is the mole then it is the perfect opportunity to flush him out?" Zeinab looked grim.

"And you suppose he will be alone and will give himself up meekly when you flash your bosom at him." I was sorry as soon as the words had passed my lips but Zeinab didn't even seem to notice.

"You certainly must not go alone." Théo was indignant.

Zeinab smiled sadly. "Thank you, but I cannot ask it," she said

Théo in turn produced his mobile, and started to dial.

'What are you doing?' Zeinab and I said in unison.

"Calling the Heavy Brigade, just as I promised," Théo replied.

"They will undoubtedly be armed!" Zeinab protested.

Théo did not reply as he was already muttering into the phone.

"They are all members of the same gun club," I told Zeinab. "I doubt they will come equipped only with pocket handkerchiefs."

"This is impossible. I cannot be responsible for a gunfight in the castle grounds!"

"I'm afraid it's too late. Everyone Théo calls will call someone else. Even as we speak, half a dozen men will be pulling on their boots and calling to their wives to unlock the gun cabinet."

"Merde!" Zeinab said explosively. "With half a lorry load of local yokels tramping about we might as well have arranged our secret meeting in the town hall with catering and a band."

"These men are also hunters, they know how to move silently and take advantage of cover," I assured her.

Théo and Zeinab looked at me. I could read their minds. I was not a hunter; neither could I arm myself with anything more deadly than a kitchen knife. I foresaw that I was going to be told to stay safely behind. I needed to forestall their arguments.

"If this is a trap then the opposition have far more knowledge than they should. They probably realise Zeinab is staying here with me, but they won't be able to fathom how much I know or have guessed. If they take Zeinab then their next move will be to come here for me. If I'm with Zeinab you can keep an eye on the pair of us. Besides, they are not going to be too suspicious if I go along with Zeinab. Who would let a woman go out alone at night when such dreadful things have been done? It will have the added advantage of focusing attention on the two of us whilst you, Théo, and your so called heavy brigade get into place."

I was proud of myself. Even to my own ears I sounded calm and confident. Only I knew that my knees were shaking in fear and excitement.

Théo grunted his agreement, and I went to get my coat. Into the big patch pockets I slipped a couple of equalisers of my own.

Théo left by the way he had come, whilst Zeinab and I exited by the front door and started to walk up the street to the chateau. We did not get a hundred metres. They seemed to come out of nowhere. A rough hand clamped over my mouth, painfully crushing my nose. I managed a pitiful squeak before all air was cut off. My arm was twisted up my back and I was propelled forward.

"Scream and I'll break your arm," he hissed.

I couldn't breathe, let alone scream, but after giving me a teeth rattling shake he loosened his hand a fraction.

I could hear sounds of scuffling from further up the street. It was no comfort at all to know that Zeinab was faring no better than me. The only thought going round my brain was that it was too soon, far too soon. Théo and his crew would have had no chance to get in place. It only dawned on me gradually that my life could end that night, very painfully.

They didn't take us down to the camp site but dragged us into the Chateau. The heavy wooden door that barred the public outside visiting hours was open. We were half pushed, half carried over the grass and down into one of the cellars. When the castle was truly a fortress the vaulted chambers were probably storage rooms. Now lit only by half a dozen candles it looked like a medieval torture chamber. I shuddered in my captor's hands and tried to suppress the thought.

There were half a dozen men already in the chamber. They looked round as the two of us and the four thugs who had captured us made our ungainly way into the room. There were the three strongmen from the harem show, a couple of guys I recognised from my tour backstage – the rest I had never seen before. One man stood out. In contrast to the others, who were wearing jeans or jogging bottoms, he wore a well cut suit, white shirt and dark tie. Despite the impressive musclemen on display it was he who was clearly in charge.

"Release them." His voice was educated and his French had no discernible regional accent. Zeinab had got her wish – she was finally about to meet one of the senior players.

The lout holding me took his hands away and then gave me a sharp push that made me fall heavily to my knees. I could feel the man tensing in preparation for delivering a kick when the boss said, "Enough!"

I looked round at Zeinab. She was on her feet and rubbing her arms. She looked sulky and sexy and quite unlike the cultured young woman with whom I had so recently had dinner. The stage had lost a great actress when Mademoiselle chose law enforcement.

"Who's the old bag?" Monsieur said, indicating me.

"She was with Zeinab, so we brought her along," the guy behind me said in a respectful tone.

"She runs the flop house I was staying in after you burned me out of my caravan. She didn't think it was respectable for a young girl to be walking the streets alone at this time of night. So she insisted on coming with me. I'd have got rid of her long before the meeting if your goons hadn't jumped me." Zeinab was contemptuous. Even though I thought it was an act, or hoped it was, the words still stung. Perhaps the anger put some backbone into me because I realised that what we needed was time – time for Théo's gang to get to the town, and time hopefully to find us amongst the ruins of the old fortress.

"Let me go, please!" I whined. "I'll not say a word. I'll go back to Scotland you'll never hear of me again." The speech earned me a slap across the head from my captor. Monsieur totally ignored me.

"You have been playing a double game, my sweet Zeinab." The suit almost crooned.

"I have been leading on that fool Delavoie, if that's what you mean." I had to give it to her – Zeinab was a cool customer. "If it had not been for the fire, Monsieur l'Inspecteur would have been so interested in me wriggling my butt that he would never have noticed our alternative hay bales. It was your thick headed soldiers who spoiled the scam, not me flirting with les Policiers. They were not doing their job – they let the opposition carry out their little tricks!"

Did the suit look slightly perturbed? I thought as much, so I decided to put in my two pennies' worth.

"Monsieur Delavoie said he was certain the mob came from Lille. He said he knows all the Le Touquet gangsters."

That at least got his attention. He turned to me. "How is it that the grim Onesime talks to you?"

"He comes into my hostel now and then. I give him breakfast. Not many people are nice to Les Flics. We pass the time."

"Did he mention his suspicions of the circus?" He was so smooth.

"Never, I saw him a couple of times. He only had eyes for Zeinab. He was obsessed."

Monsieur considered for a moment. "It looks likes you might be telling the truth, sweet thing." He went up to Zeinab took her chin in his hand and squeezing cruelly looked into her eyes. He must have been hurting her badly but she never flinched.

"But then," he continued, "a little bird, a little blue bird, tells me you are filth from Paris, sent to spy out our secrets."

"When did the clod-hopping police take dancing lessons? You know Bashir from the Kasbah Club vouches for me!"

"That is not quite true. I sent some of the boys to have a word with him. He admitted you had some very odd friends."

"A man will say what you want him to if you have his balls in a vice."

"A very graphic description, but we did not have to go that far. The bottom line is that I no longer trust you. I think you will have to disappear."

It was said quite quietly and in a matter of fact tone. I knew exactly what he meant, but Zeinab chose to misunderstand.

"I can do that! I can go back to North Africa. I still have relatives there who will help me get a new start."

"No, my dear, I was thinking of something a little more radical than that."

"You bastard!" Zeinab wrenched her face away from his hand and with an athletic pirouette landed a kick to his crotch. "Run!" she screamed.

Whilst all attention had been on the dialogue between Zeinab and the Boss I had been easing the cap off a little carton in my pocket. I threw the contents of the box of white pepper into the face of the man behind me. As he gasped and started to splutter I pushed past and headed for the stairs.

They caught us before we reached the courtyard. Our captors delivered a few punishing slaps before holding us firm once more.

I'm sure they would have liked to tear us apart but they were held in check by the Monsieur. The suit came limping up the stairs. He was still calm, still smiling. "If it were not for a good old fashioned cricket box, I fear you would have quite unmanned me," he said, his words slightly breathless.

"Strangle them and throw them over the battlements into that tangle of tress and bushes. It will hide their bodies for long enough for us to get away." He might have been ordering his morning baguette.

I started to fight in earnest and with all the strength I possessed. It was like wrestling with a set of steel bars. Slowly, I was dragged up to the ramparts. I tried to bite the hand covering my mouth. I kicked, wriggled; let myself become a dead weight, but none of it made any difference to the inexorable progress up the flight of stone steps. I prepared to scream the moment that vile hand left my mouth but all I could manage was a weak croak before the fingers started squeezing my throat again, stopping my breath again.

The pain was indescribable. My lungs felt as if they would burst and my vision was going black, but my arms were free. I scrabbled in my coat pocket, found the paring knife I had secreted there in the safety of my hostel. I thrust it forward, ramming it in and upward somewhere in the region of his gut with all the strength I had left. I was rewarded with a grunt and a slight slackening of the pressure on my throat. I twisted backwards. I saw a flash, followed by an almighty crack. The hands dropped from my throat and the man crumpled. Several more cracks rang out – I finally realised that they were shots from a gun. Someone screamed 'run' but I had no more energy left and dropped once more to my knees beside the limp form of my attacker.

There were lights, more shots, more shouting, but I stayed where I was, concentrating on getting air in and out of my lungs, revelling in the fact that I was still breathing.

Finally, I heard Zeinab's voice. "Get her out of here. Take yourself and your copains as far away as you can. Fix up alibis with wives or girlfriends. For those who live alone make up a card school. Get away – now! Leave the mopping up to us.

Arms reached for me. I knew instantly it was Théo. As he picked me up like a child I turned my face into his jumper and wept.

2

Next day we 'heard' about the battle of the chateau, how the drug dealers and the cops had shot it out amongst the ruins. A couple of men had died, more had been wounded, but none of the police officers had been hurt.

"Mainly because they were not there," I huffed.

"Hush, Chérie," cautioned Théo. "Neither were we – remember?"

"What about the guy in the suit?" I asked.

"He was rounded up with the rest. I believe he could not run very well. My 'sources' say he is singing like a proverbial bird to ensure a minimum sentence. This is a real triumph for Delavoie and his men. He will undoubtedly get promotion."

"He does not deserve it." I was determined to blame the Inspecteur for my ordeal.

"Promotion may mean a transfer, Chérie. Will you miss him scoffing your chocolate and croissants so very much?"

I laughed and then cried again. I had been terribly lachrymose ever since Théo had carried me home.

"I have been thinking, Chérie," Théo said slowly. It would be an idea if you let it be known you were bringing forward your visit to England."

"Why," I asked between blowing my nose and trying to get myself under control.

"You can wear high necked jumpers and scarves to conceal the marks on your neck. But the bruises on you face show even with make-up. A short time away from the town would be a good idea."

"And turning up at the London head-office looking like a battered wife would be a better suggestion, I take it?" I said sarcastically.

"No, Chérie. You would keep your original appointment in London. My mother has a friend who has a holiday home near Cap Blanc-Nez. You could stay there for a couple of weeks before going across La Manche to do your business in London."

"What about my hostel here?" I asked. "What about the preparations for the wedding? Are you going to abandon the work on the Cloche Blanche?"

"Rosine will run your business here. My mother and Madame Bonneau will be delighted to have a free hand in making all the necessary arrangements for the wedding." Here Théo stopped.

"The Cloche Blanche?" I prompted.

"I can't come with you. Monsieur Delavoie has asked me not to leave town until he is sure that the cover up has worked."

"Then I am not going either." I was determined.

"If too many people see you there will be talk, you know that, Chérie. If they don't connect your injuries with the fight at the Chateau they are going to suspect me of using my fists. I could not bear that."

I gave way, and set off for the bleak promontory just south of Calais that afternoon.

3

When I got there, I found that Madame Colbert's friend had stocked the tiny kitchen with groceries. I wouldn't have to go shopping for several days. I made coffee, but I didn't want anything to eat.

Later, I went for a walk on the coastal pathway, but turned back after about half a mile as I really didn't have the energy. I tried to read a book but found myself staring at the pages without comprehension. I ended up watching the grey water of the Channel and the seagulls wheeling in the huge pearl coloured sky and wondering about the future.

When dusk turned to night, I drew the curtains and lit a log fire in the hearth. Then I watched the flames licking the drift wood instead.

When I heard a knock on the door my stomach went into spasm. I remained ridged on my chair staring at the wooden panels of the door realising they didn't keep out the draughts let alone a determined attacker. I could have gone for my cell phone or taken up a kitchen knife again. What I did do was grasp the arms of my chair in total panic.

The knock came again louder. I clamped my lips together to stop the moans of fear emerging. I went into a cold sweat.

"Chérie, open the door it's freezing out here."

Théo!

I managed to stumble across the living room and fumble open the bolts. "What are you doing here?" I yelled at him.

"Easy now sweetheart," he folded me against his threadbare jumper with its familiar smells of sawdust and paint. "Do you think I would leave you all on your own? You're barely an hour's drive away. Now, what have you made for dinner? I'm starving."

"What about your instructions not to leave town?" I countered.

"What that trouillard Delavoie does not know will not hurt him. My neighbour has seen me go into my house. My van is parked outside. Donc! I am there watching my TV, which is currently entertaining my cat."

"If your van is in La Calotterie how did you get here?"

"I slipped out the back way, and one of the crew has loaned me his car for night time forays. He thinks it's very romantic and tells me I need not hurry back in the morning." Théo pretended to twirl a moustache in the manner of a pantomime villain. For the first time in ages I laughed.

"First, the little manner of dinner," he said with a sudden return to seriousness.

"I didn't feel very hungry. I was going to make something later," I said rather lamely.

"I'll slip into Escalles and get the hotel to make us a picnic. You must keep up your strength." Théo gave me a quick kiss and told me to set the table whilst he was away.

French rural hotels don't usually provide a take-away service but Théo managed it. He probably offered to fix their drains or build them an extension at a discount. All I know is that within half an hour we had a spread of whole prawns with mayonnaise, roast chicken and salad, plenty of fresh bread, and there was an apple tart on the sideboard for later. I found at least some of my appetite had returned.

In the end I did not really care how he had done it because there were more important questions to ask. As we sat once more by the fire I said, "Who fired the shots that killed those men?"

"Has it been preying on your mind, Chérie?" Théo asked gently. I nodded. "To be honest with you, no one really knows. The police are claiming it was members of the force, and there won't be any autopsies to discover the bullets. The police did in fact arrive almost as soon as we did. Someone at the Sous-Préfecture tipped off Delavoie, and Zeinab had dialled up his number again and left the phone connected in her pocket. So he knew where to go. I believe the row that followed their reunion could have been heard in Paris."

I then tried the question that had been bothering me most: "What about the man who was holding me? That was not a random shot."

"You think it was me? No, Chérie. You were so close together, I did not trust my aim. I will not say who it was, because the man is having trouble with the thought that he killed a man. He is, however, a marksman of Olympic class, and the one to do the job. I tell you, though, my love, if I had not had this man at my side, I would have tried to blow off the canaille's head without a second thought. If that had meant a term in gaol, then I would have served my time and hoped you would send me a cake with a file in it!" Théo kissed me again and I took comfort from his words.

4

The days slid by and my face healed until the marks were almost undetectable. Théo could not come every night, but he was with me often enough that I did not feel too lonely. I spoke frequently to Madame Colbert on the phone, and the endless preparations that go into even a modest wedding were being completed. I visited Madame Sophie for a few dress fittings and finally agreed after a lot of persuasion to have a horse drawn carriage as my wedding transport.

It was up to Théo to make the honeymoon arrangements. Apart from agreeing to the destination of Martinique, I left the rest to him.

Eventually, it was time to make my genuine trip to England.

CHAPTER TWENTY THREE

1

A car in London is a disadvantage, so we travelled by ferry to Dover and then took a train into the city. I discovered much to my amusement that Théo was not a particularly good sailor. However, he recovered rapidly once he was back on land. He was fascinated by everything and kept asking me about various landmarks. I explained that, as a Scot, I didn't have the geography of southern England at my finger tips, which resulted in ten minutes huffy silence.

My appointment was at 11 o'clock, so we took a taxi to the head offices of Charm & Change Continental Holidays. It was located on one of the small streets off Piccadilly. Théo came with me into the reception area whilst I announced my name and that of the person I had come to see. As the receptionist made her phone call, Théo got out his guide book, map and phrase book.

"We have no idea how long these people will keep you. If they have any courtesy at all they should offer you lunch. Give me a call on my mobile when you are done and we will find a place to meet."

I thought that it would me offering lunch rather than the reverse, but I sent him on his way with a kiss.

I had prepared carefully for this meeting. A contract with this prestigious travel company would ensure the success of the Cloche Blanche until we could stand on our own reputation. I thought we had a very good fit, but then I was an interested party.

I had dressed in a formal dark green business suit with an embroidered pale green blouse to add a touch of femininity. I had repaired my make-up and restyled my hair in the Ladies' Room at Kings Cross. First impressions are most important, but I was not relying just on impressions. I had compiled a portfolio of facts and figures, and my large document case also contained my laptop computer with a presentation on the hotel and the services we would provide to guests. I felt confident, with just a touch of excited nerves.

My appointment was with Mrs. Steel, the manager of the Northern France and Benelux Countries part of the operation.

I was kept waiting the obligatory five minutes before a rather decorative young woman came to show me into the presence. We walked through a pair of automatic glass doors and up a broad flight of stairs carpeted in thick broadloom woven with the company's logo. On the walls were art photographs of the hotels and properties I had seen in the official brochure. The Cloche Blanche would look very well in their company. I sent myself a mental memorandum to have a professional photograph taken, maybe in mid-summer when the roses would be at their best.

I was shown into a large, well-lit office at the top of the stairs. A woman rose from behind her desk, extended her hand and introduced herself as Grace Steel. Mrs. Steel was tall, very thin and grey – from her carefully coiffured hair, through the Jaeger Suit and mannish silk shirt, to her tights and t-strap shoes. She looked about fifty but could have been anything ten years either side of that age.

She had a soft, cool handshake. After a few courteous pleasantries about my journey and the weather for the time of year, she explained that the details of my presentation would be taken by her assistant, but she hoped to see me again for a short chat before I left.

If she was already thinking about my departure that was not a good sign. I was also a bit miffed that after coming so far at my own expense I was being handed over to a minion.

She got up walked to the door of the adjacent office, opened it and called: "Andreas, we're ready for you now."

A short, rather tubby man walked into the room. His crinkly hair was more grey than black, but despite the changes the years had made, I immediately recognised Andreas Christou, my ex colleague and former lover, the man I had called 'Andrew' when I had told my history to Théo.

I stood there staring at him unable to speak. Fortunately he had lost none of his presence of mind. He covered my moment of embarrassment admirably. He wished me good morning; welcomed me again to Charm & Change and took my hand as if to shake it, but instead used it as a handle to pull me into his office. Once we were alone he said, "How very nice to see you again, Genny, my dear. I have thought about you often over the years."

I was too stunned to say anything.

He went on smoothly: "This must be quite a surprise for you. I recognised your name at once when the application came in and persuaded old Steel Grey there to give you a trial. You should be very grateful to me – she's not easy to manoeuvre."

I ignored this. "What are you doing here of all places?" It was a reasonable question – how *had* a research chemist with a science degree end up in a travel agency?

"It's no great mystery, my dear. When our old company merged with that Swiss mob, they ended up with more research facilities than were economically viable. There followed a considerable downsizing of our old department. Some went to the head office in Geneva, others to the main manufacturing plant in Rouen in France, but I decided to take redundancy and use the cash payment to go into partnership with my cousins in Cyprus."

I remembered that his family had owned a detergent manufacturing plant outside Limassol. Andreas had tried to interest me in going over at one stage, but I had never even got as far as an interview. A female analytical chemist would not have gone down well with either management or workforce.

"How's the factory doing?" I asked – it was only to fill the void when he stopped speaking, because truly I had no interest in him or his career.

"The business is still going, but it isn't doing as well as we expected, and I had to look round for something else. This job is ideal. I speak French and German as well as English and Greek and it involves a quite a bit of pleasant travelling, staying in good hotels."

I tried to read between the lines. His reputation had probably caught up with him at last and our old Company had taken the opportunity to get rid of him for good. His Greek family had undoubtedly got fed up of him as well. Especially after he divorced his Cypriot wife, Olga, and took up with the blonde. More than likely they told him to move on too. A job like this suited him down to the ground. He had charm in plenty when he wanted to use it.

His looks were no longer an asset. He had put on a lot of weight since I had known him. His hair, no longer glossy black was receding, and the smooth bronze skin was showing the ravages of too much alcohol and long business lunches.

"How's Julie?" I asked.

"Juliet," he corrected. "She's fine."

I wondered if that were true; still, it was none of my concern. Now it was time to get down to business. I gave myself a mental shake.

"Despite what occurred between us all those years ago, I'm sure we can deal together in a professional way."

"I hope you have no hard feelings. There was never any real future for us. I made you no promises." He tried to look soulful. It might have worked once. It was not working now.

"That's true, you didn't," I countered. "Now, I have brought copies of my business plan and a current financial statement. I would, however, like to start with a short presentation on the hotel and the services that we can offer." I bent down to unpack my laptop.

"I don't think we need to bother with all that," he waived a dismissive hand. "I remember you were always very efficient, very thorough. Why don't I take you out for lunch? We can catch up with one another's lives. How did you manage to end up owning a hotel in France?"

"I'm afraid I can't stay for lunch," I lied. "I'm meeting my French business partner who also has an interview this morning. I would rather get this done as soon as possible." I began to get a very uncomfortable feeling that had nothing to do with seeing Andreas so unexpectedly.

"I've always liked you and I've thought about you often. " Andreas reached out to take my hand which was on the desk in front of me.

"I was convenient and easy," I snapped, "another notch on your bedpost. You didn't even have the courage to finish with me. You just left me wondering what had happened. I had to learn about Julie from office gossip."

"My dear, it was not like that at all. We had a little harmless fun and then it was over. We both moved on." He tried on a smile for size.

I was so angry. I could feel the pressure building up in me. I wanted to take him by the tie and tell him how he very nearly ruined my life. I tried to hold onto my temper and attempt to retrieve something from the catastrophe.

"We parted a long time ago and, yes, we have both created new lives. I would however prefer to deal with someone else. I'm sure if you explained to Mrs. Steel that we once worked for the same company she will either conduct the interview herself or appoint another of her assistants to deal with my application."

"I could, but I don't want to." He stood up and came to stand behind me, putting his hands on my shoulders. "You are even prettier now than you were then. You have a different air about you. I can see you are angry, but that will pass. If you are nice to me, I will ensure that all the Charm & Change travel business comes to you. It could be a very valuable contract."

"Do you think I would sell myself for a few miserable hotel room bookings?" I had completely lost my temper. "I'm going to see Mrs. Steel." I marched into her office but it was empty. I could not, would not go back. I ran down the stairs to reception. Halfway down I realised that I had left everything behind – handbag, laptop, document case. Perhaps I could persuade the receptionist go and get them for me.

There was no receptionist in the office, but Théo stood by the glass front doors looking a little lost. He saw me and came in.

"I could not find–" he started, but then took a closer look at me. "What is the matter Chérie? Who has upset you?"

I didn't have any reserves left, tears were running from my eyes and I clung to Théo.

"Andreas Christou. The man I told you about, the one from my past I called Andrew? He's here, he tried to... he said..."

Théo seemed to know just what Andreas had said. He pushed me gently to one side. "Where?" Théo asked. Helplessly, I motioned in the direction of the offices. He pushed through the doors and took the stairs two at time.

I don't know what happened next. Théo would never say and I never spoke to Andreas again. Perhaps five minutes passed, there were some thumps, a bang and a high male cry. People came out of their offices, asking one another what was going on. Théo appeared at the top of the stairs. He had Andreas dangling by his collar from one meaty hand, my property in the other.

"Tell your colleagues there is no problem," Théo said in French.

"A bit of horse-play, got a bit out of hand, no need to fuss, go back to your offices please," Andreas complied. One of the watchers was Mrs Steel. She did not move.

"Tell the nice lady what you told me Grec," Théo said pleasantly. Andreas moaned, Théo shook him, not gently, "Come on!"

Andreas shut his eyes and recited like a child. "I am very sorry ..."

"Let's have it in French so we can all understand," Théo insisted.

"I'm very sorry for any misunderstanding. Madame Sinclair has, of course, secured the contract. She will deal with someone else in future."

"And the rest!" Théo urged again.

"I will, however, always make sure she has the best possible deal."

"That was not too hard, was it?" Théo smiled, and even I took a pace back. There was no merriment there at all. The pair of them descended the stairs, Andreas dangling like a puppet, his toes just brushing the carpet.

"Remember," he said to the shaking Andreas again, "I know where you live. If you go back on your word I will find you. He took a vase of flowers off the reception counter and stuffed the blooms down Andreas' trousers and emptied the water over his head.

"I think we should reconvene in my office." Mrs. Steel's voice was a hard as her name. We progressed back up the stairs.

"I believe you can leave Andreas where he is for the time being," she said as Théo reached down for the little man.

Once back behind her desk she said in heavily accented but grammatical French, "I would like a reason why I should not call the police."

The sight of Andreas being made to look ridiculous had helped me regain my control.

"I would like to know why, when my appointment was with you, I was shunted off to an assistant. I would also like to know when sexual favours became part of your management fee!" I snapped back.

Mrs. Steel crumpled visibly. "Oh!" she mouthed.

Her lack of shock made me think that this was not the first time she had been forced to deal with this complaint. But if so, why was Andreas still employed here?

She answered my unasked question. "He is some sort of relative of the Managing Director. The complaints made to date have not been so..." she paused, "...dramatic!"

"I'm afraid you can't hold us to promises made under duress, as I'm sure you can understand, but I'm prepared to start again with an open mind if you will," she said evenly.

I looked at Théo who shrugged back at me.

'Why not?' I thought, so I retrieved my document case from Théo's care and opened my presentation once more.

"I have brought copies of my business plan and a current financial statement. I would, however, like to start with..."

2

After I had gone through my prepared speech, and Mrs Steel had asked the right sort of questions, she concluded the interview by letting us know that confirmation one way or the other would be with us within a fortnight.

As we were ushered to the door, Théo said, "What about Le Grec?"

"If I know my colleagues, our Managing Director has had the information about the flowers in the trousers minutes after you entered my office. A lot can be forgiven of family members, but becoming a laughing stock is not one of them. He will be found a rather more low profile job in a remote office – probably one that does not involve contact with members of the public."

With a warmer smile than I had seen so far, she wished us goodbye.

As we walked down the street to Piccadilly I asked Théo why he had returned to Charm & Change so soon.

"I could not make head or tail of this stupid map. I started to wander and came to a very strange area. The women were obviously prostitutes but so aggressive. They scared me to death. I thought I would try to get some directions from that pretty receptionist to a place I could go that would leave my manhood intact."

This was the man who had led the attack on armed drug dealers! Still, the girls of the notorious Shepherd's Market were a pretty scary proposition.

"Now, Chérie," Théo said tucking my arm through his. "Protect me whilst we go and find something passable to eat in this impossible city."

We went off in search of steaks.

CHAPTER TWENTY FOUR

1

One minute it seemed as if my wedding day was so far into the future that it would never come. The next, the Mlle. Ophelie from the Salon de Beauté had done her very best with my hair and make-up and Rebé Suss was making last minute adjustments to my gown.

Outside my door, an old fashioned barouche was standing with a placid-looking horse who was trying to get the last of his oats from the corners of a nosebag.

Madame Colbert, dressed in a very frivolous pink tulle coat and dress, had finally gone over to the church. The bridesmaids had also departed to take up their positions. There had been the usual stream of near disasters common to any grand occasion, such as when little Mei-Lin had spilled orange juice over her white silk dress and burst into floods of tears. Fortunately the admirable Rebé had made the dresses out of a washable fabric, and tragedy had been averted with a quick spin in the washing machine and work with a warm iron.

We had started to panic when the flowers had not arrived. The Florist's assistant had sent them to Madam Colbert's house by mistake, but Captain Christophe had done a rapid relocation with true military precision.

My bouquet was a small round posy of tiny dark blue flowers with a white saltire worked in amongst the blooms. We had drawn the line at miniature tricolours for the bridesmaids; they had sprays of lilies of France decorated with more of the unusual dark blue blooms.

Some of the invited guests failed to turn up, but some unexpected relatives had arrived, so it balanced out more or less.

Madame Colbert's sister, Soeur Emmanuelle, had travelled from Rome. She had come to visit me the previous evening to give me her blessing and a missal bound in white leather with a few words penned by the Pope himself inside the front cover. Madame was very impressed.

Théo's senior uncle, Father Simeon, had sent me a long letter wishing me well and enclosed a beautifully carved wooden rosary which I understood was his own work. Lovely as it was I decided I would carry the ebony and pearl beads that had appeared so strangely in my haunted cellar for my 'something old'.

Madame started to talk about heirlooms then blushed and went very quiet. Théo had obviously had a word.

Despite all the blue in my dress and flowers I had a pair of really lovely blue lace garters to comply with the old wedding verse. As I secured them below my knees, I thought of Madame's 'show and tradition'. I also thought about Théo.

M. Bertrand had come to visit me a week before the wedding. I offered him coffee and he wriggled in his chair and looked uncomfortable. Twice he seemed on the point of going before he had actually said what he had come to say. Finally he blurted out:

"Mademoiselle Geneviève, you know only too well the trouble jewellery has brought to our family. However, that chatterbox Rosine has let slip that you wish to wear pearls with your wedding gown and you have only some cultured pearls that are rather cheap, if you'll forgive my blunt words."

Before I could protest, he extracted a large jeweller's box from his inside pocket.

"These belong to my wife. We would both be honoured if you would consider wearing them on Friday as your borrowed trinket."

Trinket! They were the most beautiful set of matched pearls I had ever seen. A simple single strand, they glowed with a life of their own. He handed over a pair of pearl and diamond drop earrings that matched them. I could only stammer my thanks.

M. Bertrand coughed again. "You need not rush to return them. My wife will not be wearing them again. Pearls need to be worn to keep their beauty. Be happy, Mademoiselle." With a short bow he left rather quickly.

Now M. Delcroix, beautifully turned out in a formal morning suit, was twisting his top hat in his hands and muttering to Rebé, "Mademoiselle, please finish your ministrations. The gown is perfect, and if we do not leave now we will be late."

"A bride cannot be early for her wedding – it is not done. Besides, I have now adjusted the errant seam and all is well."

I looked into the mirror and saw a stranger. This beautiful, elegant creature in the wonderful gown could not be me.

"I have seen many brides during my long life in Montreuil-sur-Mer," M. Delcroix said slowly, "but I do not think I have ever seen one as lovely or as radiant as you. I am very honoured to give you away today. I wish you and Théophile every happiness in your life together and success in your enterprise at the Cloche Blanche."

"Thank you, Monsieur," I said simply. He offered me his arm and we went together out to the carriage. Rebé fussed with the folds of the dress and the photographer took another battery of shots. He had been well primed by Rebé, who was more interested in the presentation of her dress than she was in my nuptials.

Finally, nosebag removed, the pretty dappled horse began to clip clop towards the church. There, in the wonderful old porch with its rows of grim faced saints. Rosine and the little girls were waiting for me.

As we walked into the dim interior with my attendants carefully placed behind me, the organ filled the church with the sounds of Handel's 'Entry of the Queen of Sheba'. Madame Colbert had chosen my wedding music in consultation with M. Delcroix fils, who was playing the organ on this occasion.

I could see Théo standing with his cousin Christophe at the steps to the high altar. The London-bought jacket fitted his massive shoulders to perfection. The hair and beard and been trimmed but were already beginning to escape from their pomade and start to curl. He looked wonderful.

The church seemed full – full of bodies, full of the fragrance from the many sprays of flowers used for decoration at the end of each row of seats and the incense used at mass, and full of happiness. Behind the dark crowd of people, dozens of candles blazed at the feet of the saints in the side chapels, each one a prayer for Théo and me.

The impressions were fleeting. I was only just aware of them and the people in the pews on either side of me, for I only had eyes for Théo. For the rest of the service my attention was on him as we made our vows and exchanged rings.

Finally the service was over and Théo raised my veil and kissed me – rather more soundly than 'show and tradition' demanded.

We walked back down the aisle to more Handel. This time 'See now the conquering hero comes' from Saul. Madame obviously enjoyed a joke.

The members of the congregation began to come into focus. I saw a line of uniformed policemen with M. Delavoie and a very demurely suited Zeinab. A row of Sapeurs-Pompiers glittered in their best uniforms. Three members of the English Veterans Association stood to slightly wobbly attention in their regimental blazers and medals. I just about recognised members of the gun club as they were all spruced up in their best suits. Madame Couroyer from the bakery stood next to Madame Binet from the Charcuterie. There were several other shopkeepers or their wives from the town. However, I doubted that anyone would need serving this morning; they were all in church watching me. Mme Sophie and Rebecca sat together at the back looking very pleased with themselves.

Family members and friends beamed at us. I hardly recognised

Madame Bonneau who had changed her habitual black for a very fetching lavender outfit. Even Eric had been persuaded into a suit.

All my life in Montreuil was there to witness Théo and me making our vows. It was very important to me that they had come and that we had made a public declaration of our love and intent to live as man and wife.

Outside, the Spring sunshine was almost blinding after the dim interior of the church. The barouche had been replaced with a horse drawn wagonette. Théo and I were handed into the places of honour whilst the bridesmaids, best man and ushers were fitted in round us. Rebé twitched my train carefully into place once more and rearranged my veil.

We then made the traditional ride around the town. Those few citizens of Montreuil who had not squeezed into the church stood along the route and waved. Our wagonette was followed by a long procession of cars, all decorated with net bows, the drivers pounding on their car horns in the way of French weddings everywhere to chase away bad luck.

The Civil Ceremony only took a few minutes, and then we went to the cemetery so I could place my bouquet on the Calamier family tomb – as my mother had done all those years before. I shed some tears for the fact that Mum and Dad could not be there; but there were just a few and quickly dried.

At last, we arrived at the Cloche Blanche. There was another long session of photographs in the garden until even Rebé was satisfied. I thought I could smell strong pipe tobacco. I probably could – all the smokers were having a quick drag before going inside once more.

Then it was time to eat. I imagined I would be too excited, too nervous to want anything. I found instead that I was ravenous. The wedding breakfast had been one of the few things to which I had really given some serious thought. There were canapés and aperitifs whilst everyone milled about, and Théo and I thanked people for coming. I had made a list of who had given me what, and I discretely consulted it from time to time. I would, of course, send formal letters later.

When the caterers gave me the thumbs up we moved to table. We started with hot oysters on the half-shell with a champagne sauce. Then came a cold salmon mousse with a cucumber dressing. The main course was pre-sale lamb grilled over a wood fire. The caterers had set out a sort of sophisticated barbecue in the garden so as not to fill the kitchen with smoke. The meat was served with a redcurrant sauce and primeur vegetables: new potatoes, tiny carrots, asparagus and petits pois.

When the plates had been cleared away, Waiters pushed cheese trolleys around loaded with a dozen different cheeses and all the usual accompaniments, celery, grapes, olives and bowls of walnuts. Finally we had ice-cream gateau decorated with fresh fruit.

The wedding cake was wheeled in and yet more photographs taken with Théo and me wielding a sword above the top tier. The caterers then took the elegant structure to the kitchen to cut it up professionally and put in tiny white boxes for the guests to take away.

There were speeches from just about everyone, then an hour or so of more or less quiet until the evening guests started to arrive.

The children who had been good for so long were allowed to run about. The family groups settled down to gossip and I was enjoying a glass of champagne and talking to Rosine and Edouard about how we would develop the Cloche Blanche.

Suddenly there was an almighty whoosh like an evil wind from hell, followed by a bang loud enough to deafen. The Marquee set up just beyond the porte-fênetres of the dining room went up in a huge orange explosion.

The dining room curtains caught and instantly began to blaze. Flames licked the wooden window frames and spread to the table drapes.

There were cries and shouts and a rush for the front doors, but people on the whole were behaving well, and the old folk and children were being ushered out first. The members of the police and fire brigade instantly returned to duty.

Then there was the most terrible scream I have ever heard. Fleur Duval tried to rush into the fire.

"Mei-lin, Delphine, they are out there! They are burning! They will die!" she howled.

Fleur was restrained by her husband Maurice and her brother-in-law Albert. But Théo, crazy, brave Théo, ran straight into the inferno.

I tried to catch him, fell over my stupid dress and measured my length on the floor. It probably saved my life. One of the helium cylinders that had been used to fill balloons flew over my prostrate body like a rocket and buried itself in the wall. I struggled to my knees. The firemen were deploying extinguishers and beating at the flames with rugs and fire blankets. A dozen mobiles were being used to call in more help. I stared into the dancing, crackling flames. There was nothing but churning smoke and gouts of flame. Then a shadow darker than the smoke seemed to stand for a moment in the middle of the bonfire before staggering forward. Théo stumbled into the dining room with a limp figure in dirty blue and white silk under each arm. His hair and beard were on fire and the velvet jacket was burning on his back, but he was alive.

Théo was smothered under a torrent of expensive jackets beating out the flames. The girls were removed from his clutching fingers and given mouth to mouth resuscitation. In the distance I heard the wail of an ambulance. I dissolved into tears.

Somebody, I don't know who, took me to the hospital in the wake of the ambulance. I spent hours on hard hospital seating gaining startled looks from the doctors, patients and relatives who passed through the casualty department. It finally dawned on me that it was not the dirt or the smell of smoke, these were normal for an emergency unit, it was the fact that I looked like a medieval queen – albeit one who had narrowly escaped being burned at the stake.

Nurses came and went saying things like, 'The doctor is with him,' and 'We'll tell you if there is any change'.

Rebé and Zeinab arrived with some more practical clothing.

"I can't," I muttered. "What if the nurse comes for me whilst I am away, they never wait."

"I'll stay here in your place," Zeinab soothed. "If anyone arrives with news about Théo she won't get away from me even if I have to arrest her. I'll send someone to come and get you immediately; I swear it by St. Michael. Remember, I eat drug dealers for breakfast."

Rebé led me to the ladies room, as she helped me out of the ruined gown she said, "Why was Zeinab banging on about St. Michael?"

"Patron saint of police officers," I said shortly.

I saw tears in her eyes. With bitterness, I thought they were probably just for her expensive dress! But she had the patterns, there was insurance money – dresses at least could be replaced.

"Genèvieve, I am so sorry," she said after her tears had subsided. "He is a good man, one of the best. I will pray for him and for you."

I didn't think I could feel worse, but I did.

2

Around midnight, Fleur and Maurice came out of the children's unit. Fleur was laughing and crying both at once. She ran over and embraced me.

"They are scorched and suffering from smoke inhalation, but they will be all right. We owe Théo so much, how is he?" I had no answer for her.

She chattered on, "The nurses are trying to get them to sleep. Would you believe it, they are upset because their beautiful dresses are ruined?"

Maurice tugged at his wife's arm. "Fleur ma petite, come away."

She was towed down the hospital corridor still talking. Her precious children had survived. I wanted to be glad; I so very much wanted to be glad.

The hospital settled into its night time routine. The bright lights and scurrying personnel took on an almost surreal aspect.

Someone put a cardboard cup of some drink or other in my hand. I held it till it went cold then someone else took it out of my grasp again.

Mme. Colbert came to join me on the bank of chairs. She was wearing a hospital gown. I remembered that long ago in another life someone had told me she suffered from asthma. She had just escaped from medical care.

We sat together. She offered me a rosary; I grasped it more or less as I had the coffee cup.

A nurse appeared at the treatment room doors. "Madame Colbert?"

We both stood up.

"You can see him now, but we can only allow one visitor at a time until there is no further danger of infection."

Mme. Colbert and I looked at one another. She nodded and sat down. "Give him my love and tell him I am here if you will, Genèvieve, ma fille."

I surged forward. "How is he?"

"He's in a bit of a mess but we don't think there will much lasting damage," the nurse said briskly.

Théo was in a high sided cot in a side ward of the isolation unit. I had to put on mask, gown, gloves and shoe covers. Théo was on his belly, naked except for a small cloth over his hips. His entire back was pink and blistered. Someone had painted his face and head with some sort of garish ointment. The lovely curly hair had all been cut away and the beard was a ruin of stubble. But he had never looked more handsome.

He raised a hand to me. "Where is your lovely dress, Chérie?" The rasping voice was a grotesque parody of his soft tones.

"Théo, Théo, my love!" I wanted to hold him tight to me, but I did not dare touch him for fear of giving him more pain.

"Chérie, hold my hand"

Both hands were wrapped in bandages, but the tough calloused fingertips seemed intact. I pressed them to my lips.

Théo tried to smile at me then winced as the skin of his cheek bones pulled tight.

"Mei-Lin, Delphine, have they survived?" he croaked.

"Not only survived but are mourning their bridesmaid dresses."

"Ah, les jeunes filles."

Théo's eyes closed and my heart fluttered in panic. But I saw that his chest continued to expand and contract regularly.

A nurse approached. "We have given him a strong sedative. He will sleep now for several hours. We would recommend you go home now and come again in the morning."

I stayed by his bed for the rest of the night. I did, however, go home the following morning when the nurses shooed me away telling me they needed to change Théo's dressings and I was in the way.

I was back at the hospital just after noon. I had to wait whilst the Consultant did his rounds. I ambushed the great man as he came out the ward.

"Théo Colbert, I am his wife, tell me how he is, the nurses are just giving me the usual relative soothing platitudes."

"Madame Colbert, let us go to my office." The tiny brown man said taking my arm.

"Théo Colbert is strong, healthy and luckier than he deserves. He will need careful nursing for a week or two and a longer period of rest whilst his burns heal. He will, I assure you, make a full recovery. You may want to take the opportunity to get him to shave off his beard. When he came in he looked a bit like photographs of my late grandfather."

"I wonder what your grandmother might have said to such a suggestion, Monsieur Le Docteur."

"You have a point, Madame," he said as he escorted me back to the ward. "I must tell you there is some damage, and I fear he will never again look like un flibustier. Perhaps you might consider the Monsieur Le Professeur look?

It was foolish and comforting at the same time. If the consultant was talking about how Théo might wear his beard in the future it meant then he was going to have a future.

During the day, Théo drifted in and out of sleep. Nurses relayed messages from well wishers and a mountain of cards, flowers and even soft toys began to grow in the reception area. I asked the staff to distribute the flowers and toys to the other wards.

About five o'clock a nurse came to tell me that M. Delavoie would like to speak to me. I can't say that I had not been expecting this visit. I touched Théo's fingers and went out, depositing my protective clothing in the basket provided.

The detective looked careworn and harassed. "Let me take you out for a cup of coffee, Madame. I hate hospitals."

"Very well, Monsieur, but I do not wish to be away long." I was beginning to hate hospitals myself.

"The fire was set deliberately," M. Delavoie began without recourse to a preamble, his no nonsense manner a boon on this occasion. "We suspected as much, but the fire investigation team have confirmed it. The catering Johnnies barbecuing your lamb gave us good descriptions of some characters they had seen hanging about who seemed to have nothing to do with the wedding. We already have them in custody."

"Why?" I asked, although I already thought I knew.

"Théo was identified the night Zeinab was captured."

'I was there too,' I thought.

"We did a lot of damage to the organisation that night, but elements who wanted revenge remain. It will not be a great deal of comfort to you, but this latest escapade has put many more of the gang behind bars and given us a lead on some of the real brains behind the scenes. They moved in anger and at short notice. They did not take as many precautions, and we were waiting."

"You mean you knew they were going to attack us?" I could not believe my ears.

"No, no, Madame, I would have had more men at your wedding if I had known that. It was just that we were waiting for some reaction. In fact, I was almost sure they did not know about that... I mean Théophile," M. Delavoie said, eyeing the coffee pot. "It means we have more than one traitor in the Montreuil office – but we will find him, never fear Madame."

"What will this do to our insurance?" I blurted.

"I will have a word in certain ears. I don't think you need worry."

"Well if that is all, I need to get back to the hospital." I stood up but could hardly feel the ground under my feet.

"There is one more thing I'd like to say, Madame. Please sit down."

I collapsed onto the chair rather than sat down.

"I would like to say how very sorry I am. Sorry that the little girls were hurt, sorry about your wedding, your hotel. But perhaps the thing I regret most is that Colbert almost died." He passed his hand across his brow. "You see, I was there when the explosion occurred. Zeinab wanted to be at the reception early for whatever reasons you women have. I was in the dining room looking for a drink when the place went up in smoke. I was paralysed. I stood there watching as if I was the oaf, whilst Théo barrelled into that inferno. I couldn't have done it. I want you to know that in that moment I admired the man."

It could not have been easy for Onesime to say those words. I reached for his hand.

"Monsieur, Théo is not the man you knew all those years ago. He has changed, and I think you have changed too. When visiting is allowed, why not go and make your peace with him? You are never going to be friends but if you let your hatred go, I think you will both be better for it."

Then I did leave, wanting to weep, scream and perhaps smile too.

My next unexpected visitor was Rebé Suss. She was dressed once more in jumper and jeans. She asked about Théo and the girls and I was able to give her the good news.

"I am going back to Paris now. There is nothing I can do here and

I have classes I must attend if I am to graduate. Your beautiful dress will live once more but I will understand if you never want to see it again. However, I have one thing to ask. I have been told your little nieces are sad because their outfits were ruined along with everything else. I wondered if their mother would permit them to be models for me when I give my show in September. I am sure they would enjoy it and they are well behaved children who would I think do well. They would certainly be more appealing than the brats the modelling agencies tend to send us."

I muttered something neutral but thought privately that we could not have kept the girls away from the show with a company of marines.

3

The honeymoon had to be cancelled of course. But six months later we managed a belated holiday in Martinique. And if two of us flew out, three of us came home again.

EPILOGUE

The Cloche Blanche was a success almost from the first week it opened. We achieved a Michelin star in less than two years. The partnership with Rosine and Edouard worked well.

However, Rosine eventually wanted more, which was only natural. We managed an amicable dissolution of our agreement, and the Vincent and Bonneau families went on to open a country hotel on the outskirts of Amiens. It has an excellent reputation, but I don't think Rosine will be satisfied until she gets to Paris – which I think she will. I wish them well.

Henri Olivier lost his enthusiasm for the hotel life and sold Chez Henri before moving permanently to the Auvergne. Valerie did not fancy life in the mountains and came to work for us. She still likes to keep herself to herself, but I have noticed just recently her having long discussions with our new sous-chef – how many ways can you think of to rearrange a cheese board?

Chez Henri went through several hands, each more unsuccessful than the last, until it closed for good and the premises became a recruitment agency and an insurance office.

Marie-Claire has never married. Eventually, her mother's arthritis progressed to the point where Claire Bigot could no longer live alone. Marie-Claire took her mother to live with her in her tiny flat in Paris. We see them at family gatherings, and while I am as civil to them both as it is humanly possible, we will never be friends.

Brigitte Gobert did not stay long at Le Couvent. She moved to Rouen as an assistant manager then back to Paris. She has never again secured a manager's post.

Stéphanie stayed in Montreuil and eventually came to work in the Cloche Blanche. She is quiet, efficient and modest, and I find I like her very much. She reminds me of Marie-Liesse Bonneau, whom I still miss.

M. Delavoie gained his promotion and went to Paris. He stayed there a couple of years before being moved to Marseilles to head up a new anti-drugs operation. Zeinab resigned from the police force about that time. She more or less had to, as she was six months pregnant and wished to set up a new home for her husband – in Marseilles!

Rebé Suss graduated with honours and went on to create quite a stir in the fashion world as her Aunt Sophia had predicted. I still get the occasional Rebé Suss original at a prix d'ami that I wear to celebration dinners and important banquets.

Théo has got a daughter to spoil. She has long black curly hair, deep blue eyes and the sunniest personality I have ever seen in a child. But then, perhaps I am prejudiced. We called her Blanche Edith, but she is most often known as Chouette.

From time to time I visit the old cemetery. I put flowers on the Calamier grave, then go and sit for a few minutes by the tomb of the countess. I am so very grateful for the courage I seemed to get from her when I was ready to give up everything and go back to Scotland. This is my home now, and I am content.

Today, as I arranged the roses in the dining room, I worried that my change of life might be coming early. As well as the usual symptoms I have been feeling tired, bloated and sometimes a little sick in the mornings. I think however, I might wait a few weeks before consulting Dr. Deroussant.

Théo has already ordered a model train!

THE END